"Endearing characters help make this cozy a winner."

—*Publishers Weekly*

"*Mix-up in Miniature* is my favorite book in the Miniature series. I love the characters, especially Maddie and Henry. It is good to be able to visit old friends and see what turns their lives have taken."

—*I Love a Mystery*

"I was captured at once by the likability of the main character and sleuth, Geraldine Porter, who is a hobbyist in the delicate field of building/creating dollhouses and miniatures. I was instantly fond of her boyfriend, Henry, and her granddaughter, Maddie. Grace makes the characters very real and people that I would love to count as friends."

—*Goodreads*

"This is a quick read with a well-crafted plot and a likable cast of characters."

—*Myshelf*

"Writing as Margaret Grace, Camille Minichino takes a break from math and science and enters the more accessible world of crafting. ...Make no mistake, Grace's charming Miniatures Series is no small accomplishment!"

—*Mystery Lovers Bookshop News*

"All of the mysteries are solved, and most satisfactorily, too. This is an enjoyable book, with lots of miniature craft tidbits thrown in along the way."

—*Gumshoe*

# Madness in Miniature

## Mysteries by Camille Minichino

Miniature Mysteries, written as Margaret Grace
*Murder in Miniature*
*Mayhem in Miniature*
*Malice in Miniature*
*Mourning in Miniature*
*Monster in Miniature*
*Mix-up in Miniature*
*Madness in Miniature*

Periodic Table Mysteries, written as Camille Minichino
*The Hydrogen Murder*
*The Helium Murder*
*The Lithium Murder*
*The Beryllium Murder*
*The Boric Acid Murder*
*The Carbon Murder*
*The Nitrogen Murder*
*The Oxygen Murder*

Mathematical Mysteries, written as Ada Madison
*The Square Root of Murder*
*The Probability of Murder*
*A Function of Murder*
*The Quotient of Murder*

# Madness in Miniature

A MINIATURE MYSTERY

Margaret Grace

2014
PERSEVERANCE PRESS / JOHN DANIEL & COMPANY
PALO ALTO / MCKINLEYVILLE, CALIFORNIA

This is a work of fiction. Characters, places, and events are the product of the author's imagination or are used fictitiously. Any resemblance to real people, companies, institutions, organizations, or incidents is entirely coincidental.

The interior design and the cover design of this book are intended for and limited to the publisher's first print edition of the book and related marketing display purposes. All other use of those designs without the publisher's permission is prohibited.

A Perseverance Press Book
Published by John Daniel & Company
A division of Daniel & Daniel, Publishers, Inc.
Post Office Box 2790
McKinleyville, California 95519
www.danielpublishing.com/perseverance

Distributed by SCB Distributors (800) 729-6423

Book design by Eric Larson, Studio E Books, Santa Barbara

Cover image by Linda Weatherly S.

10 9 8 7 6 5 4 3 2 1

LIBRARY OF CONGRESS CATALOGING-IN-PUBLICATION DATA
Grace, Margaret, (date)
Madness in miniature / by Margaret Grace.
    pages cm. — (The miniature series)
ISBN 978-1-56474-543-9 (pbk.)
1. Porter, Geraldine (Fictitious character)—Fiction. 2. Grandparent and child—Fiction. 3. Murder—Investigation—Fiction. 4. Miniature craft—Fiction. 5. Craft shops—Fiction. 6. Earthquakes—Fiction. I. Title.
PS3563.I4663M33 2014
813'.54—dc23
                2013035788

*To Richard Rufer,*

*my amazing husband and on-the-job IT crew*

## Acknowledgments

THANKS as always to my dream critique team: mystery authors Jonnie Jacobs, Rita Lakin, and Margaret Lucke.

My gratitude also to the extraordinary Alameda County DA Inspector Chris Lux for advice on police procedure. My interpretation of his counsel through nineteen books should not be held against him.

Thanks to the many writers and friends who offered critique, information, and inspiration; in particular: Gail and David Abbate, Sara Bly, Nannette Carroll, Margaret Hamilton, Diana Orgain, Ellen Schnur, Sue Stephenson, Jean Stokowski, and Karen Streich.

Special thanks to Meredith Phillips, my editor and inspirational co-crafter in the world of miniatures.

My deepest gratitude goes to my husband, Dick Rufer, the best there is. I can't imagine working without his support.

# Madness in Miniature

# Chapter 1

I FELT A LITTLE SILLY walking down Springfield Boulevard carrying a traditional two-story American country home, with nine rooms of highly polished wood floors. But parking downtown was impossible, thanks to the construction zone still around a new store, due to open in a few days. SuperKrafts, a giant chain crafts store, had come to town. Walking beside me, eleven-year-old Maddie carried most of the furniture for the newly painted house. A kitchen set, a flowery print sofa and matching easy chairs, and odds and ends of toilets, beds, lamps, and dressers, all piled into a tote bag that bore the slogan MINIATURISTS WORK AS LITTLE AS POSSIBLE.

"Grandma, why are we taking our dollhouse to the display? I thought you didn't like the new store," Maddie asked.

"I like the store," I said, not quite a lie. I shifted the house in my arms, glad I'd chosen to build in half-scale this time—one half inch of dollhouse for every foot of real house—making it a lot easier to carry than if I'd built in one-inch scale. "I just miss the old shops that used to be on that spot. Maisie's card shop and Bebe's ceramics were there when your dad was not much older than you."

"Dad says you don't like SuperKrafts because you taught English for so many years and they spell crafts with a *k*."

"He has a point. And don't forget the way they've put an uppercase letter in the middle of the word," I added, clicking my tongue and frowning the way Maddie would have at a serving of broccoli.

"My teacher says we could have done a boycott," my grand-daughter said. "That means we wouldn't ever shop there and the big stores like SuperKrafts would go out of business and then the small stores would come back."

Ah, the simplicity of life when you're a preteen. I wondered in which part of the fifth-grade curriculum political strategies were taught these days and whether Maddie's interpretation was at all close to what her teacher had recommended. Our own Lincoln Point, California, city council had fought hard when the controversial message came from New York last year— SuperKrafts had bought property in town, displacing two of our long-standing small businesses and seriously altering the face of our main downtown shopping district. The idea of a boycott was entertained for a while until the powers-that-be decided that the benefits of welcoming the chain outweighed the negatives. Never mind that two of the negatives were the life's work of two Lincoln Point natives, Maisie Bosley of Maisie's Card Shop, and Barbara "Bebe" Mellon of Bebe's shop, DIY Ceramics. Bebe, a potter herself, accommodated other potters as well as do-it-yourself customers whose work Bebe glazed and fired.

Another factor in the council's decision to welcome Super-Krafts to Springfield Boulevard was the good work of Catherine Duncan, SuperKrafts' public relations emissary. How smart of them to send a woman who just happened to be a native of Lincoln Point to smooth things over. The Duncans had moved to New York City soon after Catherine's graduation from Abraham Lincoln High, to be closer to family. As a native of the Bronx, I remembered being slightly envious at the time that my student was moving back to my hometown, until memories of winter, with frozen toes, barely adequate down jackets, and shivery walks to the subway came flooding back. Better to be a fair weather friend to that climate.

"I'm hot. I hate summer," Maddie said, drawing my attention away from reveries of white Christmases to the current weather conditions. Lincoln Point in June was hot and dry, and would stay that way for months.

"I like summer because I get to spend more time with you," I said. If I'd had a free hand I'd have ruffled her red curls, handed down from the Porter side of the family. All I'd contributed to her genetic makeup was her skinny legs and insatiable sweet tooth.

I'd been thrilled when Maddie's dad, my son Richard, had accepted a position at Stanford Medical Center and moved his family from Los Angeles to nearby Palo Alto. It was now an easy drive for me to pick Maddie up from school and I saw her often, but summers were even better for quality time with my only grandchild. We'd worked together on the pale blue dollhouse that was now headed, albeit grudgingly on my part, for a miniatures display and raffle at the new store. I consoled myself with the fact that the SuperKrafts inventory included more miniatures supplies and accessories than other stores of its kind.

Maddie leaned against me, nearly knocking the cumbersome house to the ground. "Mmm," she said. "I'm glad I have this whole week here with you, too."

"And you get to hang out with Taylor," I said.

"Nyah," Maddie answered, pulling away.

Uh-oh, something was up between Maddie and Taylor. The unladylike grunt was Maddie's newest version of "whatever," also known as "who cares?" The girls' play dates and close friendship were very handy for Taylor's grandfather and me—Henry and I had become the adult version of BFFs, our families meshing nicely. I wasn't eager to have trouble on the home front.

"What do you mean, 'nyah'?" I asked, doing a poor imitation of Maddie's response.

"I might not see her so much this summer. School's out but I still have a lot to do. My class has to read a whole book and write a report for September, and I'll be starting computer camp pretty soon, so I'll be spending a lot of time writing computer programs."

All of which Maddie could accomplish sooner than I could fashion a twin bed out of a kitchen sponge and piece of white cotton. I hesitated to query Maddie, but figured I could give it one more push.

"Is something wrong between you and Taylor?" I asked as we trudged in quick succession past Seward's Folly, our local coffee spot, and Railsplitter Nursery, our plant and flower shop.

"Tell me again, who was Seward?" Maddie asked.

She knew as well as I did, but I gave in to her stalling tactic. I explained as I'd done since she was four, that the café was curiously named after what was considered an unwise purchase of Alaska by William Seward, one of Lincoln's former cabinet members. And to preempt her, I added a note that "Railsplitter" was one of Honest Abe's nicknames. It always took a while for newcomers to Lincoln Point to catch on to the proliferation of businesses, streets, and celebrations named after people and events in the life of our sixteenth president, but Maddie was no newcomer, and she was wise beyond her years when it came to manipulating her grandmother.

"It's okay if you don't want to tell me about you and Taylor," I said. "I'm sure it will all work out."

"Nyah," Maddie answered.

I let the matter drop. For now. If things went as usual, before the end of the day I'd hear about the issue that had driven a wedge between the two friends. I could think of a few possibilities— Maddie had spilled liquid crafts glue on Taylor's favorite book, or vice versa. Pieces of a jigsaw puzzle were lost and blamed on one or the other. A jewelry project had come apart and dozens of tiny beads had ended up on the floor, another blameworthy event.

"Nyah, nyah, nyah," Maddie chanted with each step as we made our way to SuperKrafts, as if she were vetoing all of my unspoken guesses.

I didn't want to think about the expressions that were on their way as Maddie grew into her teen years.

WITH only a few yards to go, we stopped in our tracks as the doors of SuperKrafts flew open and Maisie and Bebe, former shop owners, came out fighting. I stared in amazement as the two women, sixty-something Maisie and mid-forties Bebe, who'd been friends and business neighbors for years, duked it out verbally in front of a gathering crowd of Saturday afternoon shoppers.

"I can't believe you agreed to the idea of a billboard the size of California," Bebe yelled. "SuperKrafts will be the only thing people see of Lincoln Point from the freeway."

"They're nice enough to include us in these meetings. I think we should be supportive," Maisie said.

"They're nice? We should be grateful and supportive? All hail the megastore? That's okay for you to say," Bebe shouted. She stood with her hands on her slim hips, her head pushed forward. "You were ready to sell your shop and retire anyway." She poked her own chest. "Me? I have a lot of years left."

"Are you saying I'm an old lady? That I might as well cash it in?" Maisie's chunky body stood firm while her hands flailed in front of her.

"That's exactly what you did. Cashed it in," Bebe said.

"So did you. And for a pretty penny," Maisie said. She folded her arms across her full bosom.

"Only because I had no choice after you signed off many meetings ago."

It wasn't the first time the two women had had this argument. I'd been present at some of the contentious meetings, but this was the most public display. By now there were about two dozen people, standing around for the show, some using cameras, some with phones to their ears, to cover up their voyeurism, I suspected. I wouldn't have been surprised if there were a betting pool in progress on the side, as to which of the strong-willed businesswomen would come out ahead. Or alive. I tuned into snippets of conversation among the crowd.

"Bebe's right. There goes the town when these giants move in," from a woman I recognized as a clerk at Abe's Hardware.

"They're not all bad. They hired my sister and her boyfriend," from a young woman with a toddler. "It's not like they're bringing hazardous waste to the town."

"They even took over the alley between the old stores. We have to go all around Civic Drive to get to the mortuary," from an older man, hands in his pockets, sunglasses wrapped around his eyes.

"How often do we have to go to the mortuary?" from the woman standing next to him.

"You can still get to the Ten-to-Ten okay." This from a teen who probably made daily trips from Abraham Lincoln High School to the convenience store across the street for energy drinks.

I spotted members of my miniatures group in the crowd, as well as a couple of former students. My family joked that wherever two or more were gathered in Lincoln Point, there was sure to be a former student from my nearly thirty years' teaching at ALHS or my ongoing tutoring at the Lincoln Point library. But the two women who were fighting now were not among my alumni or my current high school equivalency students. They continued their back-and-forth tirade, with the body language among us spectators ranging from questioning looks to disapproving frowns. *Tsk-tsk*s filled the air. Yet no one left the area. We really needed more to do in this town on a weekend.

The hubbub of conversation came to a halt when Super-Krafts' doors opened again and a tall, slender woman exited. Catherine Duncan stepped with confidence onto the sidewalk, looking like the PR professional that she was, even without a navy pinstripe. She'd known enough to leave her chic Manhattan wardrobe behind and blended into the crowd with a tasteful summer dress, costume jewelry, and sandals. Nothing too loud or expensive-looking, except her bright red toenails, which screamed "fancy pedicure," and the rich leather briefcase slung over her shoulder. I tried to figure Catherine's age by working forward from her year of graduation. With my strange way of doing math, I placed her as a senior some time after the groundbreaking of the new high school gym and before Maddie's birth. I came up with thirty-three or -four years old for Catherine, and at the same time remembered her B-plus paper on women in the works of William Shakespeare.

"Ladies," Catherine said, addressing Bebe and Maisie in a

clear voice. "I wish you hadn't run out of our meeting. Can't we talk about this, please?"

"You," Bebe said, facing Catherine down. "You think you can come back here as if you're God's gift to your lowly hometown?" Bebe's long, narrow face was so red, I feared for her survival. "And don't think I'm alone in my opinion."

Catherine began another plea. "If we could all just take a breath and talk calmly. I'm here to help you."

I cringed. Right out of the playbook for hostage negotiators, I thought. As I expected, Bebe's response was the opposite of calm.

"It's a little late for that, isn't it?" Bebe said, flinging her long hair over her shoulder. She pointed to the larger-than-life Super-Krafts sign atop the sprawling one-story building, with its zigzag letters in crayon colors, and the oversized posters announcing the Grand Opening. "There's nothing to talk about anymore."

I'd stepped back, taking Maddie with me, our bodies pressed against the enormous SuperKrafts window and our dollhouse safely at our feet. Not as invisible as I'd hoped. Catherine spotted me, and waved me over. It was no use pretending I didn't know what she wanted. I'd become the reluctant liaison between her and the good people of Lincoln Point since her first trip back in a professional capacity. She'd wooed me with a line no one in her right mind should fall for.

"Everyone likes you, Mrs. Porter," she'd said, reverting to her student–teacher relationship with me.

At early meetings, I'd managed to get a few concessions from SuperKrafts in exchange for a peaceful transition, but clearly our efforts weren't enough for Bebe. Catherine turned to me now. "Gerry, help us out here," she said. "I've been meeting the merchants in small groups so we can work together on the new look of downtown, and—"

"Our downtown was fine with the old look," Bebe said. "All you want is publicity for yourself and your"—Bebe drew quote marks in the air—"'Grand Opening.'"

Maisie gave me a pleading look. "We need you, Gerry. Bebe's

ready to kill anyone who steps foot in SuperKrafts when it opens next week."

"Let's talk about it at Sadie's. My treat," Catherine said, indicating the ice cream shop across the street. Like me, Catherine was of the persuasion that no one could be unhappy while eating ice cream.

But, like Bebe, I wasn't sure what there was left to talk about. SuperKrafts was a done deal; Maisie's and Bebe's shops were history. During the long negotiations, we'd extracted a verbal promise from the corporation to hire locals and sell crafts from our artists, to use green technology for their ceramics classes, and to expand business hours to accommodate crafters who worked nine-to-five jobs.

All that was left was to try to hold the corporation to its promises. Along those lines, I'd picked up hints from Catherine that her boss might not be so easy to deal with, but we could take only one step at a time. I wondered if VIP Craig Palmer III would ever ride into town and face his project and its fallout head-on. So far he was just a name and a signature to me.

While I was adjusting to the idea of yet another meeting— and admittedly wrestling with whether to order an ice cream soda or a hot fudge sundae—teenager Jeanine Larkin came out of the store, probably summoned by a text from Catherine's busy thumbs. Jeanine, who baby-sat Maddie in the days before she considered herself too old to need one, wore a strange combination—shorts cut so high that the linings of the white canvas pockets hung below the hem in the back, and a narrow, multicolored SuperKrafts apron that reached almost to her ankles. I hoped that her working attire when the store was officially open would be more businesslike. Most likely, not.

Jeanine's slight build was deceiving. Without signs of struggle, she picked up the dollhouse from in front of Maddie's feet. "Hey, Mrs. Porter. Hey, Maddie. I'll get this set up for you in the display area," Jeanine said. "I'm excited. We already have three other houses."

"It's going to be a great display," I said. "Are you putting the open sides facing out?"

"They're on turntables, so it doesn't matter," she informed me. "Each turntable has its own unique landscaping," she added, a note of pride in her voice. "Like, one has a garden with flowers, another has this stone walkway, and one looks like it's in the middle of a city. Like that." I was impressed. The houses would be raffled off on opening day, the proceeds going to local charities. I had to say, SuperKrafts was making a great effort to be neighborly.

I knew my next negotiation would not be as successful. Maddie was a tougher customer than any big city corporation. I took a breath and addressed my granddaughter. "Maddie, will you go into the store with Jeanine and set up the furniture in our house?"

She gave me an incredulous look. "Now?"

"You're the best at arranging all the rooms."

She looked over at Sadie's and stared for a moment, as if its pink-and-white awning were calling to her. "Now?" she asked again, her voice coming out as a high squeak.

I stood my ground. "Yes, please. Don't forget to place the mirrors over the bathroom sink and the dresser. They're—"

"I know," she said, peeved. "They're wrapped separately and the glue's in the blue zipper bag." She flashed a pout at me, turning her head rapidly from me to Sadie's shop and back again. "I never get to have any fun."

I returned her gaze with a serious look of my own, one meant to remind her of the immaturity of her remark and its inappropriate timing. There were those, including her parents, who claimed that I spoiled my granddaughter. Now was the time to prove them wrong.

Maddie's look went from sullen to pitiful. I braced myself for delivering tough love, but felt myself caving. "We can have ice cream together later," I said. Good thing neither her parents nor anyone else was close enough to witness my weakness.

"It's not just the ice cream," she said.

I knew that, of course. Maddie was as curious as any eleven-year-old, and then some. If something interesting was going on, she wanted to be part of it.

"This meeting is going to be very boring. All kinds of business stuff."

"I don't think so."

"If you want, I'll tell you all about it later," I said. "Now, get in there." I faked a scolding tone and was rewarded with a quick kiss before she ran off, the tote full of furniture swinging at her side. I mouthed, "Keep her busy," to Jeanine, who'd already come back from depositing the dollhouse in the store. She gave me a thumbs-up, and I turned to the adults who wanted my attention.

While I'd been in the tug of war with Maddie, the three businesswomen, Maisie, Bebe, and Catherine, had pulled themselves together enough to start across the wide street.

"Let's go before a giant SuperCreamery swoops in from New York, kicks Sadie out, and takes over," Bebe said. "Or, I know, why don't we bring in a casino?"

"As long they offer Sadie a good deal," Maisie responded.

I heard a growl from Bebe, exasperated sighs from Maisie and Catherine, and recalled Maddie's last, desperate, whiny "Have a good time." Four females in bad moods. I followed along toward Sadie's thinking I might be wrong about the healing powers of ice cream and hot fudge.

# Chapter 2

EVERYONE IN MY miniaturists circle had been ambivalent about SuperKrafts, although for years we'd longed for a place near home to buy our dollhouse building materials, miniature furniture, and general crafts supplies. In our dreams, we saw a well-lighted space where we could hold workshops without intruding on our own living rooms. We didn't know that we'd have to sacrifice the homey feel of our downtown or the disruption of the careers and livelihoods of our friends.

Over many months, through short visits and correspondence, Catherine had done a reasonable job convincing the majority of us, and Lincoln Point citizens in general, that in the long run, the megastore would serve our community well. Hadn't we already seen the rise in employment opportunities, from inventory clerks to sales reps to assistant managers? We'd been assured of increased revenue from sales tax, and SuperKrafts had offered a generous stipend to each of the shops along Springfield Boulevard, as a "thank you" for their patience during construction. It was hard to argue with the advantages of the new presence on the boulevard. Many of the shop owners had used their windfalls for sprucing up their storefronts and offering special deals to make up for the inconvenience to customers. There was a definite upside to the megastore.

The downside of SuperKrafts had gathered around me now. The out-of-business Bebe had taken a seat as far away from Catherine as she could, given the small round table Sadie's daughter had directed us to; Maisie looked forlorn, as if she'd sold out her best friend; Catherine had shed some of her cool and now seemed nervous and unprepared for this meeting. All were silent. At least no one was fighting. Yet.

I decided it was up to me to speak the first words. "Heavy on the whipped cream, please," I said, describing my dream hot fudge sundae (the smell of melting chocolate had tipped the scales in its favor) to our pink-cheeked waitress.

The ladies followed suit, ordering a double chocolate malt (Bebe, ditto on the whipped cream), a single scoop of toasted almond (dieting Maisie), and a super-size banana split (Catherine, getting a laugh even from Bebe).

"What?" Catherine said. "I didn't have lunch today."

"You're all so lucky," Maisie said. "You can eat anything. I wouldn't be able to fit into my muumuus if I ate the way you did."

The usual diet-and-exercise conversation ensued, a nice buffer before the topic that brought us to the table. Once the delicious calories were delivered and nearly half consumed, we began in earnest, Catherine taking the lead. She looked across the table and addressed Bebe directly.

"I talked to Leo Murray," she said. "He's—"

"Leo, the almighty manager." Bebe's interruption included elaborate bowing motions as well as she could accomplish from a sitting position. "The guy from New York who acts like a big shot. Like you can't trust a local to be in charge of the store." Bebe then drew a large box in front of her face, to illustrate Leo's boxy physique and above-average height and girth.

"It's a temporary appointment, until he can train someone from here," Catherine explained. "Believe me, Leo is not going to want to stay in Lincoln Point any longer than..." Catherine caught herself, but not in time.

"Why would anyone want to live in Lincoln Point any longer than they absolutely have to? Is that what you're saying?" Maisie asked. "You got out pretty quick yourself, didn't you?" Whether or not she was aware of it, Maisie, who'd been born and raised within a few blocks of Sadie's, leaned her round body away from Catherine, toward Bebe.

I wanted to call "foul," since leaving town hadn't been Catherine's choice, but her parents'. All the grandparents and extended families on both sides were in the New York–New Jersey area and it hadn't been an unexpected decision to move back. I decided not to pursue this line of discussion, however, since we were already off on a tangent from what I knew was Catherine's original plan for the meeting.

"Leo's going to count on his workshop leaders," I said. "Is that what you started to say, Catherine?"

She nodded and made another attempt to address Bebe. "I know you don't want to work for us, but I'm glad you're willing to give it a try. I think we can make it worth your while. You're starting with ceramics, but you can also lead classes yourself or find good teachers for scrapbooking and card-making, and whatever else you want."

"Like miniatures," I said, though no one paid much attention.

Catherine continued, "You can choose your hours and make a decision once you see how the ceramics offerings go. We'd never be able to find anyone better than you."

"You'll have all new equipment," Maisie said, warming up again to the new regime. "Greener than your old stuff. Good for the planet."

"Since when are you a fan of the planet?" Bebe asked. "It took me all these years to get you to take recycling seriously."

"I've been recycling my newspapers since before you were born," Maisie said.

"Pssh," Bebe uttered, reminding me of Maddie. "Not even possible."

Here we go, I thought. Another intervention needed. So far, we'd kept our voices low and I hadn't noticed any eavesdropping or curious looks from surrounding tables. Most were filled with teenagers with loud voices and hormonal issues to fret about. I steered the conversation toward other advantages for Bebe, which kept us all on an even keel for another few minutes.

By the time our dishes were almost as clean as they were when they'd come out of Sadie's dishwasher, there was conciliation, if not smiles, around the table. Catherine took care of the check. She'd been playing with a straw from a container on the table. Now she bent it in half and let go. The straw snapped out of her hands, flew into the air and fluttered to the floor. The teens one table over burst into giggles and not even Bebe could hold back laughter.

Ice cream had worked its magic once more.

WHEN I stood to leave a few minutes later, along with the two former small-business owners, Catherine put her hand on my shoulder. "Another moment, Gerry?" she asked, still seeming not quite comfortable calling her former English teacher by her first name. I took a seat and asked our waitress for a cup of coffee, too embarrassed to order another scoop of ice cream. I would have liked a taste of Sadie's new mixed summer berry flavor, just to refresh my palate, but I had to leave room for my return trip with Maddie.

"It will all work out," I said to Catherine. "I think Bebe is actually happy with the idea of leading crafts workshops in the new store. She'll have all the fun of teaching without the headaches of running a business, though it will probably be a while before she'll admit it. That's just the way she is. And your asking Maisie's advice on sources for locally made cards was brilliant."

Catherine's face was somber. "I wish they were my biggest problems."

I raised my eyebrows, an expression that welcomed sharing, I hoped. "What *is* your biggest problem?"

"Where shall I start?"

"At the top."

"At the top in more ways than one is my boss, Craig Palmer." She smiled. "The Third. He comes from a long line of CEOs. I know you haven't met him yet, but he's the one who's been here in spirit."

"The one Bebe has been sending letters to."

"Uh-huh. Letters, phone calls, emails, making her position heard any way she can. Craig arrived in town last night and will be around some time today."

"I'll bet you can't wait for them to meet in person," I said, leading Catherine to roll her eyes. "You mentioned that he's not the easiest person to get along with."

"That would be the understatement of the week," she said.

"What's he likely to do? Wipe out all the promised perks?" It was clear what my focus was on.

"Possible, but I hope not. There's a personal aspect, too." I waited. Catherine sighed, then began again. "We were an item for a while. A very short while. I thought it was over, but you know how those things go."

Not really. I'd lived a life of charmed relationships. I'd been married to the same wonderful man, Ken Porter, for more than thirty years until he died of cancer. Henry Baker, the grandfather of Maddie's now seemingly estranged best friend, Taylor, was the first man I'd gotten close to in the years since Ken. If there was a rocky relationship in my past, it would have been in my teen years and I'd long since forgotten.

Still, I nodded, as if my life had been a daytime soap opera. "I understand," I said, which was more or less true. I certainly understood pain and loss as any person of a certain age would, as a woman would who'd watched her cherished husband die a long, painful death. "Do you think Craig will continue to give you a hard time about the break-up when he arrives?"

"I have no doubt."

"Is your job at risk?"

She shrugged. "It could be, but I have an excellent résumé and I've even had some interest from a number of headhunters."

"Craig must be a smart man to get so far in management at a big company and my guess is that he wouldn't want to lose a valuable employee. Surely, he'll be able to move on?"

Catherine laughed. At that moment she might have realized how naïve I was when it came to the comings and goings of romance. "There's another complication," she said.

"Someone other than your boss or Bebe?"

Catherine nodded. "But a member of Bebe's family. Goes back a long time."

To high school, I guessed, and remembered. "Jeff Slattery? Bebe's younger brother?"

I took Catherine's momentary silence for a "yes." When she spoke, her voice was low, her eyes cautious, as if a member of the Slattery clan or its armed surrogates had entered the ice cream shop. "Jeff's divorced and since I've been coming back here so often this past year, we've gotten together again. Sort of."

I sat back. And here I'd thought Catherine was all business when she was in town, except for the few evenings when she'd been invited by me or one of her old friends for a meal. I should have known better. Apparently, Jeff had stepped in to fill her social calendar. Jeff, an unremarkable student, had graduated a couple of years ahead of Catherine. Instead of going to college, he worked in town and eventually bought a corner shop on Springfield Boulevard and changed its name to Video Jeff's. The shop had begun as a videotape rental market back in the Dark Ages of the seventies and now, under Jeff, was almost exclusively a game store. You could buy or rent any number of new war games or revisit the old ones.

"Does Bebe know you and her brother have gotten together again?" I asked. I felt it was safe to use the term Catherine herself had used to describe their current relationship.

"We don't think so. Jeff and I have been very careful." Catherine blew out a long breath. "Bebe blames me for the fact that Jeff didn't go to college. In a way she's right. He was waiting for me to graduate, and we were going to settle down somewhere away from all this." I tried to imagine the "all this" she was referring to, and came up empty. Unless she meant Lincoln Point—was it that bad? I let her continue. "But..." She held her palms open, fingers splayed.

"Instead you left town, leaving him behind."

"Uh-huh. At the time, I was as devastated as he was, but I was seventeen and didn't see any options. I know I could have stayed here, maybe gone to college nearby, but my parents wouldn't have supported that decision. I wasn't strong enough then to buck them, and I couldn't imagine being on my own financially."

"Few seventeen-year-olds would have been able to do that," I said. "Did you and Jeff break it off then?"

"We drifted apart emotionally. Truthfully, I may have recovered from the separation sooner than Jeff did. I liked big city life. Going to college in New York was a blast. Being back here now though, seeing Jeff, I have some regrets. But can you imagine if Bebe did know we're seeing each other again? I'd be toast."

When I was in the classroom, I was pretty good at picking up things like this. I could sense immediately that a certain fifteen-year-old boy was more interested in the girl in front of him than in the Athenian lovers in *A Midsummer Night's Dream*, for example, and I'd make it a point to call on him and the object of his affection. And I had hawk's eyes when it came to catching the time-honored ritual of passing notes across the aisle. But Catherine and Jeff had reunited right under my nose and I hadn't suspected. I'd even felt bad that she was spending so many evenings alone in a small hotel room. Clearly, I'd lost my touch. Retirement had taken away my edge.

Maybe if I'd been sharper now and paying attention, I'd also know why Maddie and Taylor were on the outs. My mind went into free-association mode, as it sometimes did. What if Henry let the Maddie–Taylor situation affect our relationship? What if he took his granddaughter's side against Maddie and we argued? Broke up? Was I about to become a member of the Unlucky in Love set?

I shook away my own worry and came back to Catherine in the present. I needed clarification of Catherine's problem, or list of problems.

"Is it your boss and old flame, Craig Palmer, or Bebe Mellon who's in the way of your riding off into the sunset with Jeff?"

"I'm not looking forward to Craig and Jeff meeting, but there's no reason they need to. Anyway, I should be able to keep them apart. The real question for me and Jeff is—do we stay with the sunset, or move toward the sunrise?"

It took me a moment to catch on. "Ah, the dilemma of the bi-coastal couple. I don't imagine you'd want to give up your life in the big city."

"It would be hard, but even harder would be leaving my parents. Neither one of them is doing very well physically. And Jeff doesn't want to leave Bebe. They're very close, and all they have is each other since both parents died." Catherine waved her hands in front of her face and shook her head. "But me and Jeff are not there yet anyway. And he's definitely not pushing me."

I was proud of myself for not correcting Catherine's "me and..." grammar, which seemed to be the norm these days, though I did consider a retroactive lowering of her grade for senior year. I had the feeling we were talking around Catherine's reason for asking me to stay at Sadie's even though the ice cream was gone. I reviewed what she'd told me—Craig's hanging on was a nuisance and a potential threat to her job, but she could deal with that; Bebe was cantankerous and might be even more so if she knew Catherine was in a position to lure Jeff three thousand miles away; Jeff was staking his claim, but not being pushy. Nothing that required my assistance.

"Is there something else?" I asked.

Catherine rubbed her arms as if a chill wind had blown through the room. As far as I noticed, the temperature in the shop hadn't changed. In fact, I could have done with a little more A/C.

"I've been getting notes telling me to leave town," she said. "Not signed, of course."

I sat back. No wonder Catherine was chilly. "Do you think they're from Bebe?"

"She was the first one who came to mind, but after giving it some thought, I doubt it," Catherine said. "It's not her style, for one thing. Bebe's all in-your-face."

I nodded agreement. "And besides she knows SuperKrafts is not going to suddenly pull out and rebuild her shop, no matter what you do."

"Uh-huh. So what would be the point of telling me to leave, other than just another hassle?"

"You're right. Bebe's already told you to leave, in so many words."

Catherine gave me a weak smile. "No kidding." She frowned, getting serious again. "These notes are slipped under the door at my room in the inn. The old couple who are on the desk most of the time have no idea where they're coming from." I refrained from mentioning that the "old couple" who ran the inn were my longtime friends Loretta and Mike Olson, who were about three years older than I was. "Whoever it is goes right up the elevator or stairs to my room and leaves the envelope, avoiding the few working cameras in the place. It's happened twice on this trip already, and twice on the last one."

"Are they threatening you in some way?" I stopped lest I go in a direction worse than she'd already considered.

"Yes, I'd call them threatening. I've gotten my share of nasty letters in New York; it goes with my job. Someone is unhappy with a decision the company makes and my office is blamed. I represent SuperKrafts at business meetings back home and I might get dumped on if a competing retailer doesn't like a promotion we're running or thinks a contract violates fair practice. That's normal."

Normal? I was glad all my teaching career had brought me were complaints about pop quizzes and the occasional unhappy parent who tried to negotiate a daughter's or son's grade. If there were any threats against me as a teacher, they were made in the lunchroom or whispered in the hallway, teen to teen. I chose to assume they were few and far between.

"What's different about these latest notes?" I asked. "More personal?"

"It feels that way. First, coming right into my bedroom, essentially. And they're not specific to a business decision I made or had to implement. I remember one that was sent to my office in New York last year that was detailed to the dollar. It said something like, 'unless you lower your rate by fifty-five hundred dollars, you'll be sorry.' That kind of thing. You always know it's some lackey trying to make his mark."

"Do you have the latest notes with you by any chance?" I asked, wondering why I hadn't asked for them right away. Too much ice cream and thoughts of ice cream.

Catherine nodded, reaching into her briefcase and pulling out the offending notes. My first reaction, from being the aunt of Lincoln Point's finest homicide detective, Eino (Skip) Gowen, was disappointment that Catherine had placed the notes in plastic bags, as if they were peanut butter and jelly sandwiches or cookies for Maddie's lunch box. Didn't everyone know that evidence should be handled with gloves, and small items should be put in paper bags? Skip had long ago informed me that only TV cops used plastic, for dramatic effect, so viewers could see the smoking gun or the bloodstained cloth. I'd forgotten the details, but he'd explained how plastic interacts with most substances and could contaminate the evidence.

"Paper breathes," he'd told me. And that was the extent of my knowledge of forensic chemistry.

"I didn't touch them except at the edges, once I knew what these little white envelopes contained," Catherine said now. I allowed her to be proud of herself for that. She'd spread the four bags on the table, but I pushed them together, one on top of the other. We'd already drawn enough attention from the teens around us with the flipping soda straw, without luring them with a mystery.

I read the top note through the plastic. The handwriting had great flourishes, probably written by a left-hander, or someone who wanted us to think he was a left-hander. The initial capital letters were much larger, proportionately, than the lowercase letters. Again, that could have been a deliberate attempt to be misleading as to who was the author.

YOUR NOT WANTED HERE. YOU BETTER LEAVE SOON.

A shiver went through me, and not only because of the poor grammar and usage. The fact that Catherine could be mistaken—the notes might have been general messages to her company—did nothing to relieve my mind.

I slipped the note under the pile and moved on to the other three, all similar in tone, message, and handwriting, with only small differences in the level of threat:

IF YOU KNOW WHATS GOOD FOR YOU.

YOU SHOULDN'T HANG AROUND.

PACK UP AND LEAVE TOWN NOW.

I tried hard to study the phrases dispassionately, considering that the writer had possibly faked the errors as well as the handwriting, to further obscure his or her identity.

After I read them all, I neatened the stack, as I would any set of documents or letters, except that these made me jumpy enough to look over my shoulder and out the window at passersby. Was there a gun in the innocuous-looking shopping bag from Abe's Hardware carried by a man in cargo pants? A knife in the oversized purse slung over the shoulder of the young woman in jeans? Evil in the eyes of the kid in the wrap-around sunglasses and New York Yankees baseball cap, so far from home?

"Have you thought who else besides Bebe and Maisie were put out of business by—"

"They weren't exactly put out of business," Catherine said.

"I'm sure you have another term for it, but you know what I mean," I said, revealing only part of my annoyance.

"I'm sorry," Catherine said. "I'm just nervous, Mrs. Porter."

*Uh-oh.* I'd upset my former student, who seemed to have taken my slight reprimand as a blight on her GPA. I had a flashback to the young Catherine Duncan, with waist-length hair in many shades of brown and blond, and no lack of high school boys eager to carry her books. Now she'd graduated to a stylish shoulder-length cut and a complex social life, but I was still Mrs. Porter, one of the people responsible for her early education.

It wasn't Catherine's fault that she was confused by my reaction. I'd been on SuperKrafts' side for all practical purposes during the long months of meetings, and never expressed my ambivalence outright. Yes, I approved of the boost to our economy, but no, I didn't want to spoil the look of our lovely downtown. Yes, I wanted the enormous stock of crafts supplies at my fingertips, but no, I didn't want to put old friends out of business. It was time I stopped trying to have it both ways.

I returned to Catherine's immediate problem. "Have you thought of taking the notes to your boss or to the police?" I asked. Conciliatory, if too obvious a suggestion.

"I'd rather not go public or make a big deal out of them right now."

I interpreted the reasoning as a reluctance to bring her bosses in on the situation. I knew little of corporate politics, but I figured the negative publicity, whether aimed at her personally or professionally might not reflect well on a performance evaluation. I assumed there were in-house policies in place for this kind of communication.

"Actually, I was hoping you could ask your nephew to look into it," she continued. "Would you take them, Gerry?" She gave the pile a little nudge in my direction.

Like anyone who had more than casual dealings with me, Catherine knew about my nephew, Skip, the shining star (my term, and his mother's) of the Lincoln Point Police Department, though as far as I knew, she'd never met him. And it wasn't the first time I'd been approached, not for my great wisdom or reputation for good advice, but for my close connection to the police department. Not only through Skip, but also through his mother, my sister-in-law and best friend, Beverly Gowen, a civilian volunteer with the LPPD who was about to marry a retired LPPD detective. Quite a family affair, now that I thought about it. I wanted to remind Catherine that one didn't need to be related to our police force to receive serious attention and the benefits of their excellent work, but she was already in distress, from the notes and from my impatience with her euphemisms.

"It would be better if you took the notes to Skip yourself." I nudged them back toward her. "You can provide the context, and he'd have to deal with you eventually anyway."

"Okay," she said, her voice weak, her resolve doubtful.

"Now back to my question. Who else was adversely affected by your doing business in town?" I hoped that was euphemistic enough for her.

Catherine closed her eyes, as if reading a list in front of her face. Hard as it was to suspect my fellow Lincolnites of evildoing, I did the same.

"The alley between Bebe's and Maisie's shops was eliminated, to accommodate our large structure," Catherine began. "So the easy access to Miller's Mortuary and Ed Carville's convenience store is unavailable."

More PR-speak. I had to admire Catherine's ability to let it flow. Most of us would have said that access was cut off permanently to make room for the giant store's takeover.

"I heard people in the crowd mention that," I said.

"But construction is on the books for a new road to pass right in front of them, and there will be increased parking at the back instead of just the gravel that's there now. Mr. Miller and Eddie have both signed off and seem satisfied."

"How about the other stores on the boulevard?"

"Well, there's Video Jeff's, of course"—either Catherine's face reddened or my imagination projected a blush—"and this place"—she spread her arms to indicate Sadie's customers and well-stocked ice cream chest—"which I don't believe have suffered, except for some inconvenience during construction. The hardware store might even have done better, as our workmen often needed a quick stop for tools and supplies. There's the flower shop, bookstore, fast foods—none of them made a fuss once they accepted the stipend we offered as a gesture for inconveniencing them."

That about covered the main shopping on Springfield Boulevard. At the southern end of the road was Civic Center, comprising the library, the police building, and city hall. I couldn't imagine that anyone in those facilities would be driven to protest the new store or its most visible representative, especially at this late date. The other end of the boulevard, to the north, led past Rutledge Center, a community hall, and then on to the residential district where I lived.

"We have to think outside the box. Sorry to use jargon," Catherine said.

Rather than tell her the expression was familiar even to a layperson like me, I smiled. I picked up the top note again, in case I could glean something from it with a second look.

In a swift movement, Catherine reached over, grabbed the

pile of notes, and swept them all into her briefcase, scratching my hand in the process.

"What...?"

"Sorry," Catherine whispered, tilting her head toward the window.

A tall man with hair about an inch longer than Skip's bona fide buzz cut, wearing a dark suit despite the ninety-plus-degree weather, strode toward us. He traversed Springfield Boulevard on a diagonal course from the end of the block to Sadie's, without regard for the pedestrian walkways.

Behind him trailed a young woman, so much shorter that she was almost jogging to keep up. Halfway across the street, the man said a few words to her and held his hand out, looking like a crossing guard. The young woman dipped into a folder, pulled out a sheet of paper, reached up and placed it in the man's hand.

Craig Palmer III, I presumed. And I was lucky enough to be in a position to meet him.

# Chapter 3

ON SECOND THOUGHT, as the SuperKrafts regional manager approached Sadie's Ice Cream Shop, my initial desire to meet him receded with each step. Hadn't I already spent enough time and energy on SuperKrafts issues? I thought about Maddie, and how wrong she was about who was having all the fun. I wished I were the one setting up the furniture in our new dollhouse, perhaps adding an accessory or two from the new store's stock, enjoying all the other dollhouse entries. It was time I joined my granddaughter. I had enough to do these days, like helping Bev pick out her wedding shoes and starting a new crafts project with my group. I didn't need to become enmeshed in Catherine's complex relationship with the guy at the top. Catherine's boss, aka former lover, probably didn't want to meet me either.

I stood to leave. And was held back once more, with Catherine pressing on my hand. A signal: *Wait, Gerry. Not so fast.*

Craig Palmer pushed through the entrance to Sadie's the way movie cowboys of yore swaggered into saloons, leaving the half doors swinging behind them and stopping all conversation cold.

I was surprised he didn't say, "Howdy," but rather, "Catherine, I've been trying to call you. Your phone is off."

"Oh, I muted it," Catherine said, adding a nervous apology.

"And someone left the door to the street open."

"I'll take care of it right away," Catherine said.

"I locked it myself. You know we had to send the cameras back to the alarm company, so it's even more important to keep all the doors locked." He lowered his voice once he realized that the hoods of Lincoln Point might be listening and ready to take advantage of an unmonitored store.

I found myself channeling Bebe, thinking, *Maybe if you'd used a local alarm company instead of signing a contract with New York...* I was glad Craig was paying no attention to me.

Catherine, looking deflated, with good reason, stood and tried to make a comeback. She cleared her throat and announced, "Craig, this is Geraldine Porter. I've told you about her invaluable assistance with this project."

At times like this, I was grateful for my height. My taller-than-average build came in handy when there was potential for intimidation. Palmer and I were almost at eye level. I could tell he was much younger than I was, about the same age as Catherine, but I noticed that the patches of gray in his brown hair were a close match to mine. Aging quickly, I thought. If I were disposed to wear heels higher than two inches, I'd have passed him up.

Palmer gave me a distracted smile and offered his hand. "Yes, Catherine tells me you've been a big help with the locals," he said, looking over my shoulder. Was he choosing an ice cream flavor from the chest? I doubted it. Thinking up more perks for the locals? I doubted that, too. More like reviewing whatever agenda he had with Catherine.

I shook his hand, then quickly withdrew mine and offered it to the young woman in his wake. "I'm Gerry Porter," I said. "Did you just come in from New York also?"

The small woman seemed surprised to have been noticed but recovered in time to nod and say that her name was Megan Sutley. "Mr. Palmer's administrative assistant," she said. As if I couldn't tell.

"This isn't exactly the place for a business meeting," Palmer said, looking around at Sadie's latest attempt at a lighthearted ambience.

I wholeheartedly disagreed, but I had to admit that Sadie had gone overboard, using her extra money for over-the-top redecorating. She'd never intended her ice cream parlor to be used for serious boardroom talk. The most extreme new attraction was a large booth at the back of the shop. Formerly bright pink vinyl, the booth was now the color and design of a waffle cone, adorned with a giant molded plastic replica of the top of a sundae, including fudge sauce dripping over vanilla ice cream topped with whipped cream, multicolored sprinkles, and a huge cherry. I decided it should be called a maxi-sundae, the opposite of miniature, and thought of the latest room box project Maddie and I had started: a miniature ice cream parlor, of the black-and-white-tile floor variety, with posters of mouthwatering treats on the walls.

While I was mentally shaping tiny scoops of ice cream from polymer clay, Palmer had decided to take the meeting back to SuperKrafts. I wondered why the big man had bothered to cross the street in the first place, instead of sending his admin to fetch Catherine. Unless it was to embarrass her. I cut off my speculation—who was I to try to understand the corporate world?

I said good-bye and placed an order to go—a small cup of summer berry for me and a brownie sundae with extra nuts and no cherry for Maddie. I added a chocolate shake for her baby-sitter-turned-clerk, the ever-patient Jeanine, assuming shakes were on everyone's list of acceptable snacks, and called Maddie on her cell while I waited.

"How's it going over there, sweetheart?" I asked. "Are the houses all set up?"

"Yeah, I had to glue on a few shingles that fell off and Jeanine wanted me to add some grass to the outside. While you were having ice cream."

"I'll be over in a minute with yours. We can take it home and watch whatever video you like."

"And order Sal's pizza for dinner?"

"Only if you eat something green, too." Who said I spoiled my granddaughter?

WHILE Maddie watched, for the fourth time this year that I knew of, a movie that featured a thirteen-year-old girl who was a spy, I snuck out of the room and called Henry.

Henry Baker had run the woodworking shop at ALHS, where he developed and taught in trade and vocational programs while I was teaching English. Between us we probably knew every student who passed through the halls of the high school for a span of three decades. We'd been on the same faculty for all those years, but we'd seen each other rarely, in the lounge or at the occasional full faculty meeting. Then our paths intersected in a big way when we met at a reunion of our students, thirty-year alums, in San Francisco. We'd both been through long ordeals as our spouses passed away, and we both had brilliant, adorable granddaughters the same age—that is, not counting the four-month difference that mattered only to preteens. The rest was recent history.

"I'm giving in to pizza tonight, if you're interested," I told Henry.

"I almost beat you to it, but Taylor vetoed the idea," he said. "Says she has too much homework. I'm still reeling."

"I was afraid of that," I said, and told Henry of Maddie's funk when I mentioned Taylor.

"Trouble in preteen city," Henry said.

"Do you have any clue what it might be about?"

"Nope. I'll see what I can find out. But I don't expect a great outpouring of information."

"Too bad. I ordered an extra-large," I said.

"I could still come over. Kay's here."

"I was hoping you'd say that." Taylor's mother, Kay, was a lawyer. Maybe with some time alone with her daughter, she could cross-examine Taylor and let us know what was going on.

I hung up to find Maddie at my heels. "Is Mr. Baker coming by himself?" she asked.

*Mr. Baker.* Bad sign. Not long ago—yesterday—he was Uncle Henry. "Taylor has a lot of homework," I said. "Funny, don't you think, since it's summer vacation?"

Maddie shrugged. "Nyah."

We settled into our dinner routine, setting placemats, napkins, water glasses, knives and forks. I made a salad for two, plus an extra leaf for Maddie.

"Are you sure there's nothing you want to tell me, sweet-heart?" I asked.

"Is Mr. Baker going to be invited to Aunt Beverly's wed-ding?" she asked.

"I'm sure he is. Is that your real question? You know, you can't keep on—"

*Buzz, buzz. Buzz, buzz.*

Either Maddie was lucky or I needed to pay attention to signs from the universe telling me to mind my own business. I felt a little better when I heard Maddie's, "Hi, Uncle Henry," and not "Nyah." "How come you have the pizza?" she asked him.

"I pulled up at the same time as Sal's delivery boy. I wrestled him to the ground and stole all the pizza in his car." He swung the wide flat box up over his head, causing panic and giggles to erupt. "Ta da!"

We were off to a good start. I was pleased that Maddie vol-untarily piled two pieces of lettuce and a curl of carrot onto her plate. We chatted about Maddie's girl spy movie, our sum-mer projects, and upcoming short trips with great ease, and then Henry tested the waters.

"Taylor can't wait to go to Tahoe in August. How about you, Maddie?" he asked.

Maddie's face tightened. She sucked in her cheeks and drew in a long breath. "I just wish we had a swimming pool," she said.

At least it wasn't another "Nyah." But where had that come from? Maddie was much more of a land-based girl, preferring to ride her bike or click away on her mobile devices than splash around in water. I tried to recall discussion of a swimming pool by her parents, but no such talk came to mind.

"I thought you didn't care much for swimming," I ventured.

"Nobody likes me," she said.

Now I was really worried. Where was my self-confident granddaughter, the one who aced all her classes and lit up even a room full of strangers? "Maddie," I began, at about the same time that Henry, bless him, said, "I like you."

"I can't think of anyone who doesn't—"

*Rumble, rumble. Rumble, rumble.*

An all-too-familiar thundering noise cut me off. At the same time, the chandelier above us began an ominous swing on its gilded chain; the coffee in Henry's mug splashed to the brim and over; a hardback book with a slippery cover on a small table slid ever so slightly in the direction of the dining room window.

*Rumble, rumble. Rattle, rattle. Rumble, rumble. Rattle, rattle.*

An earthquake. The only question was: Is this the Big One?

Maddie gasped and pushed her chair back. "Drop, cover, and hold on!" she yelled, and fell to the floor. A few seconds later, the three of us were crouched under the long dining room table, holding on to its legs. We heard thuds and breaking glass, but no large crashing. Maddie repeated the long form of the mantra she'd been taught. "Drop to the floor, duck under a table or a desk, and hold on even if it moves. Do not run. Do not go outside," she said, on autopilot. "Keep away from bookcases, windows, or anything that can fall on you," she mumbled, then announced, "We're in an earthquake."

Maddie had been drilled well, as all California schoolchildren were. But she hadn't yet experienced enough quakes to take this one in stride. Her eyes were wide, her knuckles white as she held onto her table leg. Henry released his hold on his post and moved over to Maddie's, adding his body to the protection the tabletop offered.

"I think we're clear," I said. "But it's so cozy under here, shall we stay for a while?" A better suggestion than reminding Maddie of the possibility of immediate aftershocks.

Maddie's laugh sounded like a great release of tension. I could tell she was okay when she began to instruct us in what she'd learned from a significant study unit on earthquakes last year. "They used to use pendulums, like the chandelier, only really big, to measure how the ground shaked"—she waved the word away. It seemed Maddie herself had been rattled—"...I mean *shook*. And the San Andreas Fault has made the ground move by two inches every year and in fifteen million years, Los Angeles and San Francisco will be next to each other." She took a long breath, as if she were gasping for air. "I used to live in Los Angeles, Uncle Henry."

"I know that," Henry said. "I'm sure glad you live here now."

"Me, too," I said, from my perch one table leg over.

"Are we ready to guess what magnitude it was?" Henry asked. "When I was in school, we'd all take a guess and the one who came closest would get a prize."

"What kind of prize?" Maddie asked.

"Well, back then a new ruler or a protractor was a big deal."

"Or a composition book," I offered, remembering how I loved the look and feel of a new, blank notebook.

"I think it was a five-point-seven," Maddie said, apparently forgetting that anything that big in magnitude would have caused considerably more disruption. Depending on where the epicenter was, we'd have experienced windows breaking, plaster falling, and even heavy furniture moving. But it made sense that anything that sent us under the table would impress Maddie and be accompanied by a large number.

"I'll say two-point-three," Henry said.

"My turn?" I asked. "You know me and numbers. I have to think. I hate the Richter scale."

"I taught it to you last year," Maddie said.

She was right, but it was hard for a math-challenged person like me to comprehend that a magnitude of five was ten times greater than a magnitude of four, a six was ten times greater than a five, and so on for each step up. But each step also represented more than thirty times as much energy. Huh? It went against all the math I learned in grade school. Maybe I'd have caught on more quickly if I'd grown up in California instead of on the East Coast, where hurricanes were the threat. Whoever was in charge for that first hurricane did it right: call them by first names. I remembered Beulah, Camille, Anita. No math involved.

I screwed up my courage. "Three-point-one," I said.

"Okay, everyone remember what their number is," Maddie said. "I wonder what broke?" she asked, but made no move to find out. Neither did she race to her computer to find out the reported magnitude, as she did whenever any kind of question came up, even in casual conversation, from how many games were played in last year's World Series to how long it took to

cook a twenty-two-pound turkey. It occurred to me that she was
nervous about making the trip from the north end of the house
where we were gathered in the dining room, clear down to the
southeast corner where her computer was stationed.

No sooner were we on our feet—a little wobbly in my case
after all that squatting—than:

*Rumble, rattle. Rumble, rattle.*

Brief gasps all around although the little aftershock was much
shorter and less intense than the main event.

"Whoa," Maddie said, and dropped again anyway.

Henry and I stood under the doorframe for a minute, just in
case. "Once again, I think we're okay," Henry said, then shouted
in mock–SWAT-team mode, "Clear!"

The standard post-earthquake drill began, the "Recover"
phase, after "Prepare" and "Survive," the steps in the manual every
Californian had read, in one form or another. Henry instructed
us to stay put while he inspected the house. He clicked a number
on his phone while he walked and I knew he'd be calling home.

From the noises I'd heard in my home, I expected a few pieces of broken pottery, but no fallen bookcases or large objects. My
late husband, an architect, had been religious about earthquake
safety. Our bookcases were bolted to the walls; major appliances
and the water heater were strapped to studs; our smaller collect-
ibles, potential projectiles, were secured with earthquake putty or
gel. Ken knew what he was doing.

Henry returned from his house tour reporting good news,
except for two casualties, a vase that was part of my collection on
a table in my atrium, and a large serving bowl on a shelf in my
kitchen, both now smashed to smithereens.

The news would travel fast and I figured I'd be contacted by
friends and relatives from near and far. Maddie had already received an "Everything okay?" text from her mother, who was in
Los Angeles for an exhibit of her paintings, followed by a phone
call from her father, from his office at Stanford Medical; Beverly
and Nick, who were at a criminal justice workshop in San Francisco, called with "No movement here for a change"; Henry's

daughter, Kay, the mother of the out-of-favor Taylor, assured him, "We're okay here"; and several friends on the East Coast, who I know pictured a giant crevasse in our living room floor, suggested, "Come back. At least hurricanes give you warning." I was constantly telling my Bronx peeps, as Skip called them, that our quakes were of the ground-rumbling kind, not the movie kind where the earth cracks open and swallows up a semi-truck and a family of six in an SUV.

"Must be a slow news night all over the country," Henry said. "They're making a big deal out of a very small quake." We both noted that years ago, before instant networking and the means to tell the world what we ate for breakfast, news of a small quake wouldn't even have made it as far as the border between California and Oregon.

We reassembled in the living room, silently declaring the dinner party aborted since a topping of dust from the swinging chandelier now covered the pizza. I wondered if our new Super-Krafts store survived, but didn't care enough to make the calls necessary to find out. I hoped that didn't make me a bad person.

"Mom says her paintings are on the good wall at the show," Maddie said, explaining the way seismic waves traveled. We noted that the two items that toppled in my house were on the same side, the west wall of each room, though the atrium and kitchen were overlapping, side by side and shifted with respect to each other. Objects that were hung or shelved on the other walls were undisturbed. Maddie made it clearer than my science teachers in the Bronx those many years ago. But then, the Bronx wasn't known for its earthquakes.

When the calls and texts died down, we finally turned our chairs to face the TV and clicked on the news, where already facts and figures were scrolling across the lower edge of the screen. An estimated half million detectable earthquakes occur in the world each year. The largest recorded earthquake in the world was of magnitude nine-point-five in Chile in 1960, when two million people were left homeless. The famous San Francisco earthquake of 1906 was of magnitude seven-point-eight with an epicenter two miles off shore. Moonquakes occur less frequently but at greater depth, on the moon.

"Fascinating," I said.

"What about today's magnitude?" asked Maddie, not a big fan of history. "Who won the prize?"

"How do they compile the data so quickly?" I wondered aloud.

"They probably have it all ready for when the Big One comes," Henry offered.

Maddie and I shivered at the thought, but reports of local accidents were barely worth a bandage. A man in nearby Sunnyvale had an injury to his toes when his toaster oven fell from the counter, and a retired teacher in Los Altos was hurt when she lost her balance and her arm banged against a file cabinet. I was impressed that the young woman reporting was able to contain herself and kept her smile in check.

"I hope my teacher is okay," Maddie said.

Henry grabbed the remote. "Here it comes."

Back at the anchor desk, a middle-aged man with curly locks and glasses informed us that "Today's earthquake in the South Bay had an epicenter in Cupertino. At six thirty-two this evening, it weighed in at a magnitude of three-point-one."

Maddie gasped. "That was exactly Grandma's guess," she said, doing a heroic job at being happy for me. "I can't believe it."

I couldn't believe it either. I remembered a favorite expression of Ken's: "Sometimes it's better to be lucky than good."

"Didn't we say the one who was farthest off would win the prize?" Henry said.

"That's how I remember it," I said.

With not a trace of embarrassment, Maddie held her hands out, ready to accept a prize for coming up with the number that was most off the mark. Henry flipped a dollar bill into her open palms.

Maddie skipped around with glee. Not a single "Nyah." So what if it had taken an earthquake to brighten her mood?

———

"MAYBE I should sleep with you tonight," Maddie said at bed-time. "In case, you know, something happens, and then we'd be together to help each other."

No argument from me, as I tucked her into one side of my queen-size bed. She settled on the pillow. "What's the biggest earthquake you were ever in?" she asked.

I told her, with some hyperbole, where I was and what I felt during the six-point-nine Loma Prieta earthquake, which famously interrupted the World Series in 1989. That quake, with an epicenter south of San Francisco, lasted fifteen to twenty seconds and was felt as far away as San Diego, five hundred miles south.

"Wow," she said. "Did anyone die?"

"Sadly, yes. Somewhere between sixty and seventy people, but thousands were injured or left homeless."

"That part's very sad," Maddie said, by which I assumed she meant that all other aspects of earthquakes were kind of fun.

"What's this about wishing you had a swimming pool? And that no one likes you?" I asked, hoping to catch her off guard in this special quiet time.

Smarter than me by far, Maddie stretched her long arms above her head and came out with a wide and loud yawn. "I'm really sleepy, Grandma. G'night."

"Sure you are," I said, and tickled her where I knew it would count. Then I left her alone. We'd both had enough for one day.

A QUICK *buzz, buzz.*

My doorbell. Just when I thought the day was over. I should have known better, since my atrium lights, visible from the street, were still on. I clattered to the front door in my noisy clogs. I checked the peephole but I'd already guessed who'd be cruising about for coffee or tea and my special ginger cookies at eleven o'clock at night. My nephew Skip, another fun-loving Porter family redhead. And I would never shut him out, no matter what the hour.

"Hey, Aunt Gerry."

I looked at Skip's attire—khakis, a light blue shirt, and a

windbreaker, about halfway between "on the job" and "officially off duty." "Hey, yourself," I said. "Are you on earthquake patrol?"

"You could say that. Such a small one, there's not much damage anywhere, just a lot of spilled drinks and crooked pictures. And false alarms everywhere, like in a bad comedy. It's almost a joke on Facebook, too. Someone posted a photo of a tipped-over lawn chair, with a caption, 'We will never forget the Lincoln Point 3.1.' Like that."

"I'd think they'd be counting their blessings."

"Not so much. Not my Facebook friends anyway." Skip had already located the cookies and munched away while he helped me set up and then pour from a pitcher of iced tea. "But you never know about that one little thing, or big thing, that falls over that might be hazardous, and no one is around to check it. So the brass like us to go to selected locales and informally inspect. We look in on empty public buildings, houses where people are on vacation, closed shops, folks who live alone, that kind of thing."

"You mean old folks," I said, exaggerating the motion of my atrium rocking chair.

Skip smiled. "Sort of."

"And even big-shot detectives like my favorite nephew get to help out."

"Your only nephew, and it's better than sitting with my feet up on my desk."

"So this is an official earthquake call for your report?"

"Could be, if I need the points."

I smiled. "How comforting. Did you find anything interesting in your rounds?"

"Not so far. Like I said, unless you count spilled coffee."

To illustrate, and to make me nervous, Skip tipped his glass so the tea nearly ran out onto my new area rug. Too bad Maddie wasn't awake to laugh. In fact, I was surprised the doorbell hadn't awakened her; usually even her sleeping radar was tuned to the arrival of her first cousin once removed, aka Uncle Skip, day or night.

We'd hardly had time to catch up on his mother's wedding

plans (Skip's sixth stint as best man, he informed me) and on his own love life (currently uncommitted after a recent breakup with my lovely next-door neighbor), when his cell phone rang. I heard one side of a familiar conversation.

"Uh-huh." Pause. "Where?" Pause. I handed Skip a small notebook and pen I kept handy for such occasions. He nodded thanks. "Uh-huh. Name?" Pause. "Tonight, huh?" Pause. "On my way."

"Don't tell me," I said. "It's 'gotta go' time."

He flipped the notebook shut and stuck it in his pocket. I didn't ask for it back. "There's an earthquake casualty after all," he said.

I pulled a plastic bag from a cabinet in the kitchen and filled it with cookies to go. "Something serious?"

"Uh-huh. We spoke too soon about the benevolent quake. A guy was killed when a large knickknack or some heavy object fell on his head."

"How awful. Is it anyone we know?"

"You're asking, is he a former student of yours? Not this time," he said, on his way out the door. "He works for that big new store downtown. Poor guy just flew in today from New York." Skip kissed my cheek. "This is one case you won't have a connection to."

*Don't be so sure*, I said under my breath.

# Chapter 4

I STOOD WITH my back to the closed door, listening to Skip's car drive off. I could hardly forget his short visit and go to bed. As I made my way back to the atrium chair, I reviewed the conversation I'd heard. There was only one "big new store downtown" as far as I knew. SuperKrafts. And how many guys who worked for them had flown in from New York today? It had to be Craig Palmer. Catherine's boss and ex-boyfriend was killed in a tiny temblor. What were the odds? Would any New Yorker ever come to California again? How would Catherine get through this disastrous turn?

I couldn't erase the image of the strong, in-charge leader as he was earlier today in Sadie's Ice Cream Shop, now lying limp on the floor of his newest project.

On a more personal level, I regretted every bad thought I'd had about Palmer during the few minutes I'd known him. I thought how this might have been his first trip to the West Coast. He'd probably survived all manner of snowstorms on the East Coast, perhaps even a blizzard or two, only to die in a quake that hardly disturbed the teacups in my dining room hutch.

I had my hand on my phone to call Catherine before I realized there was a possibility that I was way off. I'd heard only a quick summary from Skip as he'd run out the door and that was hearsay from someone on the phone. That's how rumors got started and stories got twisted, I reminded myself. It wasn't such a leap backward to think that each fact had become convoluted in the telling, and the unfortunate victim was instead a woman from New Jersey or New Mexico who'd flown in last week and worked for any of the giant chain stores between San Jose and Palo Alto, making a stop in Lincoln Point for a quick bite at the fast food restaurant next to SuperKrafts.

As Ken always told me, my imagination was suited for fiction, or miniatures, which were a kind of fiction themselves. What dollhouse decorator didn't think of herself as lounging in the elaborate Victorian living room she'd created, reading from a richly bound book, listening to lovely music from the ornate harp in the corner? That was the romantic fiction. The truth was that the sofa was made from a wooden block, the leather volume was a piece of Styrofoam that didn't open, and the harp strings were dental floss, but that didn't stop a miniaturist from seeing luxury and comfort, and hearing beautiful sounds.

I turned on the TV news, at low volume so as not to wake Maddie, but the earthquake had already receded into history and there was no mention yet of an out-of-town victim in Lincoln Point.

I wandered back to my bedroom and squeezed in beside Maddie, who'd be sorry she'd missed her Uncle Skip and a lot of speculating.

WHEN my phone rang at one-fifteen in the morning, I had the feeling I'd soon have the answer to which of my speculations held merit. I picked up quickly and carried the phone into the atrium, hoping Maddie, who'd jolted up at the sound, would fall back on her pillow and continue a sweet dream.

"Mrs. Porter…Gerry…you'll never believe this," Catherine said. She spoke in halting phrases. "Craig…Craig Palmer, my… my boss…he's dead. The earthquake." Catherine seemed oblivious to the fact that she'd awakened me, with no clue that it wasn't the middle of the day. "Something in the store fell on him. I'm not sure what, but it must have been heavy…something from high up, I guess…I don't know. I just know he's dead."

My hopes that I'd misinterpreted Skip's summons dashed, I walked to the kitchen and put on the kettle. It might be a long night. "I'm so sorry, Catherine."

If I was worried about finding the right words to say, I needn't have. Catherine hadn't called to listen. She continued on her own. "Megan and I left him in the store going over some books with Leo. He wasn't very happy about some of the perks we've been handing out and I can't believe we actually fought over stupid things like whether the store would be open or closed on Labor Day, and all the while..."

I heard an opening and was about to offer to go to her hotel if she wanted to talk. I was in my "cookies cure everything" mode, packing a few treats for her in my mind. No one should be in mourning in a bare, foodless hotel room. Then I remembered Maddie. As much as she'd insist that she was old enough to be left alone, I wouldn't leave her, especially after the traumatic shaking—of the house and her body—that had gone on this evening. I explained it all to Catherine.

"But if you can get yourself here, we can have some tea," I added.

"Oh, really, Mrs. Porter? That would be so great. I need to get out of this room. If you're sure it won't be too much of an imposition."

"Not at all."

My new plan for the night, rather than sleeping, was to change out of my nightclothes into something more suitable for company, and arrange cookies on a plate. What else did one serve a guest who was expected at nearly two in the morning? Cheese and crackers? A ham sandwich? I'd have to be ready for anything.

CATHERINE had the presence of mind to remember Maddie and knock on my door instead of ringing the bell. She was also well put together for someone who'd been in such a state over the phone. She wore loose pants, a short top, and a dark shawl against the cool night air. I figured the act of dressing and having somewhere to go had distracted her and calmed her down, which was part of the reason I'd invited her over, the other part being to console a woman who had been my student, and then a colleague of sorts.

Catherine fell onto my shoulder, a little tricky, given my extra inches in height. I did my best to hunch over to make it easier for her. I felt rather than heard her sobs. When she pulled away, she reached into her large tote and pulled out a bottle of wine. Apparently she was concerned that I had only tea in the house. Not far from the truth, though there was probably a bottle of wine somewhere in my cupboard, brought by a guest during the last holiday season.

"Put this away for the next time I visit," she said, handing me the bottle. "Or for yourself. I realize I shouldn't drink any alcohol tonight. Do you have something cold?"

"Iced tea coming up," I said, following her wise instruction to stash the wine for now. "Can I get you anything else? A sandwich? Fruit?" She blotted her face with a tissue and shook her head. While I prepared my second after-hours tea service, Catherine talked about her own late-night phone call.

"Leo phoned me. He said the police found Craig around eleven o'clock. They were patrolling downtown and the store was on their beat. They went in to make sure everything was okay, just routine, and they found him." She paused for a breath. "They called Leo and..." Her sobs took over.

Leo, the temporary (he hoped) manager, the large, vocal man who'd only recently joined the team at joint meetings between SuperKrafts and town reps. In spite of reported enmity between Craig and Leo (as there seemed to be among all the store's New York crew), he must have been stunned by the news.

Catherine's sobbing ceased; she took a deep breath, which ended in a moan. I wished I could do something to comfort her. For now, refilling her glass, pushing the plate of cookies toward her, and letting her talk would have to do.

"Leo got the call from the police, maybe because the manager's name is on some list? I don't know how they figure these things out. And Leo called me," she repeated. She looked up with a sharp movement. "Megan," she said. "Someone needs to call Megan. Craig's admin. I can't believe I walked right out of the hotel, not even thinking of Megan. She got in last night. You met her today. I need to call her." Catherine had gone into harried mode, as I suspected was normal for her in the halls of her New York office building.

"Let's not worry about Megan right now," I said. "I'll bet Leo already called her."

"I don't know. They were pretty mad at each other at the end."

"Leo and Megan were angry with each other?" I was having trouble following Catherine's pronouns. I blamed the late hour for my foggy brain.

"Craig, too. It was Craig and Megan against Leo. It was awful, and now he's dead. Craig's dead."

"What was the argument about?" I asked, wondering how long we should continue on the topic of Craig and his death. Maybe instead I should be asking Catherine questions about her parents, her life in New York, what was new on Broadway these days.

"Leo is anxious to get home to New York and Craig was pushing for him to stay here until the end of the year. Craig isn't Leo's boss, not technically, and that's been a problem in itself. And Megan was on Craig's side because, you know, she's his admin."

"Six more months? Why?" I thought of the promise SuperKrafts management had made, that a Lincoln Point resident would be put in Leo's job very soon. No specific date was given, but we town reps assumed "very soon" meant three or four weeks at most.

"Are you asking me why Leo wants to go home?" Catherine asked.

"No, why did Craig want him to stay?" I wasn't ready to hear how Leo wanted to leave Lincoln Point because the town was a cultural wasteland and he missed the Carnegie Deli, MOMA, the New York Philharmonic (though the ALHS orchestra wasn't that bad, which was how people characterized most amateur performances), and perhaps his family.

"Leo says it's because he's up for a promotion above Craig, and the longer he's away the more likely it is that Craig would be promoted to that job instead. They've always been competitive like that. And Megan would probably get a promotion either way, so I don't know why she was so much on Craig's side, except, like I said, she sort of has to be."

Office politics. Henry and I, two retirees from ALHS, talked about it sometimes, how neither of us could abide all the machinations and jockeying for position that went on in our little corner of academe. I could only guess how much more brutal things would get when the stakes were high, as they must be in the corporate world of New York. It was a strange juxtaposition at SuperKrafts: bickering and infighting among those who provided the materials for hobbies that were meant to be soothing, community building, and—in the case of miniatures—adorable.

Catherine closed her eyes. Coming to terms with Craig's death? "Well, Leo won't be getting any competition from Craig," she said, through tears. "Not anymore." She drew in her breath. "And me and Craig, too. We fought so much when we broke up and I thought it was cooling down, but yesterday he started in on me again, wanting to give us another chance, and I blew him off. I mean, not that I'd want this for him anyway, but it feels so..."

"It's awful," I agreed, reaching over to put my hand on hers. We'd taken seats in my atrium, across from each other at a small table. I'd thought it would help to be in an open area, with my grand ficus and my skylight window to the stars. Maybe there were some happy memories to unleash. Now I had the thought that the living room might have been better, in case she wanted to lean back and fall asleep on my couch.

"Do you know Craig's family?" I asked.

"His parents live in Manhattan. I've met them a couple of times. They travel in different circles from my mom and dad. And he doesn't have any siblings. He really is a good guy, you know." She paused. "I mean he was. He could be tough but that's because he wanted the best for the company, and for us. When he had to, he could mellow out."

It was hard to picture a mellowed-out Craig Palmer, but I'd had only the slimmest of interactions with him.

*Tap, tap. Tap, tap.*

Another thoughtful guest. As I got up to check, the door opened slowly. I'd forgotten to lock it after Catherine released me from our hug. Catherine tensed now at the sound of someone entering, but as I expected, it was Skip who poked his head in.

"I saw the light on. Everything okay?"

"Do all Lincoln Point citizens get this treatment, or am I special?" I asked.

"Both," he said, with a teasing smile. "But there's more attention when there are cookies involved."

As much as she'd heard about Skip, I didn't think Catherine had met him. I introduced him as LPPD's star homicide detective, and Catherine as a former LP native who was now a successful businesswoman in New York City. A round of small talk revealed that the two young people, the same age, plus or minus a few years, had just missed each other at ALHS.

"I'm sorry about your friend," Skip said, when I mentioned Catherine's connection to our earthquake casualty. "It must be quite a shock, but you've come to the right place for comfort." Skip had poured himself a glass of tea and pulled up a chair. "I hope the earthquake itself didn't spook you."

"Not really. As Gerry says, I grew up here. I was almost eighteen when I left, so I've been through a few quakes," Catherine said.

"Where were you when it hit today?"

"In my hotel room. I felt it, and the alarm clock on the night table shook and sort of slid for a sec, but nothing was damaged."

"That must make it seem all the more strange that your friend was killed."

Where was Skip going with this? I knew my nephew and this wasn't his usual line of social interaction, especially when meeting someone for the first time. Someone who was grieving the loss of a friend.

"Yes, it seems incredibly strange," Catherine said. "I still can't believe it."

"Say, Catherine, I know it's late, but if you could answer some questions regarding your association with Craig Palmer"—Skip made this seem casual, an off-the-wall thought—"it would be a big help to us, filling out our reports for the bosses and all. While things are fresh in your mind."

"Of course, but I don't really know anything. I wasn't there when it happened."

"Did you see Mr. Palmer today?" Skip asked.

Catherine closed her eyes, perhaps to hold back tears, perhaps to check a mental clock to help her answer the question. "Yes, we had a meeting in the back room, what will be the employee's lounge, at SuperKrafts."

"It would help if I could get a few details. Nothing proprietary, of course, just what was the agenda, who was there, when did the meeting start, when did it end? Like that."

Catherine took a deep breath. "There was Craig, Megan, who's his admin, and Leo, our manager. And me." She looked at me. "We started soon after the gathering at Sadie's, Gerry. Around three o'clock?"

I thought back through the many hours. Maddie and I had arrived home a little before three, ready to run her first video. "That sounds about right," I said.

"My part of the meeting was over by five-ish," Catherine continued. "But the others continued while I went onto the main retail floor to help Jeanine, our associate."

"Associate, that's a salesperson, right?" Skip asked.

"Uh-huh."

"Jeanine Larkin. You know her," I said to Skip, trying to slow him down. I could see that Catherine was beginning to get uncomfortable, calling up disturbing memories. "Jeanine used to baby-sit a lot for Maddie. She just graduated high school and is going for her community college degree at night."

My rude nephew made no comment other than to give me a nod that said, yes, he did remember Jeanine, followed by raised eyebrows that asked why it mattered and why I was interrupting him.

"What was the meeting about?" Skip asked, returning to his straight-on face-to-face position with Catherine.

"Just business stuff. The Grand Opening celebration coming up, various sales and specials."

"So you helped Jeanine for how long?"

"Maybe an hour."

"And the other three were still there when you left?"

"I...I'm not sure. I never went back to the meeting room."

"And where did you go when you left the building? Around six was it?"

"Yes, Jeanine left first and I left soon after."

"To go...?" Skip asked.

"It was still kind of warm so I walked around for a while, down by the library."

"So, you left the meeting with Mr. Palmer at about five, left the store at about six, then walked around?"

"Maybe it wasn't that late, maybe I left earlier. What does it matter?"

"Okay, but in any case, you were back at the hotel by six thirty-two?"

"Excuse me?" Catherine said.

"Six thirty-two. That's when the earthquake hit, and you said you were in your hotel room when it hit. Where did you say you were staying again?"

Catherine hadn't said, and Skip knew it. She looked rattled, as if there'd been another quake, which is how I was feeling also. She folded her arms across her chest, adjusted her shawl, and fidgeted in her chair. And why wouldn't she be flustered? She was being interrogated by a homicide detective. Why? I wondered. Craig Palmer had been hit by a falling object in an earthquake. Hadn't he?

"More tea, anyone?" I asked. "I can cut a fresh lemon."

Catherine looked at her watch. "I really should get going. I've kept you up long enough already, Gerry." She stood and brushed invisible specks from her pants, and picked up her tote. She seemed annoyed enough to ask for her wine back. "Nice to meet you, Skip. Good luck with the reports," she said, with an insincerity that I could taste.

Skip reached into his jacket pocket and pulled out a card. I winced. I'd hoped he wouldn't do that. "Take this, please, Catherine. And call me if you think of anything else."

Catherine plucked the card from Skip's hand, and without looking at it, dropped it into her tote. She gave me a small wave and headed for the door. I joined her in the short walk past the ficus.

"I'm so sorry if we made you uncomfortable," I said, assuming part of the blame, for not interrupting Skip sooner.

Catherine shook her head. "I'm just tired," she said. "Thanks for…" She seemed to be struggling to think of something to be grateful for.

"Call me or come by any time," I said. I heard no response.

As soon as the lock clicked into place, I turned to my nephew.

"Speak," I said.

"What?"

"What, indeed. What was that about? You were grilling her as if she were a suspect in one of your murder investigations."

Skip raised his eyebrows and bit his upper lip, a sure sign of pressure. He spread his palms, as if to say…

And I finally saw it. I drew in my breath. "Craig Palmer was murdered, wasn't he?"

A slow nod and a sigh were all I needed for a reply. I put on more water, for coffee this time. The day was getting longer and longer.

# Chapter 5

SKIP INDULGED ME with an explanation of his behavior toward my guest. He'd just learned that Craig Palmer's death wasn't caused by the three-point-one, though his killer apparently hoped that would be the assumption. Once Skip realized I might know the victim, he'd come by to tell me, though he claimed he wouldn't have awakened me if my house had been dark.

"But when I saw the car outside, I asked myself, 'Who could possibly be visiting my aunt at this hour, if not a suspect in my case?'" he said.

"How can you say that?"

"Because you're, like, the Lincoln Point Guide to Everything and Everyone. You're at most one degree of separation from anyone in town. More sought after than the mayor probably."

"It's my connection to you that sends everyone my way," I said. "I'm the go-to person for anything that involves the police or might involve the police."

Ignoring my disclaimer, Skip went on. "So I thought, 'Here's my chance.' I wanted to get as much as I could out of whoever was visiting you before they knew that we knew we had a murder on our hands."

"You didn't have to be rude to her."

"I wasn't that rude. You have to admit, Catherine Duncan is a good candidate. Employee, former lover."

"You know that already? You work fast."

He stood briefly and took a bow. "Glad you noticed."

"How do you know for sure it was murder?" I asked.

"I'll explain later. After all you're a suspect, too"—he was saved by his grin—"but for now, I'd like your take on the principals, the people meeting in that back room."

Teasing aside, I knew I'd soon be giving my statement, along with everyone else who was connected to Craig Palmer, especially on the day of his murder.

I reviewed what I knew for Skip. There had been three meetings that I knew of—first, the one in the store, with Catherine, Bebe, and Maisie, then the impromptu Sadie's meeting, and finally, the late afternoon meeting among only the SuperKrafts employees. I assumed Skip was most interested in the last one, the gathering that seemed to have ended in murder.

"But I wasn't at the three o'clock meeting, so all I know is what Catherine told me," I said.

"Understood." He reached for his fifth or sixth cookie and though I didn't ask why, he offered a defense. "They're smaller than usual, Aunt Gerry," he said, then, "Go for it. Just give me a rundown on whatever you know about the meetings."

It had occurred to me while Skip was badgering my guest that Catherine didn't mention the argument that had erupted at the final meeting with Craig Palmer, nor the fight she and Craig had over their relationship. I could understand why she wouldn't want to share the details, since at first she didn't think of herself as being formally questioned by the police in my atrium. But I decided I'd be sorry if I didn't dump everything I knew onto Skip, right now. I told him what I knew about Leo's wanting to go back to New York to claim a possible promotion, and Craig and Megan's wanting him to stay in Lincoln Point for the rest of the year. Maybe to thwart Leo's upgrade, maybe for some other reason. I ended by making light of a possible ex-lovers' quarrel sometime during a break in the three o'clock meeting.

"As far as all the career maneuvers, I don't know how much clout Craig had, but I gathered it was significant enough to cause stress among them," I added.

"That much trouble in a crafts store?" he asked.

"Politics," I said. "It's everywhere. Except in the Lincoln

Point Police Department, which I suppose runs on brotherly love." Skip pretended to gag. "There's also the local front," I said, taking a big gulp of air.

I hated to speak ill of my neighbors, and surely wouldn't have if I'd been talking to any other officer of the law. The fact that I was telling my nephew made it different somehow. Skip was thoroughly honest and dedicated not only to his job but also to the citizens of his hometown. I knew he would use the information carefully. Skip was a modest guy in spite of his meteoric (my word) rise in the ranks of the LPPD, the youngest homicide detective in the squad. So what if he used "Hail to the Chief" as the ring tone on his cell phone.

"There's something else," I began. "About that earlier meeting, before we all went to Sadie's. I'm not sure who else was present, but certainly Catherine, Maisie Bosley, and Bebe Mellon."

"Yes? "

"Did you happen to hear anything about a public display of anger?" I asked.

"You mean the fight between Bebe and Maisie on Springfield Boulevard?" he asked.

"You are good. Let me put that in context for you."

I recapped the tensions around SuperKrafts' taking over the spaces formerly belonging to Maisie and Bebe. "Maisie seems to have adjusted, but it's been hard for Bebe to let go. Not for a minute do I think she'd hurt anyone over it."

"I'll take it all under advisement. Thanks a lot, Aunt Gerry. We need to get you on the payroll."

"I'll stick to being the official baker."

"Works for me. Anything else come to mind?"

"There's one other little twist. Video Jeff."

"The game store Jeff? Jeff Slattery?"

I nodded, and though I was beginning to feel like the worst kind of snitch, laid it all out for Skip—the high school romance between Catherine and Jeff, Bebe's little brother; how the relationship went south fifteen years ago when Catherine left town with her family, but might be heading north at the moment.

"This is over and above Catherine's not-quite-ended romance with Craig?"

I confirmed his assessment, but drew the line at telling Skip about the notes Catherine had been receiving at her hotel room. Whether pertinent to the love triangle or not, the threats in the notes were directed to Catherine, after all, not to the murdered Craig Palmer. If Catherine wanted the help of the police with the letters, she could ask for it herself, as I'd recommended in the first place. Besides, if I blabbed any more, I'd never hear a secret in this town again.

Not surprisingly, Skip sensed my discomfort. "I know this is hard for you, Aunt Gerry, and believe me, I won't abuse this. Kidding aside, you know I value your insights."

No wonder I loved my nephew.

When my atrium clock struck three, we both stood up, taking the chime as an ending bell of some kind.

"Are you going to be able to get any sleep?" I asked Skip, whose eyelids were at the lowest still-awake position I'd ever seen.

"Not likely. This is an unusual situation in that some of the prime suspects could get on a plane to JFK any minute."

"I hadn't thought of that."

"Maybe if we're lucky, a local will be the guilty party," he said with a grin.

"Skip! Are you trying to annoy me tonight? This morning?"

"No, but I am a little grouchy." Skip indicated the object of his grouchiness by tilting his head toward my neighbor on the left, his on-again, off-again girlfriend, June Chinn, a tech writer in a Silicon Valley software firm. Fortunately, June and I stayed friends no matter what the weather was between her and my nephew. His mother, Bev, and I had been rooting for June from the beginning of their dating life.

"How big is this tiff with June?"

Skip sighed. "Dollhouse size."

Whatever that meant.

———

"I FELT another shock last night," Maddie said at breakfast. Although we were eating later than usual—nine o'clock—both morning and breakfast seemed to come fast on the heels of my post-midnight snacks.

"Really? An aftershock?" I asked.

"Uh-huh," Maddie said, between gulps of orange juice. "And I woke up and you weren't in bed."

"I must have been raiding the fridge."

Maddie gave me a sideways look. "Then I thought I heard Uncle Skip's voice."

"Imagine that."

"I wanted to get up, but my legs were, like, I couldn't move them, so I just zonked out again."

"I'm glad you were able to go back to sleep."

"Is there a case, Grandma?"

I should have known. I couldn't remember exactly when Maddie became obsessed with cases. Before she could say the word properly, it seemed to me. More than once Skip had used her extraordinary computer skills to help in an investigation, which thrilled her. I was proud of her, but also worried that she was headed for a life of crime. Crime fighting, that is. It was enough to worry about my nephew in his professional role; in my dreams my granddaughter was in a much less hazardous occupation. Like building dollhouses, for example.

"Uncle Skip is busy with his job," I said.

"Anything I can help with?"

"I'm sure he'll call you if he needs you. Don't you have a book to read for school?"

"I thought the case might be about the man who died in the earthquake."

"What man?" A lame response but I'd been startled by Maddie's remark. Had my granddaughter been eavesdropping last night? It wouldn't have been the first time, but generally she made an appearance eventually when she heard something interesting and wanted in.

"It's on the Internet. It said a man in Lincoln Point was killed when a big vase fell on him. That must have been awful."

A vase was the murder weapon? Maddie already knew more than I did. Maybe Internet news, rather than via a cop nephew, was the way to get information. "Did they say how he died?" I asked her, wondering if the word "murder" had come up.

"I told you. A big vase fell on his head. From the earthquake. That's why I was confused. If it was an accident then Uncle Skip wouldn't have anything to investigate, right, Grandma?"

"If it was an accident, that's right."

"Hmm," Maddie said. "You're making it sound like it wasn't an accident."

"You know, we should check our earthquake kits," I said.

"Grandma, you're not answering me." She paused. "Oh, never mind. Let's check our kits and then if we need supplies we can go downtown and buy them."

Downtown, where the action was. How had I allowed this to happen? What normal eleven-year-old would rather see crime scene tape than visit a theme park? On the other hand, her grandmother had the same preference.

*Dum dum, da da dum, da da dum.*

My cell phone, a Sousa march programmed by Maddie in honor of the next holiday, the Fourth of July. I was treated to (or subjected to, depending on her choice) a new ring tone whenever she felt the need to fiddle with a mobile device.

"Mrs. Porter? This is Jeff Slattery. It's been a while since I've seen you or talked to you."

Video Jeff, Bebe's kid brother. "Jeff, of course. Congratulations on the new look for your shop. I've only seen the outside, but I can tell that you've put a lot of work into it."

"Yeah, thanks. I guess it looks less like a dive now, huh?" Close to what I was thinking, but no need for me to confirm it. "Mrs. Porter, the police have picked up Bebe. They didn't say it but I know they think my sister killed Palmer."

Jeff sounded fraught with worry. I didn't know him or his store very well. I'd had him as a student only in a freshman composition class, and hardly ever set foot in his arcade. I felt a massive pang of guilt—wasn't I the one who'd steered Skip toward a disgruntled Bebe?

"I'm sure they're questioning anyone who had anything to do with Craig Palmer and all the negotiations for the store."

"I don't know. They went to her house early this morning. She called me about eight o'clock."

"Have they actually arrested her?"

"I don't think so. They let her call me and I saw her for a couple of minutes. That's a good sign, isn't it?"

"It sounds good," I said, hoping I sounded convincing.

"But they're saying she can't go home yet. I know you're connected to the police department." At that moment I wished Skip could have heard this confirmation that my so-called claim to fame in town was due to him. "Is that normal procedure?" Jeff asked.

Only if they expected to find something within a certain time frame that I couldn't remember. I tried to recall Skip's tutorials. Twenty-four hours? Or was it forty-eight, and then they had to release a suspect or charge her with the crime, and they wouldn't do that unless they thought they had enough evidence that pointed to her. I decided not to share that much with her brother.

"Jeff, if Bebe didn't hurt Mr. Palmer—"

"She didn't, Mrs. Porter. She couldn't have. You know her. She can sound mean sometimes, but she's all talk. She's really a very gentle person."

I wondered if Jeff had ever seen his sister angry. Or heard her vitriol against SuperKrafts and those who represented the store.

"Would you like me to see what I can find out, Jeff?" I wanted to take back the offer almost as soon as it left my mouth. Who was I to pretend to hand out hope with respect to the dealings of the LPPD and their investigations?

But when I heard Jeff's response, a deep sigh that I took as great relief and gratitude, the reason he'd called me, I couldn't retreat. "Would you, Mrs. Porter? I hate to impose on you or your nephew, but that would be so great. Thank you, thank you."

"I have to ask you something, Jeff."

"Shoot."

"Did your sister know that you and Catherine were seeing each other again?"

A long pause. I figured I'd caught Jeff by surprise with my insider knowledge. "Not until yesterday," he said when he came back on the line. "Bebe came into the shop, which she hardly ever does, and found me and Catherine in the back. We were arguing, but she could tell that we were, you know…together."

Interesting that lovers could argue in a way that someone knew they were…lovers. Another mystery. Besides that, I was building a new image of Catherine, arguing with her current ex-boyfriend and also with her former ex-boyfriend, who was now her current boyfriend. Busy life. I wondered how she kept it all straight.

"How did your sister respond when she saw you two?"

"She was mad, but she knew there was nothing she could do about it. I'm not seventeen anymore. Or even twenty. What does this have to do with Palmer's murder?"

"I'm not sure, Jeff, but if I'm going to help Bebe, I want to know as much as possible about her state of mind."

"Okay, sure. I get it."

My next question should have been, "Where were you when the vase crashed onto Craig's head?" but I couldn't bring myself to ask it. There must have been some reason the police picked up Bebe and not her brother. If Jeff knew of Craig's reluctance to accept the end of his affair with Catherine, then Jeff had a strong reason to want the former lover out of the way.

"I'll do my best, but I can't promise anything, Jeff."

"I know, but just try. That's all I'm asking."

Only when I hung up did I notice that Maddie had been a silent partner in the phone call, her attention glued to my side of the conversation. She held her cereal spoon as if it were a pitchfork, her eyes wide and expectant.

"You're going to help him, right, Grandma?"

"I'm going to try."

"Are you expecting to drop me off at Taylor's?"

"The thought crossed my mind."

Maddie shook her head with great passion. "Uh-uh."

"Are you going to tell me what's wrong between you two?"

"Nothing's wrong. I just want to go with you. You know I love seeing Uncle Skip and his friends at the station."

It was hard for me to argue since Maddie did always want to accompany me to the LPPD. Wasn't that a thrill for every pre-teen? But I knew this time the scales were tipped against being with Taylor, no matter what the alternative was. I decided not to push it. It was true that all of Skip's coworkers in uniform loved her and I could count on at least one of them giving Maddie a tour of a corner of the building she hadn't yet visited, or failing that, giving her free access to the food in the lunchroom.

"Be ready in a half hour," I said, and she skipped off.

BEFORE I slithered into the police station and skulked around for information, I needed to call both Bev and Henry to reschedule dates. I called Henry first. We'd planned to work this morning on a miniature ice cream parlor for the ALHS auction. He was building and painting the box that would hold tiny tubs of crafts clay-cum-ice cream and a counter with the world's smallest tip jar. I had another reason for calling him—Henry was also likely to know Jeff better than I did. He was too modest to brag about the classes full of students, mostly boys, who for one reason or another didn't have college in their future, but needed a mentor and a creative outlet for their talents. Henry was the man, and his woodworking shop was the place.

It was immediately clear that Henry had the same facts that I had about Craig Palmer's murder, his liaison with the Internet being Taylor. His granddaughter and her hardworking attorney parents lived in the house that Henry owned and Taylor's mother grew up in, a convenient arrangement for all.

"How about this turn of events, huh?" Henry asked. "A murder disguised as an earthquake, and a small trembler at that. It's tragic and so hard to fathom."

I agreed. "Craig's family is in New York. I can't imagine how hard it is for his parents, learning that their son is dead, and his body is all the way across the country. I hope things will be cleared up so they can at least have some closure."

We both paused and I realized I hadn't taken the time to acknowledge the death of a man barely out of his youth. Henry and I had each suffered the loss of a spouse and knew the toll it took. The death of a relative or a friend or even a business associate changed everything, and a violent death was like an earthquake, rattling the foundation of life for so many people. I couldn't imagine how much more difficult it would be to lose a child.

I heard a long sigh from Henry, getting ready to move on. "You were with him yesterday, weren't you? Before dinner?" he asked.

"We were introduced; that's about it, though his name has come up a lot." I briefed Henry on the after-hours visitors I'd entertained, and then got to my question. "How well do you know Jeff Slattery?"

"Video Jeff? Nice kid." I didn't remind him that the kid was now in his mid-thirties. For most of us, our students were forever "kids" no matter how many children of their own they had. "He hung around the shop a lot," Henry continued. "In fact, I thought for sure he'd go into woodcrafts more seriously when he graduated. I got him a spot at a school in Oregon where an old pal of mine started a special program that Jeff would have fit right into. He could have gotten an associate's degree. He kept saying, maybe in a couple of years, but he ended up taking over the arcade instead."

"Apparently he had a Plan A that didn't work out," I said. "After two years, when his sweetheart, Catherine Duncan, graduated, they were supposed to run off to make their fortune together."

"In a land far away," Henry said, in a tone that called for cueing romantic music.

"Or in Oregon."

"What's up with you and Jeff? Why are you asking about him?"

"He called to tell me that Bebe was taken in for questioning this morning, about Palmer's murder. That's what I'm assuming, anyway. Jeff isn't clear on whether or not she's been arrested."

"And he wants your help, I'll bet."

"Uh-huh."

"Uh-oh."

"What is it?" I asked.

"I'd be offering to take Maddie, but with this sudden summer freeze between our girls, I'm not so sure that's a good idea."

I agreed and explained that Maddie had already covered that possibility with a plea to accompany me. "I'm sorry I won't be able to keep our date to work on the ice cream parlor this morning."

"I'm glad it's not because our fickle granddaughters are on the outs."

I laughed as if I hadn't thought of that myself. "I probably won't be long with Bebe, but I feel I have to do my best."

"I'm free all day except for chauffeuring duty. Taylor has a pool party this afternoon at a classmate's house. Call me when you get back? Maybe we'll still have some time."

"That should work. I hope I'll be able to talk to Bebe. Granted, she is high-strung and stubborn, but I can't see her beating up anyone physically. And certainly not killing someone. In fact, if she's angry at anyone, it's at Catherine. Bebe has more reasons to want to dispose of her, on both a business and a personal level."

"But Palmer was Catherine's boss, wasn't he? Wouldn't he be more to blame for the loss of her shop, in Bebe's eyes?"

"I'm not sure Bebe saw it that way. Plus there's the double whammy, with the rekindled romance."

"I see your point. But Catherine is still alive."

*Beep, beep. Beep, beep.*

My call-waiting signal. I checked my screen. "Catherine is alive and on my other line."

"We'll talk later," we said together.

Catherine's voice was calmer than I'd heard it since her first appearance in Lincoln Point for the SuperKrafts project. "It looks like the mystery is solved," she said. "The police have Bebe. I'll bet she's the one who's been sending me the crazy notes, too."

I wondered if Catherine's new-old boyfriend knew how she viewed his sister's situation. "I understand she's being questioned, as I'm sure many of us who saw Craig yesterday will be," I said. Including you, I thought.

"Yes, but the police actually went to Bebe's house and took her downtown. I just got a phone call asking me to drop in at the station sometime today. And Megan and Leo got the same call. That's different, isn't it?"

"Do the police claim to have evidence of Bebe's guilt?" I asked.

I felt a tug at my arm. "Who's guilty?" Maddie whispered.

She would choose this morning to be on time for departure. I cupped my hand over the phone mic. "Ten minutes," I said.

"I didn't talk to her myself, but Jeff said she didn't mention evidence," Catherine said. "Gerry, I've been thinking of showing the police the notes I've gotten. Now that they have Bebe, maybe they can use them." *Against her* was unsaid, but hung in the air.

I was torn between agreeing with Catherine that the police should see her notes, which I'd recommended as soon as I'd seen them, and my slightly miffed feeling that Catherine had already made herself judge and jury against Bebe. I tried to figure out why she would take that stance. Was she genuinely relieved that her feeling of vulnerability over the notes was now gone? Happy that not only was Craig out of her life, just one more annoyance she didn't have to deal with, but that his killer was someone who'd also been in her way, professionally and personally? Could Catherine be that selfish in her thinking? Where was the sympathy and empathy I might expect if the sister of a boyfriend, or even simply a friend and colleague, was being accused of murder?

It wasn't my job to advise Catherine, I told myself. I was no longer her teacher, making a recommendation for a research paper or advising her on an essay for her college applications. I didn't envy my nephew and the LPPD, whose job it was to sort it all out.

"If you're worried about the notes, you should certainly show them to the police," I told Catherine.

"What notes?" Maddie asked, still under foot. I gave her a smile and a gentle shove.

"Will you see if you can find out what they have on Bebe?" Catherine asked.

"I'm on my way to the station now," I said. If she sensed that I was distancing myself from her many quandaries, and committing to nothing, she didn't say.

I MADE a quick call to Beverly's cell to tell her our shoe shopping would have to wait.

"I'll just stay at work, then," she said. "Maybe tomorrow? Mondays are less crowded anyway."

"That should be fine."

"You know it's not too late to think of a double wedding."

I laughed. "It's a great idea, and I'd do it in a minute, Bev, but what if Maddie and Taylor don't make up? It might be awkward."

"All the more reason for you and Henry to get married. We'd all be family then."

"I'd love to chat some more, but, as your son would say, 'gotta go.'"

I hung up and wondered why Bev's idea didn't sound as crazy and out of the question as it used to.

I changed out of shorts into a sleeveless dress and better looking sandals. Maddie had dressed in a clean T, a sign of great respect for where she was headed. Not enough to have brushed her unruly red curls, but I was sure she didn't see it that way, and she was beautiful as-is.

"Do you have a stamp, Grandma?" Maddie asked as we were almost out the door.

"Sure, what do you need?"

"A stamp. For a letter."

"Do you need any help with the letter?"

"Nope."

Maddie followed me back to my desk, in a corner of my crafts room. On the way, I stretched my neck and strained to read the address on the envelope, but Maddie held it close. Spy Girl at work. I peeled a stamp from the roll and held out my hand for the letter, ostensibly to place the stamp on it. Maddie grinned and held her own hand out. I gave her the stamp.

"I'll drop it in the box in front of City Hall," she said.

I imagined myself a sleuth—locating the pad on which Maddie had written the letter, and rubbing a pencil over the top page. But Maddie had probably used her computer and my printer, so that wouldn't work. I might be able to find a file if she'd saved the letter, or even if she hadn't. I knew files could be dug out somehow after they'd been deleted, but I wouldn't know where to start. At times like this, I'd call on Maddie's computer skills to help me. How ironic.

Nostalgia took over for a moment. There was a lot to be said for the days when hard metal keys made impressions on a typewriter platen. I also longed for the days when my granddaughter couldn't reach the mailbox.

# Chapter 6

I PARKED MY CAR in the police station lot and walked toward the building. Since Civic Center was a relatively new complex, the trees were young and useless for badly needed shade. I was glad I'd worn my floppy white cotton hat, unfashionable but necessary on a hot, dry day like today. Maddie's fair complexion was safe under a baseball cap with the logo of her Palo Alto school soccer team. Did that make it a soccer cap? I shook my head at the question, marveling at how far afield my mind could wander some days.

Coming back to the task at hand, I felt compelled to warn Maddie. "You know you can't stay in the office while I talk to Uncle Skip."

"I know, I know, but I'm expecting you to tell me everything right after, like always."

"Of course."

I'd almost made a deal with Maddie before we left, that if she'd tell me what was up with Taylor and her, I'd keep her with me, but that would have set a very bad precedent. I didn't need to add mutual bribery to her already full bag of borderline-acceptable tricks. I had to stick to the routine we'd established for times like this, when I had a private matter to discuss with Skip or some other adult. Maddie eventually resigned herself to the fact that she wouldn't be in on those conversations, but at least she'd be in the environment where things were happening. I suspected that she longed for the day when she'd be considered eligible for inclusion. For now she seemed content to be handed off to anyone with a badge.

We climbed the wide concrete steps to the front door of the police station, with no lack of greeters on the way, some headed down the steps, others passing us on the right or left in the same direction during the upward trek. We heard "Hey, Red," from a female officer and "Hi, Squirt," from a male in uniform (no female could get away with that); we said, "Good morning" to office workers and maintenance staff. Inside the building, Maddie thrived on comments about how tall she was getting, how she must be glad to be out of school for the summer, and how it was about time she got her own badge. Some people even said, "Hi" to me.

When we entered the large, cubicle-lined area that held the working crime fighters of the LPPD, the first welcoming sound was the voice of Skip's mother, Bev Gowen. She was coming from the direction of her son's cubicle, her red hair signaling that another Porter family member was in our midst.

"I'm trying to make it absolutely clear to my son that a tux is required for his role in his mother's wedding," Bev told me. She made it sound like a tough job and I had no doubt that it was. Bev and Nick's wedding was in a month. Besides Bev's shoes, there was my own dress to shop for. "I heard you two were coming today," Bev said, after bear-hugging Maddie. "I can't wait to go shopping for our outfits. Besides shoes, I need something for my hair. Maybe tonight at the mall?"

"Grandma's busy. She needs to talk to Uncle Skip about who's guilty and who's getting notes." Bev and I looked at each other. It had been a tough sell getting Maddie excited about what she was going to wear. We'd hoped she'd warm up to it as the date approached. Not yet. "Also," Maddie continued, "I need someone to take me to the mailbox so I can mail a letter. I could do it myself, but"—she tilted her head in my direction—"I'm not allowed."

"I'm sure we can take care of that," Bev said. "Shall we dump Grandma and see what's up downstairs in the jail?"

Maddie's eyes brightened. "Really? We can go down there? I've never seen a jail cell except on TV."

"I don't know…" I said, dragging out the words, questioning her television habits in my mind.

"Just kidding," Bev said.

"I don't deserve this," I said, wandering toward Skip's cubicle, leaving them in the dust of the hallway. I wished I could have signaled Bev to check out the address on the envelope Maddie was about to drop in the mailbox. Since I'd given her only one "Forever" stamp, the only thing I could be sure of was that the letter was staying in the United States. I had to count on my sister-in-law's good sense and ability to pry.

"Hey," Skip said. "I thought I heard you, Aunt Gerry." He scratched his red-stubbled chin. "Hmm, I wonder what your agenda is. Want to weigh in on whether I have to wear a tux to the big wedding?"

"Wise guy." Skip would know I had no opinion on clothing but quite a few on criminal proceedings.

I headed down the hall toward his cubicle, entered, and waited for him to catch up, mentally as well as physically. I took a seat and looked around as I usually did for any new decorations or change of photos. The first thing I noticed was that June's picture was still on his desk, though pushed back a bit, half-hidden by a mug of pens and pencils. It could have meant something. It could have meant nothing. Skip entered the gap in the partitions, caught my eye, and smiled. He reached to the photo and moved it next to the mug, both now an equal distance from the edge of the desk. He was a detective, after all.

"Look, Aunt Gerry, I know my mom and dad had a quick wedding in an office somewhere because he had to leave for some army outpost."

"I remember," I said. None of us ever forgot that Eino Gowen, Sr. shipped out and came back several times during his military career, but he never came back from the first Gulf War. Ken and I, but especially Ken, stepped in to help his sister parent her eleven-year-old boy. Skip and our son Richard became like brothers and were still very close.

"So I kind of understand why this time Mom wants to go

all formal," Skip said. He took off his jacket, revealing a short-sleeved shirt, as if to emphasize his desire for informality. "I can't believe my good buddy Nick is going along with all this. He's not a tux-and-shiny-shoes kind of guy."

"Bride's choice," I said, hoping to end the topic.

"Isn't there some maximum age past which you can't be called a bride?"

"Now you're really annoying me." We needed to get down to business. "No one seems to know whether Bebe's been charged with anything," I began.

"They're executing a warrant for her house and car as we speak," he said. "I'm only telling you because if you were her next-door neighbor you'd know this anyway."

"I understand. What else would a next-door neighbor know?"

"That's about it. Until further developments, we're just asking her to be a cooperating witness."

"But you think you'll have something?"

"We're waiting for fingerprint results on the vase. But she has no alibi and she openly fought with and threatened SuperKrafts employees."

"But not Craig Palmer. As far as I know, she only met him once."

"Here's another 'but.' From what I understand, she's been harassing him or the company by mail, for almost a year. True?"

"You mean interacting with him as one of the Lincoln Point citizens with a role in the restructuring of our downtown."

"Man, you've really picked up on the PR lady's jargon. Whatever. Bebe's our best bet."

"I hope you can do better than that." I wasn't sure why I was so adamant about defending Bebe. She hadn't been shy about exploding in public and condemning SuperKrafts to all kinds of nasty fates when she lost her store. Maybe just because she needed someone on her side at the moment. "Why would she kill Palmer? SuperKrafts is a lot bigger than Craig Palmer. Their policies and tactics don't die with him," I reminded Skip.

He shrugged. "Craig Palmer is as big as Bebe can get. A bird in the hand. He's bigger than Catherine Duncan." He raised his arm and marked off a tall man—or building—in the air. "Bebe's not about to fly to New York to find the top guy."

"What about Leo Murray, the temporary manager, and Megan Sutley, Palmer's admin? They were all arguing not long before the earthquake. Palmer had a lot to say about their jobs and promotions." I wasn't as sure as I sounded about the inner workings of SuperKrafts, but it was a definite maybe.

"We'll get to all of them. I'm not saying we're going to arrest Bebe before lunch. You asked and I'm telling you how the cards are stacking up."

"Can I talk to Bebe?"

"If she wants you to."

"Her brother wants me to."

"I'm sure he does."

Skip picked up the receiver on his desk phone, a somewhat old-fashioned model with buttons that linked the whole building, I assumed. Maddie would have been displeased since, as usual, his side of the conversation revealed nothing of interest. When he hung up, he motioned for me to follow him. Either the call had done its job and I was on my way to see Bebe, or Skip was leading me out onto the grass of Civic Center.

"She's this way," he said, giving me hope.

I WAS well aware of the two kinds of rooms in the LPPD building, one for witnesses and the other for suspects. Bebe was in the windowless, uncarpeted version. She looked as I would have expected after a rough few days making a last stand against City Hall and spending half a morning in police custody, whether Skip called it that or not. Her long hair was pulled back and held together with a rubber band. I knew I had at least two of Maddie's scrunchies in my purse and wondered if I should offer one to Bebe.

"My brother send you?" she asked, making it clear that she wasn't the one who'd made the request to see me.

"Jeff is concerned, like all of us, Bebe." Uninvited, I took a seat opposite her. The cop's seat, I thought.

"Tell Jeff I'm okay. I didn't do anything, though I kinda wish I did."

I hoped she hadn't expressed that sentiment to the police. I thought of reminding her that a man was dead by someone's hand and flip remarks weren't going to be appreciated by anyone.

"I'm sure you don't mean that," I offered. "But I can see why you're stressed—"

"Who says I'm stressed?"

I bit my lip and tried another expression of sympathy for her plight and added a word of comfort I had no right to speak. "I'm sure this will all be straightened out quickly."

Bebe shrugged. "Whatever."

It was a good thing I was used to Bebe's crusty manner or I might have thought she didn't want my help.

"Would you mind answering a couple of questions?"

"You sound like the cops. They're also pretending I have a choice. They're saying there are fingerprints on the vase, the one Palmer was killed with. And they're expecting them to be mine." Bebe blew out her breath as if she had just taken a drag on a cigarette. "Of course my fingerprints are on the vase. Like I told them, my prints would be all over the place in the store. Especially on the vases. I'm a ceramics artist. A potter. I wanted to check out the new vases, look at the features, see where they were made and all. We've had practically free rein of the store for the last month." She paused and rolled her eyes. "Really big of them SuperKrafts VIPs."

"So your fingerprints could have gotten on the vase at any time."

Bebe opened her palms to me. "Duh."

"When was the last time you saw Craig Palmer?" I asked, apparently unable to stop sounding like a cop or a lawyer.

"Never met him."

Another line I hoped she hadn't used with the police, who could easily verify her meeting him, albeit briefly, yesterday at the store. I needed another tack. I reviewed the events of last evening in my mind to pinpoint a time for when Palmer's body had been found. I recalled that Skip had received the notice when he was at my house, a little after eleven P.M. If the vase that killed him had been wielded by a person and not by Mother Nature via a three-point-one, the murder could have taken place any time between the end of the late afternoon meeting and about ten forty-five at night. I decided to use the shaker as a benchmark, until further notice.

"Bebe, where were you at the time of the earthquake?" I asked.

"Why are you still questioning me?"

"I'm trying to help—"

"Did I ask for your help?"

"Bebe, your brother and your friends"—I was guessing here—"are worried and want to help you. Is there anything you can tell me about last evening, when the man you never met was killed?" Two could play the sarcasm game.

"Look, just tell Jeff not to worry about me. That's the only reason you're here." I figured she meant that's why she'd agreed to see me. "Anything else is none of your business."

Bebe was right. In fact, Bebe had a more realistic view of my alleged role in this investigation than anyone else. I was not a cop, simply the aunt of a cop, and if all she'd wanted was a messenger between her and her brother, that was that.

"Okay, Bebe. I understand that you don't want my help," I said, standing up. I headed for the door, sure that Bebe would call me back. But I didn't hear the "Wait, wait," that I'd heard so often in TV interview scenes where the cops fake out the witness. Bebe was willing to take her chances without intervention. I hoped that her next visitor would get more cooperation. For now, I had no choice but to leave.

I opened the door and nearly ran into Megan Sutley and Leo Murray. They'd been walking down the hallway, headed to interview rooms I knew were more plush than the one Bebe had been consigned to. We all apologized for our parts in the collision and each expressed our surprise and dismay at Craig Palmer's murder.

"I don't know what's going to happen now," Megan said, a light scent of lavender wafting in the air between us. "I'm waiting for word from Corporate on whether we should go ahead with the Grand Opening, or just have a soft opening, you know, no fanfare."

"Works for me," Leo said, towering over the petite Megan. His attire was casual but not off-the-rack, and not from one of many nearby sports clothing outlets.

"Then there are all the other projects back at the head office and around the country," Megan said. "Craig was overseeing an expansion in North Carolina"—I couldn't help wondering if they were expanding into a row of perfectly good small stores—"a potential new store in Nevada, some new contracts…"

"I imagine it will take a while to fill his position," I said.

I heard a "Yes" from Megan and a "Not really" from Leo, at about the same time.

Leo shrugged. "Frankly, I'm expecting that Corporate will call me back to New York any minute. I'm ready to step up." He looked over Megan's head and past my shoulder at an officer at the end of the corridor. "I think I heard my name," he said. "I'm in Interview Two." Leo sauntered down the hallway, his "Excuse me" barely a mumble.

From the way Megan screwed up her mouth, I gathered that she wasn't a fan of Leo Murray. It was hard to see whom she was a fan of, since Craig's absence through death didn't seem to rattle her as it had Catherine. It was possible that she was looking forward to a boss who treated her less like a servant, as I'd witnessed yesterday.

"Have you and Leo worked together a long time?" I asked.

"Me and Leo, no. I've worked for Craig forever. Whatever he says, Leo's not cut out for the business at the level Craig operated on. He's better off…" Megan stopped and cleared her throat.

"In a small town like this?" I was getting a little tired of New Yorkers, though I used to be one and I loved the city.

"I didn't mean anything negative, Mrs. Porter. Just"—she stopped and put her hand on the door to Interview Three—"Oh, this is me," she said. "I'm supposed to wait in here. I already talked to a couple of cops. I don't know what I can add. I didn't see Craig after about six o'clock when the meeting broke up. I guess he stayed behind and"—she frowned and shook her head—"you know."

"And an earthquake hit," I said. "Were you someplace where you could feel it?" Pretty smooth, if I did say so myself.

"I was back at the hotel, if you can call it that. The KenTucky Inn." She covered her mouth to stifle laughter. "Sorry, I know it's all about Abraham Lincoln around here, and I don't mean to make fun of it, but..."

"We all agree with you on that one," I said. "It's the silliest name in the roll books of silly names." I meant it. Although the innkeepers (a term they preferred to hoteliers), Loretta and Mike Olson, were good friends of mine, I cringed every time I recommended the inn to an out-of-town guest. Apparently they'd told their seven-year-old son that he could name the inn (as luck would have it, at the time his class was reading about the humble birth of Honest Abe in a log cabin in Kentucky) and they felt they had to honor the promise. I didn't know which was worse, the pun on Lincoln's birth state or the mid-word uppercase letter. Maybe that's where SuperKrafts got the idea to come here in the first place. The land of quirky spelling. But the place was close to downtown and charming. And at least for now, it hadn't been taken over by a chain.

"It was my first earthquake and pretty scary," Megan continued. "The coffeemaker and the ice bucket shook, and a glass broke."

"Was Leo with you?"

"No, he stayed behind with Craig. Anyway, he's in San Jose where Craig was, in a real hotel—oh, there I go again—I mean, a bigger hotel. The guys don't like small, cozy places. By the way, do you have these earthquakes often?"

"Not as often as the news might lead you to believe."

"The first one can be unsettling," Skip chimed in, approaching from behind me.

Megan shuddered, but her simultaneous smile took the edge off her reaction. "You got that right," she said, and entered the room.

Skip addressed me in a low voice. "Beverly and Maddie are waiting for you in my cubicle." I supposed it wouldn't have been cool for him to refer to Bev as "Mom" within earshot of an official witness.

"I'm on my way," I said. I was tempted to pinch his cheek in retaliation for all the grief he'd given me lately, but lucky for him, I was in an accommodating mood. Also, he slipped into Interview Three to join Megan before I could make my move. Smart guy.

"WE want to hear everything, Grandma," Maddie said.

Bev smiled. "*We* certainly do," she said, emphasizing "we" for Maddie's benefit.

"Did you mail your letter?" I asked.

"Uh-huh. And Aunt Beverly showed me where they keep all the cars she helps them drag in from the street. They're not stolen or anything, except some of them might be, but they're all abandoned. Like, the owner walked away because the engine wouldn't start, or something. Or sometimes, they're just lost. Right, Aunt Bev?"

So what if Maddie was avoiding my question. I looked at Bev who gave me a slight nod, which I took to mean that she'd seen the addressee on Maddie's letter. I'd get the scoop later from my peer. Hooray! Good old (that is, the young bride) Bev, sensing that I'd want to know about the letter without my mentioning it.

Bev glanced at her watch. "It's not even ten o'clock in the morning, too early for ice cream."

I thought about my promise to Jeff and my disappointing visit with Bebe. "Who's up for a video game?" I asked.

THE light ping of Video Jeff's door was the same alert he'd always had, left over from before his remodel using SuperKrafts money. Much of the interior was different, though dim light still prevailed. Instead of tripping over boxes and remotes in a cluttered, crowded space, I'd entered a neatly laid-out store. One wall was lined with used games for various brands of equipment; the center of the store held rows of bins with what looked like new shrink-wrapped packages. Jeff had set up monitors with headsets in one corner of the store—the modern version of the pinball machine—and that's where the wide-eyed Maddie was headed.

Jeff greeted Maddie first. "Hey, Ms. Porter, guess what? You are the one-hundredth person to walk in that door today," he said.

"One hundred? Already?" Maddie asked.

"You bet," Jeff answered. "And every day I give a prize to the one-hundredth person."

I noticed the heads of four young boys turn in our direction, but Jeff ignored them and tended to Maddie. He tore off a receipt slip, the old-fashioned kind that most Springfield Boulevard retailers still used, whether to impress the tourists or to avoid buying and having to learn new equipment, I didn't know. He wrote on the lined paper: ONE HOUR FREE FOR ANY GAME. At the bottom next to Total, he wrote PAID IN FULL TO 100TH GUEST.

"Wow," Maddie said, grinning. She thanked Jeff and stood in the middle of the store spinning around to decide which direction she'd run to first. The boys, meanwhile, had returned to their own games. If they wondered about the new hundredth-visitor policy, they didn't say.

Bev had begged off the field trip to Video Jeff's. "The life of a civilian volunteer is a hard one," she'd said. "I have phone duty during the regular girl's breaks and lunch hour. Who knows what favorite pet has been lost? Or what parking ticket was totally, totally unfair?"

Jeff was left with me and a few intensely occupied teens and preteens. "Bebe throw you out?" Jeff asked.

Wise little brother, I thought. "She's trying to stay independent, counting on her innocence to bring her home."

"We all know how well that works," Jeff said, leading me to wonder if he'd had his own bad experience with the police.

"She looks good," I lied. "They haven't charged her, so there's not much else to do."

"One of her neighbors called me. The police were at her

house with a search warrant. I ran over there, but they wouldn't tell me anything. Do you think I should get her a lawyer?"

"It couldn't hurt to have one on standby, just in case."

"Well, I appreciate you going over there, Mrs. Porter. She sent me away after about two minutes." *Now, you tell me,* I thought. "I'm sure everyone is always asking you for favors because of…"

I could tell Jeff was embarrassed to admit he was trying to use my connections to the police department to his advantage. I needed to start collecting these admissions and show them to Skip.

"My superior intelligence?" I teased.

Jeff laughed harder than I would have liked. "Yeah, that's right."

"How did you fare in the earthquake, by the way? Anything damaged?" I asked.

"No damage, just a lot of fallen boxes." He pointed to the wall of used games. "But they were a little banged up anyway, so no big deal."

"Were you in the store at the time?"

"Just closing up."

While a group of young boys came into the store (no special prize for numbers one hundred and one through one hundred and five), I mentally reviewed the alibis I'd collected unofficially for the time of Craig Palmer's murder, reciting them to myself in preparation for writing down the list as soon as I could. Catherine and Megan were in their rooms at the KenTucky Inn; Jeff was closing up his shop; Leo was still at the store when Megan left and could have gone to his hotel in San Jose eventually. He also might have killed Craig first, since they'd been the only two left in the building.

How handy for me that I could limit the suspects to a small pool of people. How tough for Skip and the LPPD that they had no such luxury. I imagined a whiteboard in a meeting room at the station with photos of everyone who had crossed paths with Craig Palmer, here, in New York City, in his travels. My head spun. I thought of former girlfriends who might have held a grudge, disgruntled employees, unsatisfied customers of Super-Krafts all over the country, unhappy citizens of Lincoln Point. How far back would investigators have to go to find people with means, motive, and opportunity?

I made a note to ask Skip to keep his promise of details on why Palmer's death was declared a murder and not an accident. It would have been so much easier if we could simply say, "The earthquake did it."

I found Maddie, surrounded by several boys, all competing for a score that I was afraid involved a high body count.

"Time to go," I said, having to use my classroom voice. Loud and authoritative.

"I haven't used up my hour," Maddie shouted back.

"There's no expiration date. You can come back any time," Jeff said.

Something told me she'd claim every minute of her prize.

Jeff walked us outside. "Sometimes it gets too noisy in there even for me," he remarked. He looked down Springfield Boulevard, toward the police station, toward the jail. "But I guess it's better than a lot of places."

No kidding.

# Chapter 7

WHEN SADIE'S DAUGHTER showed up to work at eleven she found Maddie, Bev, and me on the bench outside the family-run ice cream shop. "You should have knocked. My mom is in there," she said, her cherry-colored uniform dress on a hanger, draped over her arm.

But we were comfortable, still not dreadfully hot, and Bev had joined us for wedding talk. Skip was correct in that his mother did seem to be making up for the brief ceremony with his dad. For this wedding, Bev was going all out, with a caterer, a baker (both local independents, she assured us), and about one hundred and fifty guests.

"It was impossible to trim it down," Bev had said while we were making up the mailing list.

"Between you and Nick, you must know every cop and cop's wife," I'd said.

"And every felon and felon's accomplice," Bev chuckled. "But don't worry, I'm seating you and Henry far away from them. By the way, how are you and Henry?"

"We're both quite healthy, thank you," I said.

"No, I mean, how are you and Henry?" This time she'd crossed her index and middle fingers, and wore a silly smile above them.

I gave her a silent, silly smile back.

Maddie, sitting between us now, in front of Sadie's, repeated her assertion that she was too old to be a flower girl and she didn't want to be a bridesmaid and wear a dress, but she wanted some role in the wedding.

"You can be our photographer," Bev said.

"Don't you have a real photographer?" Maddie asked.

"Yes, but he doesn't know everyone the way you do. He wouldn't know who's really important, like your mom and dad, for example."

"And Grandma."

Bev slapped her forehead and smiled. "And Grandma. How could I forget Grandma." I smiled back and bowed from my seated position.

"I can make a movie with my phone," Maddie said.

"Wow, that would be great," Bev said. "So we're all set."

"What do I have to wear?"

"Well, if you have official duties like taking pictures, who knows what you'll have to do. You might need to kneel on the grass or climb on something to get a good shot. You can wear whatever you want, but make sure it's comfortable. Probably a frilly dress wouldn't be advisable."

Maddie sat back, her tongue licking her lips. She was having a good day. A trip to the police station, a free pass at Video Jeff's while all the boys envied her, and now permission to dress casually as an official photographer at her great-aunt's wedding. To top it off, Sadie pushed through the door.

"We're open. C'mon in."

From the way the three of us stampeded to the table, you'd think it had been years since we'd had ice cream.

AS I'd hoped, Maddie and I had time later for a relaxing crafting session. My main crafts area was the second room from the front of the house, next to Maddie's bedroom. When it came right down to it, however, every room in my four-bedroom home was a crafts room to some extent. We'd already started on the interior components of the twelve-inch-by-nine-inch ice cream shop that Henry was building for us. Not that we were addicted or anything. Maddie had carefully chosen the flavors—strawberry, chocolate, raspberry ripple, and "just nothing with mint," she'd said. After a half hour of shaping tiny balls of crafts clay and gluing them into miniature sundae glasses, Maddie made an announcement.

"This is getting boring. I'd rather do an earthquake," she said.

Maddie still seemed a bit moody, even after her treat-filled morning. Bev and I hadn't had a private moment to discuss the letter Maddie had mailed, and I wondered if her lingering grouchiness had anything to do with the missive.

"An earthquake? You mean an outdoor scene showing the geological layers?" I hoped not. Too much like a science project.

"No," she said. "Just a place where there's been an earthquake with things that fell over." She'd already told me that she'd considered finishing the ice cream shop, then shaking it as if a seven-point-nine hit it, but decided against wrecking anything that looked like Sadie's.

We sat on opposite sides of a long table, billed in store catalogs as a picnic table, but the staple of every crafter I knew. The surfaces of the ones I owned were constantly strewn with tiny objects and pieces of indefinable origin destined to be part of a dollhouse or a room box or a free-standing miniature scene. Sometimes an entire row of dollhouses occupied the table, as if I'd created a suburban street in my own home. My greatest pleasure was delivering the houses to a school or hospital for a raffle—or most recently, to SuperKrafts for the charities auction—and then starting all over with new houses. I could see that the ice cream shop was now relegated to the "unfinished" side of the room.

"Let's brainstorm," I said, having introduced the concept to Maddie when she was barely able to repeat a two-syllable word.

She closed her eyes, part of our early brainstorming ritual. "Okay."

"A schoolroom?" I suggested. "A hair salon? A post office?"

She shook her head, no, no, and no. "A swimming pool," she said. Apparently we hadn't been brainstorming at all; I'd simply been trying to guess what Maddie had in mind from the start.

I remembered her earlier complaint that she wished she had a pool. I could certainly give her a miniature pool. "A swimming pool hit by an earthquake. We can do it. We can have poolside lounge chairs tipped over," I said.

"And sodas spilled out."

"A beach ball that flew into a bush."

"Some rafts and tubes."

"A lifeguard chair?" I offered on my next turn.

Maddie shook her head. "I don't think so."

"Is this an indoor pool or an outdoor pool?" I asked.

"I'm not sure."

"You have a particular pool in mind?"

"Nyah. Let's forget about the pool. How about a police station?"

*What?* I looked at her, wishing I could get inside her head the way I'd done when she was a toddler. My family marveled at how I always knew what my little granddaughter wanted. Milk or juice? Sneakers or sandals? A bedtime story from the big blue book or one from the skinny red book? Now at only eleven, she was impossible to read. What would I do next year and those to follow?

"Okay, let's do a police station," I said.

"I mean a police station in an earthquake," she said.

*Of course.* "You got it."

"Do you think it will be too boring?" she asked.

"Not if it's been hit by an earthquake."

"I don't want it to be just desks and chairs."

"Let's think of what cute things we can add," I said. I thought a minute. "Handcuffs. We can make them from jewelry clasps."

"The silver lobster clasps," Maddie said, delighted that she remembered the technical name. "They already look just like handcuffs. And we can have, like, a lunch bag, like Uncle Skip has sometimes. He puts his sandwich on top of it when he eats it. We could make a sandwich, easy." Maddie, who never sat long in one place unless there was a computer in front of her, had left the table and skipped around the room as she brainstormed, ticking off items for consideration. "And a coffee mug. And photos, like the one of June on his desk."

We were on our way.

We started with a lunch bag. Maddie dashed to the kitchen to get a life-size brown bag, which we then unraveled, as she called it, taking it apart so we could spread it out to see the pattern. She was good at scaling down the shape and making a template for a bag that was one-twelfth scale.

*Dum dum, da da dum, da da dum.*

I resisted the urge to get off my chair and march around the room with the music. I checked my cell phone screen. Catherine calling. Probably to ask about my brief visit with Bebe.

"Are you in the middle of something, Gerry?" she asked.

I looked at the table, Maddie's sketch, the scraps of brown paper, and sitting in its cradle, my smoking glue gun. What could Catherine want that would be more important than this? Maddie stared at me, waiting to see what I was going to do and whether she'd be included.

"I am busy, Catherine. Is something wrong?"

"It's just … I was reading these notes again." She let out a loud sigh.

I carried the phone out of the crafts room, into my atrium. "Did you get another one?"

"No, but I'm trying to figure out the handwriting. Like, is it a man or a woman? If it's Bebe, then I'm safe, I guess, now that she's in custody. But then about a half hour ago someone knocked on my door really hard. I didn't answer and he went away, but the knocking was, like, angry, and scared me. I was afraid to look through the peephole. I saw this movie where a guy shot someone in the eye, through the hole." Catherine let out a noise, like a shiver, as if a wind had whipped through her room. "Finally I went to the window and after a couple of minutes I saw Leo's car drive away. At least, I'm pretty sure it was Leo's. What if Leo killed Craig? And is sending me notes. Maybe he had another one but he heard me in the room and left?"

"But it wouldn't make sense for Leo to send you notes telling you to get out of town, would it?"

"I don't know. I guess not. I'm afraid to leave the room, Gerry."

I pictured the KenTucky Inn, mentally blocking out the large sign in front. Three floors high, formerly a sprawling private home with expansive lawns that had been replaced by parking lots in the front and back, according to city ordinances.

"How good a look at the car did you get?"

Maddie entered the atrium and flopped onto my lap, as far as her long legs would allow. It was more of a reclining position these days, as if I were her personal poolside lounge chair. Her head rested on my shoulder, a handy spot for a little girl who wanted to eavesdrop on her grandmother's conversation.

"I got a pretty good look," Catherine said. "Leo's rental car is a funny shade of blue. I'm on the third floor in the back with a window onto the parking lot. He drove right under me." Another shivery noise.

"Have you talked to the police yet?" I asked, leaving off "as I advised."

She paused. "That's not the real reason I called, Gerry. I was going to call you anyway. We scheduled a meeting, Leo, Megan, and I, to make some decisions about the Grand Opening. It would be great if you could come." I noted the swift transition between being afraid to step out of her hotel room to cajoling me into a meeting. "Maisie's not feeling well and Bebe's still at the police station and we don't want to recruit someone new. But we should have at least one community rep."

"For appearances?" I asked, smoothing Maddie's red curls.

"Well, sort of, but you know we value your input, Gerry."

How flattering. "When and where?"

"At the store at three."

I looked at the nearest wall clock, hanging over my kitchen sink and visible from the atrium. "An hour from now?"

"We'd be really grateful."

"Isn't the store still a crime scene?"

"Not as of twenty minutes ago. Jeanine called to say the cops took the tape down. I guess they have all the evidence they need. Or whatever. Anyway, it's all clear. And Mrs. Porter, I don't know how you feel about the Grand Opening, given the circumstances, but it doesn't seem right to me to have a hundred balloons going up right over the spot where Craig was murdered. Not so soon anyway."

In spite of Catherine's unsubtle lobbying for my support, I tended to agree with her. Although Craig wasn't a resident and had spent little more than twenty-four hours alive on Lincoln Point soil, he'd been murdered in our town and it seemed only proper that we respect his memory. Even if someone had traveled from New York to kill him, which, I admitted to myself, was my preferred scenario. And probably the town's.

I thought about the opportunity to see the recent crime scene, an excuse to be with all three SuperKrafts suspects, as I thought of them, and a chance to help the police close their case and remove Lincoln Point from unwanted attention. "I'll be there," I said, as Maddie clapped her hands at the possibility of a field trip.

"Uncle Henry's or Aunt Beverly's?" I asked her, meaning, "You're not invited."

She hoisted herself off my lap and faced me. "You haven't told me anything about this case," she said. "Just because there's no computer work, it doesn't mean I can't help."

Maddie had a point. Also, it wasn't fair to exploit her techie talents and cut her out of cases that didn't require those particular skills. She couldn't help it that she was eleven years old going on thirty. On the other hand, a person had been murdered in the very building where the meeting would be held. What if the killer returned, or, more likely in my mind, was one of the attendees of the meeting? I didn't want her there.

"This time I promise to tell you all about the case when I get back."

"Abso-totally-lutely?" Another linguistic variation from Maddie.

"Abso-blahblahblah-lutely," I answered.

Earlier, by phone, Henry and I had considered forcing a showdown between his granddaughter and mine. If he happened to be needed to pick up Taylor from her swim party while he happened to be taking care of Maddie, well, whose fault would that happen to be?

"But it's probably better to let them set the pace," he'd said.

"Unless it exceeds a statute of limitations. Shall we say a week?"

"A week is good. We have our own convenience to consider," Henry had said.

We'd hung up on a chuckle.

BEV, my accommodating sister-in-law and the bride-to-be, came by in plenty of time for me to make the meeting.

"We might as well stay here," she said to Maddie. "Your grandma's fridge and cookie jar are a lot more inviting than mine."

Until Maddie left the atrium, we chatted about how much time wedding planning takes and what other items we could add to the police station room box. Bev had a wealth of ideas. Maddie drew up a list at this more fruitful brainstorming session as we came up with a magnifying glass, a gun and holster, and three-ring binders, plus everyday desk supplies like telephones, staplers, scissors, and file folders.

"I have an idea," Maddie said, and skipped away toward the crafts room.

Bev and I moved closer and put our heads together. "Did you get anything from Maddie about the letter or about her Taylor snit?" I asked, talking in a low voice at a rapid speed.

Bev clucked her tongue, disappointed. "Sorry, I didn't see the full address, but I did notice a large uppercase *T* and the rest of the name could definitely have been Taylor."

"That's what I guessed."

"I tried to get a better look, but our Ms. Maddie was very careful." I believed her. She looked around now to be sure Maddie was still out of earshot. It was clear who was in charge of the household.

"She's always careful," I said.

"Bummer. We have Maddie and Taylor at kid odds and Skip and June at grown-up odds."

"Do you know what that's about?" I asked, no longer whispering.

"It's a time thing, I'm pretty sure. They both put in a lot of overtime at their jobs. And I think Skip, lovely lad though he is, still has this idea that man's work is more important than woman's work, so it's okay for him to be late or miss a date, but not for her."

"Well, he is a cop."

"She has a demanding job, too. Software deadlines are serious. She's told me about the fierce competition in the business, and how important it is to meet the launch date when they have a new product."

"It's still not life and death," I noted.

"Whose side are you on?"

"Oops," I said.

Before I turned over my crafts table and significant collection of glues to Maddie and Bev, it occurred to me that Bev might be able to answer a question that Skip had glossed over last night. He never did tell me what exactly was the murder weapon. Bev cleared it up for me.

"We told the press it was a vase; actually it might have been twelve vases," Bev said.

"Meaning?"

"Skip told me that they found a wooden crate containing a dozen pottery vases, each one about ten inches high. One vase was out of the crate and seems to have been used to bash in... well, fallen hard on the victim's head. The other vases were half in, half out, lots of broken pieces. The way the crime scene guys have reconstructed things, so far, anyway—Palmer and the killer walked out of the lounge where they might have been meeting and entered the general area of the store together. They were right on the border between the warehouse side and the retail side when the earthquake hit. The killer seized the opportunity, took a vase out of the crate and smashed it...you know. Then he or she pushed or lifted the crate onto Palmer's body, and smashed a few vases afterward, to make it look like the crate had fallen on Palmer from above."

"But that didn't happen? The earthquake didn't do it?"

"No, the trajectories were all off. There was a set of shelves near the crate but it wasn't high enough off the floor to send the crate where it landed; and the widths didn't compute; and it's unlikely that anyone would have stashed the vases on the shelf like that in the first place, et cetera, et cetera. Plus, why would only one vase fall out of its mooring in the packing material and land on Palmer's head in just the right spot? They have all kinds of photos to back up this theory."

"It sounds as though the killer was sloppy."

"Probably spur of the moment. Crime of passion, as they say. The killer and victim might have been fighting and then the earthquake was handy to cover up a last burst of anger."

*Slap, slap, slap.* The sound of running flip-flops. Maddie bounded into the atrium waving a narrow streamer of some kind.

"Ta da!" Her announcement was accompanied by a wide grin, the kind I hadn't seen enough of lately.

On a closer look at the streamer, Bev and I expressed our delight with words like "wow" and "amazing," and high-fives all around. Maddie had produced miniature crime scene tape.

"I typed out the words, then I copied and pasted them over and over in the smallest font I have, then I highlighted them in yellow. If I had yellow paper, I would have just printed them on it. Then I cut the pieces…I mean, with scissors…and strung them together with glue"—she held up the newly created long strip with the never-ending phrase POLICE CRIME SCENE DO NOT CROSS—"and ta da!"

I couldn't have been more thrilled, by the result of Maddie's creativity, of course, but even more so by her increasing interest and enthusiasm for miniatures. It had taken some time to win the young soccer-loving Maddie over to the craft, and today's leap into a project all her own brightened my life considerably.

I left the house, knowing my crafts table was in good hands.

# Chapter 8

———— ✐✐✐ ————

I DROVE DOWNTOWN, my car's A/C much too underpow-
ered for the usual increase in midafternoon temperatures. My
hands were sticky on my steering wheel, my face flushed from
overheating. I hoped the not-yet-open SuperKrafts had a cooler
climate, though I had a feeling that the managers' tempers would
be flaring no matter what the weather.

At two forty-five on a Sunday afternoon, most shops were still
open. I marveled again at the brand new sidewalk on both sides
of Springfield Boulevard, all the way to the corner where Rosie's
Bookshop sat. SuperKrafts was the generous funding agency for
the sidewalk project, which included new parking lots behind its
own store as well as a small park in front of Civic Center.

Incentives worked both ways, as I'd learned. The town council had given a tax break to the giant retailer, in the form of a slid-
ing scale that was based on their profits. Theoretically, the town
would still be ahead because of the enormous income from the
sales tax SuperKrafts would generate. The vision was that when
crafters from all over the area came to Lincoln Point to buy their
supplies, they'd also send their kids to Video Jeff's while they
shopped, stop for lunch at Willie's Bagels across the street, and
pick up gifts and odds and ends at Rosie's and at Abe's Hardware
before having dessert at Sadie's. Everyone would prosper. Time
would tell.

I parked in the unfinished lot behind SuperKrafts. I had a few
minutes before the meeting and took a chance that Skip might
be available to answer a couple of questions that could be key to

the impromptu gathering I was called to. I tried his cell phone first and wasn't quite prepared for his opening. I'd always felt that Caller ID gave an unfair advantage to the person on the receiving end. A heads-up. Or a warning.

"I heard you really hit it off with Bebe Mellon," he said. "She wants you to visit every day."

"You're so well-informed. No wonder you're rising in the ranks." I realized that if that was the best I could come up with, I should stop playing the smart-remarks game.

"Yeah, I was trying to be a wise guy, but I'm also telling you the truth. Bebe put in a request to talk to you again."

"Seriously?"

"Uh-huh. She's seeing the handwriting on the wall. She knows you're the most influential person in the department." I blew a poor imitation of a raspberry into the phone. "Sorry, there I go again," he said. "But I am serious about her request. You busy?"

I gave Skip my current location, mission, and reason for calling, assuring him also that I was more than happy to return to jail.

"What's the status of Craig Palmer's body?" I asked, having no time to think of more euphemistic phrasing.

"We're done on this end," he said. "I believe he's headed home to New York on Wednesday afternoon."

The day scheduled for SuperKrafts' Grand Opening. "Do you know if Craig's family is planning to come here to claim his body?"

"Not as far as I know. They've declined the option of escorting him home. I heard they've made arrangements with Miller's for transport."

There was never a way around the awkwardness of dealing with a dead person or talking about him. I'd had my own sad business with Miller's Mortuary when Ken died, and remembered the words and phrases that were meant to be comforting: *departed*, like a train leaving the station, but scheduled to return soon; *passed on,* with the implication that the next phase was so much better for the person; gathering in a *parlor*, where soft conversation might be served along with tea; offerings of sympathy for the *loss*, as if the person might one day show up in a Lost and Found department. A cleansed vocabulary, falling short of the reality.

I buried my memories. I had what I needed from Skip. "Thanks," I said. "I'll visit Bebe as soon as this meeting is over."

"I'll have someone there to take your official statement. I kind of forgot that our little chat as the night turned into morning didn't count. I'll be at the station by then, too."

"Where are you now? With June? Nosy aunts want to know."

"Sure, that will work. Good luck at the meeting."

Apparently Skip was with June. Mending whatever was wrong, I hoped.

I SURVEYED the parking lot. There was as always a selection of trucks and vans with the SuperKrafts logo on the sides, plus the familiar rental cars—Catherine's silver Taurus, and Leo's Ford in a shade of blue they might have revived from the nineteen-fifties. I assumed one of the other cars, a red Camry close to the back entrance, was Megan's. Nice that SuperKrafts could afford to allow each employee to rent his own car.

The large metal delivery door was (theoretically) always locked and alarmed, opened by punching a code into the keypad above the handle. Catherine, or some supercomputer in New York, changed the code every day during the preparations phase. Maisie, Bebe, and I and a few other residents were on an "as needed" list for meetings that included us. I had no code for today, and with any luck, my work as a town rep was over and I'd never have one again. I rang the loud, harsh-sounding bell.

Leo, taller than me by nearly a head, opened the door. His broad shoulders and portly physique were incongruous with some of the more girly products in the store. I had no trouble believing he wanted out of cute retail and back to a sleek office with a view of the Chrysler Building. His attire would certainly be more appropriate in midtown Manhattan. He might have been the only male in Lincoln Point wearing a long-sleeved shirt and tie on this hot summer Sunday.

"We've already started," he said by way of greeting.

I checked my watch. Five minutes after three. Shouldn't I have been congratulated for showing up at all on such short notice? Not that I liked being late, but the time spent praising Maddie's miniature crime scene tape and then talking to Skip had slowed me down. I hadn't realized SuperKrafts ran such a tight ship, and in any case, I wouldn't have given up the chance to applaud Maddie's achievement, nor the opportunity for police intel, like any good operative.

"I'll try to catch up," I said.

I followed Leo inside the delivery area, across a wide concrete floor as dimly lit as my garage with its nightlight, toward what would soon be the employee's lounge. The retail area was dark, thanks to the specially coated front windows. I couldn't see the spot where I'd figured Palmer had been found. I wondered how long I'd have to wait before reasonably being able to excuse myself to use the rest room, conveniently located a few yards into the main part of the shop where crime scene tape had been up not long ago.

One short wall of the meeting room was set up with a kitchen counter; two other walls were lined with vending machines, lockers, and a bulletin board. Catherine and Megan sat across from each other at a long table, stacks of paper in front of them. I arrived just in time to hear Megan's position on the agenda item Catherine had prepared me for on the phone—to open grandly or not to open grandly on Wednesday.

"I say we proceed as planned," Megan said, tapping her pen on one of the small notepads on the table. "I vote Grand Opening on Wednesday."

"I'm not sure why you even have a vote," Catherine said. "You know nothing about this store. Have you even walked into the retail area?"

"I don't have to. I've seen a million like it. I don't see why we can't have the opening. It's not as if Craig's body is still here in the store," Megan said.

Catherine's face took on a horrified look. "How can you be so callous?" she asked, her voice high and shaky.

"Oh, really, Catherine. We don't need to impress Mrs. Porter," Leo said, pulling out a chair for me and taking the one at the head of the table.

The room gave off an eerie ambience, with a warehouse-high ceiling and low-level lighting. The hum of the refrigerator and the vending machines competed with the crackling of the fluorescent lights. I was acutely aware that beyond us in the vast store full of merchandise was a particular spot on the floor, where Craig Palmer's body had lain for several hours. I had too vivid a picture of him in my mind. I regretted the highly effective air-conditioning and wished I'd worn a sweater.

Catherine crossed her arms, ready to speak again. "I'm sorry if a little respect is too much to ask of you both. Craig Palmer was our boss—"

"Your boss," Leo interrupted.

"—and our colleague," Catherine continued.

I cleared my throat. All three turned to me, seeming to take the sound as a maneuver on my part to enter the skirmish, which was not my intent. My intent was to clear my throat.

"What do you say, Mrs. Porter?" Megan asked.

I cleared my throat again, this time to stall before I spoke. "I understand that Craig's remains will be sent to his parents on Wednesday." I had to admit I enjoyed the surprised glances that were sent my way. I wished I'd been able to impress my ALHS students as easily with my inside knowledge of Shakespeare. "Mr. and Mrs. Palmer won't be coming to town," I continued, "but in my opinion, it seems in bad taste to have any kind of celebration until their son's body is back with his family."

"See," Catherine said, as if something had been proven, or as if my opinion mattered.

Leo and Megan looked at each other. I thought I detected slight nods. "I suppose postponing the event would be okay," Megan said. "We can open for business, low key, on Wednesday, so we don't have to change the schedules of the workers and do a truckload of paperwork, but we won't have the balloons and cake, et cetera, et cetera, until Saturday."

Nods all around.

"Not as good as Wednesday, but better than waiting a whole week," Leo said.

"I don't understand," I said. "I would have thought a weekend would be the obvious choice for a Grand Opening."

The three professional retailers shook their heads. "Too much competition on weekends," Megan explained. "The outlet malls around here are a big attraction—you can hit more stores at once. The idea was that we'd have Wednesday all to ourselves."

"Also, crafters tend to be retired ladies"—Leo kept his eyes on me as he spoke—"and they're not going to be working on a Wednesday. On the other hand, their kids or younger friends will be at a job so the crafters will have nothing to do but shop."

I wondered if Leo realized the incongruities in his final thought—putting *crafters* and *nothing to do* in the same sentence. I could have taken the time to point out that the crafter in front of him also tutored adults studying for their high school equivalency diplomas and worked year-round on fund-raisers for local causes. But I was used to the stereotype, and didn't resent the profiling as much as Catherine seemed to. She shot Leo a look that said, *Do you realize who you're talking to?*

We moved on to important topics like balloons and refreshments, all of which had been ordered, but now would have to be stored longer (the balloons) or rescheduled for delivery on Saturday (food and drink).

"I think it would be nice if we had a little memorial service with the ribbon cutting," Catherine said.

"Listen to yourself," Leo said.

"I mean, just a few words to acknowledge that a person very important to this project has been...was..."

"Is no longer with us," Megan said.

"Oh, for heaven's sakes," Leo said, probably straining to keep his response G-Rated.

"Everyone knows Craig was murdered on this spot," Megan said.

"Not on this spot," Leo said. "Out there." He pointed to the space beyond the meeting room. "And now you're afraid to even walk that far."

"I'm not afraid. There's just no need to. Maybe that spot will be an attraction. But let's not flaunt it."

"Flaunt it?" Catherine yelled. "What's wrong with you? You think I want to use Craig's death as a marketing tool? How can you think that?" She was hoarse by the time she finished.

I'd had enough of SuperKrafts on what should have been a relaxing, crafting Sunday. I felt I'd given enough input. The rest was about politics, marketing, and sales, none of which I was adept at.

"Excuse me," I said. "I'm going to the rest room. I'll stop by before I leave to see if there's anything else I can help you with."

I wasn't surprised that I got no argument.

WALKING out of the lounge into the store didn't help me erase the image of a departed, deceased person who had passed away. On the floor a few yards in, I saw bits of packing straw, the kind that was really plastic and familiar to me from shipments of miniatures to my home. I figured that was where the crate of vases had been. I assumed that the vases themselves had been taken into evidence and tested for blood and fingerprints. I pushed away the idea that they'd one day be back on the shelves, and I vowed never to buy a vase in SuperKrafts.

In front of me, the aisles of the store were beautifully organized. With the equivalent of sunglasses for a storefront and only dimmed overhead lights on, the merchandise was in shadow, but it wasn't hard for me to make out items I'd seen accumulate on the shelves over the past months. Scrapbooking paper, stickers, rubber stamps, glue, and special pens were in one section; beads, string, and jewelry-making tools in another. The miniatures section held more items than were in the entire inventory of dollhouse stores I'd visited, which of necessity had given over square footage to other kinds of merchandise.

When I thought I'd reached the spot where Craig had been killed, I squatted and peered at the tiles in the floor, looking for signs of the struggle between Craig and his killer, a scene that would forever be associated with SuperKrafts in my mind. I ran my fingers along the grout, sniffed a piece of straw, squinted at a tiny shard of pottery. Except for my lack of official jacket, anyone watching might think I was a bona fide crime scene investigator. I wondered how the professionals decided what to pick up and bag for evidence, what to photograph, and what was useless and unrelated to the crime. Clearly the ceramic shard and bits of straw left behind were considered negligible.

I stood for a broader view, trying to guess how much of the area would have been marked off as a crime scene. I wished I'd gotten a look before they removed the tape. My survey took in more ceramics and straw, and at the outer limits of my view, something that caught the light of a low-level safety lamp—a stray blue-green bead on the floor. I walked over and picked it up. I squinted, and thought it might be a metallic-coated bead, with many facets. It was close enough to a rack that held beads in different sizes and colors to have fallen out of a package. Putting it in my purse made me feel useful, as if I'd just saved someone from slipping and falling. Failing that, I'd neatened up the store a bit.

Toward the front of the store was the display of dollhouses, their tiny roofs forming a miniature city skyline against the tinted windows that faced Springfield Boulevard. I easily picked out the one Maddie and I had built since there were only two half-scale houses and the other was a turreted Victorian. I nudged the mirrors that Maddie had glued to the walls above the bathroom sink and the dresser in the main bedroom. The miniature mirrors were solidly attached. Even in her snit about being banned from the meeting at Sadie's, she'd done an excellent job on her assignment. I allowed myself a moment of pride in my granddaughter.

I wandered the aisles, past Floral and Home Décor; knitting and crocheting yarn, books, and needles. I wished I was getting this preview of the nearly complete store under different circumstances. I checked out the art supplies and thought about buying a sketchbook and charcoal for Taylor, who showed great interest in drawing. Maddie could give it to her on her next birthday, if they were on speaking terms.

I spotted a flyer advertising SuperKrafts' classes. Stacks of the ads were piled in wire holders at the ends of the aisles. When I noticed one of the workshops on the list was Ceramics with Bebe Mellon, I snatched a couple of copies to take to her at the police station. It might lift her spirits to know she was appreciated and labeled "a master at ceramics." With any luck, she'd be released from jail in time to show up.

I walked back toward the exit to the parking lot, deciding not to check in on my friends at the meeting. If they'd needed me, they'd have come to get me. Then again, they thought I'd gone to the rest room. Maybe they were waiting for the sound of a flushing toilet.

*DUM dum, da da dum, da da dum.* My cell phone, ringing as I walked past the three SuperKrafts' employees' rental cars. I entered my car and turned on the ignition and the A/C. I'd think about fuel economy and the environment when summer was over.

"Hey, Mom," my daughter-in-law, Mary Lou, said. "Still picking up the pieces after the big quake?"

"In a way, yes."

"I was kidding. Wasn't it barely over a three?"

I gave Mary Lou a "Yes, but…" and an update on the quake-related murder. "In a way, the earthquake was a handy weapon," I said.

"Wow, I'm sorry. I read about it, but didn't give it a lot of thought. I didn't put it all together. You, SuperKrafts, and all."

"Why would you? Tell me about the art show." Mary Lou knew I was her biggest fan, always waiting for the next new technique she'd try with her oils.

"It's going pretty well as far as networking and contacts. Not too many sales, but it's early yet. I found a great framing place to recommend to potential buyers. Makes it easier for them."

It wasn't entirely out of the question that Mary Lou would call just to say, "Hey," and to talk about the latest exhibit of her original portraits (beautiful, of course) and offer insights into marketing her work. But I sensed she had something more in mind today. Sure enough: "Have you noticed anything different in Maddie?" she asked. "Like a bad mood?"

"What do you mean?"

Mary Lou laughed. "I forgot. You're never going to admit anything negative about your perfect grandchild."

"No reason to," I said.

"Then let me do it. I think she and Taylor had some kind of a scrap. She doesn't go on and on as usual about what they've done together and when I ask her about it, she gets sullen—I know it's hard for you to believe—and shuts down."

I admitted to Mary Lou that I'd noticed the same behavior. "When did it start?" I asked.

"Not long ago. Right when school let out. I'm thinking it might be over a boy."

What? I hadn't thought of that, any more than I knew what was up between Catherine and Jeff, or Skip and June. And right under my nose. I was better with *Romeo and Juliet*, a nice clean-cut love story. I blocked out the fact the famous couple were teens and died at the end.

"What makes you say that?" I asked Mary Lou. "Did Maddie mention a boy?"

"No, but she's that age, Mom. Twelve is looming." How did that happen? I wondered. I tried to pinpoint the day I could no longer sweep her off her feet into my arms, then realized not even her father or Skip could do that now. "So, I was wondering if maybe you...you know, could bring it up? The boy thing?" Mary Lou's voice ended on a light note, as if this would be the easiest thing in the world for me to do.

I thought back to Maddie's interaction at Video Jeff's and pictured the boys who'd surrounded her at the flashy game console. If the cause of Maddie's estrangement from Taylor was a boy, as Mary Lou suggested, he'd be like those boys. Not one of those boys exactly, but *like* those boys. I remembered their contorted faces, their mouths tight with concentration, their eyes intent on the screen and the equipment in front of them. I recalled their cries of victory and defeat, winced at their warlike stances. "Oh, no," I muttered.

"What's wrong, Mom?"

"I don't think I'm the one to do that."

"You're much better with her at these sensitive things, Mom."

A picture formed in my mind: me, bringing up the topic of "boys" with my granddaughter while we glued tiny cups to saucers the size of her pinky fingernail.

"You know, Mary Lou, she still hasn't changed the décor in Richard's old room, though I've told her many times she can have it the way she wants it. She sticks with that baseball set I made for him when he was about four."

"I know, but these things don't happen all at once. There's a lot of overlap between little girl and grown-up girl. Just see what you can find out, okay?"

"I just don't think—"

"Thanks a lot, Mom. You're the greatest."

"Okay," I said, my voice so weak I doubted Mary Lou heard me. I doubted also that she needed to.

AT four in the afternoon I was on my way to jail. As I approached the front door of the police station, I called Bev's phone. Nick, the groom-to-be, my future brother-in-law answered. I thought how happy Ken would be that his sister had found someone, and I was positive the two men would have become great friends. My immediate delight was that baby-sitter Bev had adult company plus backup in case Maddie turned sour at my absence—not because she missed me, but because she was missing out on an adventure. I wished I could convince Maddie that she didn't know how lucky she was.

"Is it okay if I make another stop?" I asked, hoping the background noise didn't alert Nick to the fact that I'd made the assumption already.

"Not a problem," he said. "We're settled in, playing some board game that's not on a board."

I thanked him and before hanging up, promised a special batch of cookies.

I opened the front door of the building, and nearly banged into my nephew.

"Hey, Aunt Gerry. Where's the squirt?" Skip asked.

"With your mom and Nick." As we walked toward the stairs to the lower level, I told Skip about my meeting at SuperKrafts, and since there wasn't much to report, also about my conversation with Mary Lou, being sure to get his solemn oath of secrecy first. Then something about the environment spawned a brilliant thought. It must have been the crowd of uniformed men and women milling around, emitting authoritative auras, supported by an assortment of hardware from handcuffs to flashlights to holstered weapons.

"Maddie adores you," I began, though it wouldn't be news to him. "Maybe you should be the one who—"

Skip stopped and held out his hands as if to ward off an attack. "Whoa. You want me to give her the birds-and-the-bees talk?"

"No, no. Just see what's up in that regard. You could ask if there are any boys in her class that she especially likes."

"Not a chance," Skip said.

"Or if there any boys she does homework with during study period."

"Uh-uh."

"Or does she ever have lunch with a boy? Share her box of raisins? Then wait and see how she reacts. If this feud with Taylor really is about a boy, she might let something slip."

Skip shook his head so hard I thought he'd have a headache for the rest of the day and into the night. "Absolutely not. That's women's work."

"Now you're sounding like the fifties."

"Let's not go there. I get enough of that with…" Uh-oh. I figured I hit a June Chinn nerve. I'd have to address it later. I let Skip continue. "I'm just saying Maddie and I don't have conversations like that. We horse around, talk sports, throw balls at each other, play computer games…"

"That's what I mean. You have a kind of rapport with her that Mary Lou and I don't have. You're her Uncle Skip. You play with her."

"You play with her, too. You're always doing the dollhouse thing with her."

"The dollhouse thing? That's serious business."

But Uncle Skip had already started walking away. "Let's go find Bebe," he said, pushing the stairwell door open and heading down the stairs.

"At least stop calling her 'squirt,'" I said to his back.

I COULD see that Bebe was striving for a new attitude for this visit. She sat up and brightened slightly when she saw me, even though her face was a web of concern. Something was off, either with her or with my perception. She was still in an interview room, so her status with the LPPD didn't seem to have improved. My interaction with Skip had been so charged with personal matters, I'd neglected to ask what their long-term plans were for Bebe, who was apparently their prime suspect. Why hadn't I at least asked about the results of the search warrants for her house and car? A wave of guilt washed over me as I realized I hadn't done much except wrangle alibis out of everyone I considered a suspect. Not that it was my job to solve a homicide, but I hated to see Bebe, a friend for many years, held for so long and possibly charged with murder. As abrasive and ill-tempered as Bebe could be, I didn't for a minute think she'd killed anyone. I also bristled at the fact that an unsolved murder in Lincoln Point dominated the news in the entire South Bay. Add to that, the victim was an integral part of a project that had taken a lot of my attention over the past year, and my sense of duty took over. It was time to get myself in gear.

"Gerry, hey," Bebe said. "I knew you'd come back even though I threw you out. They let me talk to Jeff for a while, so I feel much better."

I took a seat. "I'm glad to hear that, Bebe. Has anyone given you an update on the investigation?"

"Nothing new on their end. They come in and bring me a coffee and I even got a sandwich this afternoon."

I decided to wait Bebe out. When she wanted to tell me

why she'd asked for me, she would. "I'm glad they're treating you well," I said.

"They're always asking if I'm ready to talk." Bebe lowered her voice. "And you know, Gerry, I think I am. I'm ready to talk."

"What do you mean 'talk,' Bebe?"

"Jeff is working on getting me a lawyer, and I suppose I'll need one eventually, but I wanted you to know the truth."

I felt my whole body stiffen. "Which is?"

"I killed Craig Palmer."

# Chapter 9

HAD I HEARD RIGHT? Or had I fallen asleep from the excessive heat outside and the stuffiness inside the police building? I blinked, shook my head, and the clear memory was still there. Bebe Mellon, ceramicist and sister of Jeff Slattery, admitted to killing the late Craig Palmer of New York City.

I reached over and put my hand on hers. "Bebe, do you know what you're saying?"

"I do, Gerry, and I need to get this off my chest. Off my conscience. It's not fair to my little brother, who's worried about me, or to anyone else to let this drag on. I'm ready to pay whatever price I have to and take whatever punishment is coming to me."

An empty coffee mug stood on the table next to Bebe's right arm. I had the urge to pick it up and send it to a lab for drug testing. Had the LPPD—my own nephew, perhaps—been so eager to close the case that they'd given her a little something to cloud her judgment? Nah.

"Why don't you tell me about it, Bebe," I said in a near whisper. *Before you speak to the police without a lawyer,* I added to myself.

She blew out a breath, but seemed eerily calm. "Wow, I don't know where to start."

"Just take your time and tell me from the beginning. You were in SuperKrafts with Craig?"

"Uh-huh."

"How did you get into the building?"

"I'm on the code list, remember?"

"And they hadn't canceled the code for the day?"

"They must have forgotten. Or I got in just under the wire."

"And then?"

"Okay, I was really mad at him, you know. I heard he was going to cut my workshop from the schedule. I knew he was still meeting with Catherine and the others so I waited in a corner of the store till it was over."

"You expected the others to leave the building before he did?"

"Well, I, uh, sort of figured he'd be the last one in the room. Then when he was alone, I went up to him and I asked him why he was cutting me out and we fought and I just lost it and picked up a vase, and..." Bebe finished by lifting her arms and bringing an invisible object down on the table, with a thud. I flinched at the sound though Bebe remained calm through the demonstration.

"The vase was right there?"

"Yeah, I just picked up the first thing I could, you know."

"And if the others hadn't gone out first?"

"Well, I guess I would have found another way." She threw up her hands. "Why are you asking all these questions, Gerry? I'm just trying to tell you how I did it."

Bebe had become agitated, which was not my intention. I was conscious of people—police people—walking in the hallway outside the interview room. I hoped the room was soundproofed and not bugged. If someone in charge heard Bebe, she might be arrested immediately.

I should have been relieved by our conversation. Didn't I want the case to be solved? Well, here it was, solved. The easiest way possible. A confession. But something was off. A lot, in fact. There was the detail concerning the murder weapon, which Skip had shared with me, but wasn't publicly known—that Craig's body was found in the retail area just outside the meeting room, and that the lethal vase had been pulled from a whole crate of vases in that area. Bebe's story made it sound as though, one, she killed him in the meeting room, and two, the vase was also in the room, loose and handy.

"Bebe, will you do me a big favor? Don't tell this to anyone until we talk again. Especially not the police."

"But I want to get this over with."

"I know, and I want it over, too, but please tell me you'll wait just a little longer."

"Are you going to talk to a lawyer or something?"

I hesitated. To lie or not to lie. I was getting good at finding that middle ground. "Yes," I said, as Henry's daughter and son-in-law, both lawyers, came to mind. So what if their specialty was mergers and acquisitions? And so what if I was really going to talk to Henry, who was a master craftsman, but not in law?

Bebe's face went through contortions as if it were hugely difficult for her to make this decision, or to think at all. "Okay," she said, the word coming out in a loud breath.

I patted her arm and thanked her. I hated to leave her, not fully trusting that she'd keep her specious story to herself, but I had a call to make and a lot of thinking to do.

THE last person I wanted to meet as I headed for the exit was Skip, but we ran into each other for the second time in an hour.

"I've got someone ready to take your statement," he said.

I'd forgotten that I hadn't yet been officially interviewed. I changed my mind on the spot—the last person I wanted to meet wasn't Skip, but a cop who would formally interview me and ask what I knew about Craig Palmer's murder. Not now, not after I'd been confessed to.

"Fred Bates. He's working some other cases, but he can fit you in."

I felt a little better. "I know Fred. I had his son in school."

"Of course you did." Skip scratched his head. "It's hard to find anyone around here that you don't have a connection with."

"You say that as if it's a bad thing."

"It would be nice if once you didn't have the upper hand," Skip said, his grin taking away from a remark that might otherwise have been perceived as too smart for his own good.

"I'm in kind of a hurry. Would it be possible for me to come back later tonight?"

"Sure." He pointed toward the interview room that housed Bebe. "Did you get anything useful from Bebe?"

"Nothing," I said, without hesitation, since I considered Bebe's so-called confession useless.

"Nothing," he repeated as if he didn't believe me.

"Any word on the fingerprints?" I asked, to keep him from probing. I was also hoping that someone else's prints besides Bebe's would be on the vase, someone without the good excuse Bebe had given, back when she was proclaiming her innocence.

"You know better than that. The way the crime labs are backed up we'll be lucky to have them this year." Unfortunately, I knew Skip was only slightly exaggerating. He'd schooled all his family and friends on the pitiful state of crime labs. "We're better off than a lot of states where blood results take up to eleven months and the six-month 'speedy trial' rule goes out the window," he continued.

"Sorry, I should know better."

"It's okay. Back to that other topic, I've been thinking about what you were suggesting."

My first thought was that the interview room was indeed wired and Skip had been listening in on my conversation with Bebe. What if he'd heard my suggestion—let's face it, *plea*—that she not talk to the police? Had my nephew set up Fred Bates to charge me and arrest me for obstruction of justice? *Had* I been obstructing justice?

He must have seen my panicked look. "I mean about talking to Maddie," he explained. "What did you think I meant?"

"Nothing," I said again, this time feeling my face flush.

"Well, I might be able to work it in, the boy talk," he said. "But only if it feels right."

"That's terrific," I said, relaxing my shoulders. "Only if it feels right, of course."

"I was thinking I could ask her if any boys in her class are as cute as me."

He grinned, and at that moment I doubted any boy, or man, could be as cute as my nephew. I risked a quick peck on his cheek before we went our separate ways.

IT was five o'clock by the time I reached my car. I hated to impose on Bev and Nick, but I wanted to make a private call to Henry. I needed advice about my meeting with Bebe, and couldn't very well ask Skip or even Bev or Nick. They were all officially tied to the police force in one way or another, and probably took the same oath to report any confessions, suspicious or not.

I dug around in my bottomless purse and found a chocolate ball wrapped, or almost wrapped, in red foil. I hoped it was from Valentine's Day and not Christmas. I popped the small candy in my mouth, a rush of sugar to keep me going for a little while, and punched in Henry's number.

"Another pizza, another earthquake?" he asked.

I told him that was a great idea, to try a do-over on the pizza, then launched into my troublesome visit with Bebe. I reviewed all the things that didn't add up in her story.

"That's tough," he said. "You really think she's covering for someone?"

"That's the only reason I can think of that she'd be willing to go to jail. And as far as I know there's no other family besides her brother."

"Video Jeff."

"Right. Bebe was married briefly, but her ex is long gone and there are no children. She's been close friends with Maisie for years, but I can't imagine either that Maisie killed a man or that Bebe would be that quick to go to jail for her."

"Is Jeff a viable suspect?"

"He certainly had motive for wanting Craig Palmer out of the picture. Craig was competition." Once again, I wished I'd paid more attention when I heard about romances and love affairs, especially relationships gone bad. Most people would have a sixth sense about those things. Was Catherine really "over" Craig? Had she committed to staying in Lincoln Point with Jeff? Were they still discussing it, giving Jeff the need to eliminate Craig and the pull in the New York direction? I was hopeless at figuring it out.

I tuned back in to Henry's voice. "I imagine the police questioned Jeff?" he asked.

"I imagine so."

"You'd think the favorite aunt of a homicide cop would know for sure."

"The only aunt," I reminded him. "And I wish it gave me as much of an inside track as everyone thinks it does. I know you can't tell me what to do, Henry, but I'm at a loss about my obligation, legally and otherwise."

"I can talk to Kay. It's not her field, but it might be a very simple question with a simple answer. The legal part anyway. I'll speak hypothetically, of course."

"Hypothetically, that would help a lot. Then, no matter what, I have to try to figure out who really killed Craig Palmer. Bebe is about to confess to a crime she didn't commit. I can't sit around."

"I didn't think you could."

It felt good to be understood.

I NEEDED time and quiet space to get my thoughts in order. My car was too hot; the library behind me in Civic Center was closed; my house was full of people. I could go to Sadie's but I wouldn't be there ten minutes before a friend or former student would want me to join them, feeling sorry for me because I was eating alone. At times like this, Lincoln Point seemed too small.

I was still parked in front of the police station. I wished I could march back in and sit down with Skip, ask him straight-out the facts of the case and his thoughts on it. I heard Skip's voice in my head: "Not gonna happen."

Maybe I could endure the car for a few minutes if I had a little shade. I drove out of Civic Center, around to the half-finished lot behind Ten-to-Ten, the convenience store, and parked under a tree that had survived the construction project. I bought a cold bottle of water, and sat with my windows down and a notebook resting partly on my lap and partly on the steering wheel. I breathed deeply, sifted through my questions, and wrote them down.

First, *How did the killer get into the building?* which depended a lot on *What time was the store access code changed every day?* I had no detailed knowledge of the schedule, and never cared to find out. We Lincoln Point reps came and went, assuming the managers would see to it that we had access when we needed it. If the code ran from midnight to midnight, then Bebe, or anyone with the code on Saturday, could have entered the building during the late afternoon meeting. But even if the code changed at six, which would match what was the closing time during construction, someone with the code would have been able to sneak in before the meeting. In a store like SuperKrafts, with its fully packed shelves and cartons of inventory stacked high and deep, there was no shortage of places to hide.

I made a note to ask Skip if there had been signs of forced entry, in which case, the entire population of Lincoln Point and beyond could have gotten in through the back door. The metal door and keypad had looked fine to me when I entered this afternoon, but I hadn't been focusing on them with a crime scene tech's eye.

Next, *When was Craig killed?* A question I hadn't considered until now. I'd been smugly collecting alibis for six thirty-two, the time of the earthquake, but who said Craig was killed at that moment? His body had been found at ten forty-five. He could have been killed at ten-forty. The killer could have pulled a vase out of the crate before the police arrived for their routine check. I thought it unlikely that Craig would have been in the building very late—alive, that is—but I had no way of knowing. Again, Skip would have this information. Even if the medical examiner couldn't pinpoint a time of death exactly, the police would have traced Craig's movements by now. They'd know if he'd been seen leaving the building, having dinner in town, whether he'd been alone, who'd been the last to see him. They'd also know—

*Tap, tap, tap.*

"Hey, Gerry?"

I jolted, knocking my notebook to the floor. Someone was tapping on my car door.

"Gerry? Are you okay?"

I came to and saw Maisie Bosley standing next to my car, a worried look on her face. "I'm fine," I said. "I must have dozed off." Entertaining in the wee hours would do that to me.

Maisie, not one to be easily dismissed, leaned in and put her hand on my forehead. "Your head feels pretty hot, Gerry."

"It's still about ninety degrees out here," I said. "But thank you for your concern, Maisie. I thought you weren't feeling well."

"I'm fine now. Come to Willie's with me and I'll buy you a cold drink."

At the mention of Willie's Bagels, I realized I hadn't had anything to eat but a stale chocolate ball since my trip to Sadie's before noon. I'd made a sandwich for Maddie before I left the house, but had nothing myself. "Make it a cinnamon bagel and it's a deal," I said, though my plan was to treat Maisie. And pump her for information.

WILLIE'S was named for the Lincolns' third son, who died before his twelfth birthday. No wonder Mary had issues with depression. Losing a spouse was bad enough, but I couldn't imagine the agony of losing a child Maddie's age.

Maisie and I trudged across the street toward the bagel shop, discussing nothing heavier than the weather, comparing last year's temperatures in the month of June to this year's, and moaning that this was to be another serious drought year. We both heaved loud sighs as we entered air-conditioned bliss. Willie's was already decked out for Fourth of July. The old black-and-white photos that lined the walls were festooned with red-white-and-blue garlands and paper flags of all sizes.

While Maisie stopped at the rest room, I called home and begged for another hour.

"No worries, Gerry. We're having a pizza party," Bev said. "It's been ages since I've spent any time here and we're having a ball. I'll tell Maddie you're in the hardware store talking to Abe about plumbing supplies, and she'll be fine." The one thing that made life with our precocious preteen manageable was her predictability.

When Maisie came back, she was as ready as I was to switch topics from the weather to murder.

"What do you think about Bebe's arrest, Gerry?" she asked.

"Has she been arrested?" My shoulders fell. Did Maisie have more current knowledge than I did? I considered the image of Bebe, calling for a cop, pouring out her story for the official record. I hoped her confessor would be on top of the case enough to see the holes in her tall tale as clearly as I did.

"Well, she's been at the station all day and I think she's still there."

I relaxed. "That's different from being arrested," I explained, as if I had a degree in criminal justice instead of English lit. "It means they're trying to find enough evidence to charge her with the crime."

Maisie shrugged as if there was little difference. She wasn't far off. "I feel bad for her. I knew she was mad; she's always mad about something. But I guess this time she was madder than I thought," she said.

I gave Maisie a startled, questioning look. "You don't believe Bebe killed Craig, do you?"

Another shrug, from one of Bebe's good friends. "Bebe could lose it, you know. Remember the time those hoodlums broke her front window? She chased those boys down the street and would have whipped them if she'd caught them. Then she didn't quit until the police found the kids and made them do community service. If she'd had her way they'd have been sent to Juvenile Hall."

"I remember that, but—" I began, wanting to clarify the difference between whipping a vandal and bashing someone's head in.

"And I was there another time when a crate of ceramics was delivered to her shop and the pieces were all damaged. She was ready to throw one of the cracked platters at the driver, except he was built like a wrestler and was able to stop her."

Maisie went on with more examples of Bebe's temper. By the time my cinnamon bagel with extra cream cheese arrived, I was ready to accept Craig's murder as a crime of passion with Bebe as the perpetrator. But one bite of dough, raisin, and creamy spread, and I returned to my senses. I tried to recall whether Maisie had always seemed this ready to gossip and think the worst even of someone who was supposed to be a good friend. Probably, yes. I'm sure Maisie's current attitude was also affected by the fact that some of Bebe's ire had been directed toward her during these last months of SuperKrafts negotiations.

"Those incidents are a long way from murder," I said.

"I know, and I'm sorry I went on and on, Gerry. Really, I'm worried about her."

"Did you mention Bebe's temper to the police? I assume they questioned you?"

Maisie seemed horrified at the thought. "Of course not. I would never tell any of this to the police. They asked me about the fight we had outside the store yesterday morning and I made it seem like it was a little spat between friends. I'm just telling you how bad she can be because you're her friend, too."

It wasn't the first time I didn't quite get Maisie's logic. "I'm glad to hear that, Maisie." I finished another large segment of bagel and a long sip of iced tea, then, as casually as possible, asked, "Did you feel that earthquake yesterday? I was home with Maddie and we ended up under the table."

"I was home but it was over before I could even react and run to the doorway," she said. Maddie's "drop, cover, and hold" mantra came after Maisie's time, as it did for me. We were the "stand under a doorframe" generation. The stance, which I'd assumed a number of times during the last decades, always felt silly to me, as if we were being asked to hold up the house. "Everyone's been asking about the quake," Maisie continued, "even the police, though it was among the smallest I've ever experienced. Of course, that didn't keep my daughter from calling me from

LA to be sure I was okay. Liz is the only one who remembers to do that."

Maisie droned on about which of her children checked up on her and how often. To me, the most interesting tidbit was her mentioning that, like me, the police were collecting alibis for the time of the earthquake. I decided that must mean they'd determined Craig's time of death as following soon after the earthquake. I mentally checked off that question in my notebook.

"How was the rest of your interview with the police?" I asked Maisie, remembering that mine was yet to happen officially. I'd told Skip I'd be back at some unspecified time. I doubted most citizens were given such leniency, and I was grateful for it. I really wanted to gather information first, and have more time to think about how I might help figure out who the true killer was.

"You know me," Maisie answered. "I was so nervous talking to cops. I guess everyone is. Like when you see one on the freeway, you slow down even if you're only going the speed limit. You keep thinking they're going to arrest you, never mind that you're completely innocent." Maisie gasped and nearly tipped over her iced tea. "Oh, Gerry, what if that's what happened to Bebe?"

It was about time Maisie caught on.

# Chapter 10

I ARRIVED HOME from a day of intense meetings and walked into the middle of a party. I'd meant to relieve Bev and Nick of baby-sitting duties (not that Maddie considered herself being sat), but instead found them, along with Maddie and Henry, laughing their way through a spy girl movie, pizza, and popcorn. I felt a twinge of envy. And left out. But it was my fault. What was I doing hanging around a police station, playing sleuth, which was not my job, while my family and friends were enjoying themselves on a Sunday evening? Did I have that little respect for the police? Did I not trust them to solve this crime and trust Bebe to take care of herself? I needed some serious soul-searching.

"Hi, everyone," I said, crossing the atrium floor and entering the living room.

"Grandma, come and watch," Maddie shouted, as whoever had the remote put Spy Girl on pause.

"Sit here," Henry said, setting a chair from the dining room next to his.

"This movie's a hoot," Nick said, scratching a hairless spot on his head. "Who'da thought?"

Bev said, "I knew you'd like it," to Nick, and "Let me get you a cold drink," to me.

In less than five minutes, I was seated next to Henry, my right hand holding a mercifully cold glass of iced tea, my left immersed in Henry's popcorn bowl. I laughed with the others when Spy Girl literally pulled the rug out from under the thief's feet, toppling him, thus slowing him down while the police rushed up the driveway. "Yay!" we all cheered for Spy Girl.

I supposed I should have been glad that no one asked how my day was.

WHEN Bev and Nick had left and Maddie was busy at her computer, Henry and I had a few moments. He started with an explanation for the conspicuous absence of Taylor.

"Her pool party turned into a slumber party. Kay agreed to it. She doesn't know about the trouble that's brewing."

"There might be a letter on the way," I said, reviewing the saga of the special mail drop Maddie had made.

"I'll watch for it. Maybe I'll remember my science class tricks and steam it open if it arrives while Taylor is out of the house."

"It might be about a boy," I said.

Henry's eyes widened. He nearly slammed his mug down on the coffee table. "What? Taylor's barely eleven years old."

"Eleven and a half," I said, quickly adding, "still way too young, though. I agree."

"Who is he?" Henry asked, ready to do battle.

I explained that there was no boy for sure. I shared Mary Lou's theory that a boy might be at the center of the quarrel between the girls, and Skip's reluctant acceptance of the fact-finding mission. "I doubt it's serious," I offered and we laughed. Still, if there was a boy, I pitied him.

"I talked to Kay, hypothetically, about a person's responsibility if someone confesses to a crime," Henry said, moving on to my other dilemma.

"And?" I was all ears.

"Of course, being an officer of the court, she strongly recommended that the hypothetical person tell the police what she heard. However, there is no legal obligation for her or him to do so, unless the hypothetical person actually saw the crime being committed, or has incontrovertible evidence that the crime was committed by the person confessing. Otherwise, it's considered hearsay."

"I think I got it. I'm not…that is, the hypothetical person is not committing a crime by keeping the confession to him- or herself."

"Lawyerspeak, huh? They have their own language," said Henry, who lived with two of them.

MADDIE was back in her own bed tonight. More exactly in her father's old bed, under her father's nearly threadbare baseball sheet. I took my usual place on the rocker next to her. "I didn't want to bother you and Uncle Henry while you were talking," she said.

"That was considerate of you."

"But you promised you'd tell me about your meetings today."

"They really were very boring."

"You always say that but they never are."

Except for this evening at the impromptu party, when her laughter could be heard over everyone else's, Maddie had been sad these past few days. I wished I could reach over and make everything better for her. The least I could do was satisfy her curiosity.

"Are you ready?" I asked, tickling her, getting the desired response. "Because I'm going to tell you every boring detail."

She sat up against her pillow, covered with bats, balls, and an occasional pennant. "Go for it," she said through giggles.

"First, I got in my car, put the key in the ignition, buckled my seat belt—"

More giggles, and a poke. "Grandma!"

"Okay, no more fooling around. I drove to SuperKrafts and sat in on a meeting where we talked about whether to have the Grand Opening of the store on Wednesday, as originally planned, or to postpone it. Is that more fascinating?"

"Uh-huh," Maddie said, trying to be serious.

I continued, eventually giving Maddie the bottom line— they'd wait until Saturday to put on the gala—without repeating some of the crude remarks that were on the record, and closed with, "There will be balloons and cake and lots of special deals."

"Will I still be here on Saturday?"

"You certainly will. Your mom and dad aren't picking you up till Sunday evening."

"Goody." That's what I loved to hear. "And they'll raffle off the dollhouses on Sunday?"

I nodded. "People will be able to buy raffle tickets starting on Wednesday, and the winners will be announced at noon on Sunday."

I got another "Goody," followed by "What did you do next?"

I braced myself. "Then, I went to visit Mrs. Mellon at the police station."

Maddie pushed herself up, the better to pay attention. Clearly this was her favorite part. "Is she under arrest for killing the SuperKrafts guy?"

"No," I said, thinking, *Not yet.* "You know how the police always question everyone who ever knew a person who's been killed."

"She's the only one they're keeping, though, isn't she?"

I wondered how Maddie knew that. But, of course Maddie was always on alert for information, whether the adults were aware of it or not. "That's true. I'm sure it will all be straightened out soon," I said, hoping to rush on past this part of my day.

"Are you going to straighten it out for her?" she asked. I laughed and checked the state of her eyelids. No sign of sleepiness. "'Cause I could help," she said.

"You know if I needed anything, I would come to you first."

Maddie clapped and said, "Okay. I have an idea. But I want to hear what you did next."

I thought it wise to omit the part where I cajoled Skip into having the boy talk with her. "I ran into Mrs. Bosley. I was hungry by then, so I went to Willie's with her and had a bagel. Then I came home and joined the party."

"What did you talk about with Mrs. Bosley?"

"Nothing special."

"Grandma!"

"I don't like to share too many sad things with you," I explained. "We talked about how awful it was that someone died, and that it was in our town, in the brand-new store that we'd been looking forward to."

"Yeah, but not everyone was happy about the store, like Mrs. Mellon. I'm not saying she killed the boss, but someone else who didn't want the store probably did it, don't you think?"

"That's possible," I said. "But it's nothing either of us should be concerned about."

"I was thinking of how I could help. Do you want to hear my idea?"

Nothing was easy with my granddaughter. That seemed to be the price of brilliance in the family's next generation.

"Of course," I said.

She wiggled a bit, preparing to make her pitch. "Mr. Palmer died right when the earthquake hit, didn't he?"

"The police think so, yes."

"We could get everyone's alibi for where they were during the earthquake and ask them what fell. Then we could figure out if that thing would have fallen, because stuff gets knocked off walls according to what direction the wave comes from, and maybe one of them is lying. There are sites that tell you what kind of quake it was. I can draw charts and maps." She finally took a breath. "What do you think?"

Where to start? Were earthquakes really that simple? Weren't there many layers? How could we tell what happened deep down among the layers? Even if it were a simple process, not everyone used falling objects to describe their alibi. I couldn't imagine that Maddie's chart would amount to anything.

"That's a great idea," I said. Maybe Maddie would forget this plan in the morning. And maybe the sun would rise in the west.

"Do you have any data for me yet?" she asked.

"Yes, I already know where some of the people were."

"You know where they claimed they were," Maddie, the budding interrogator, corrected. "You can just give me the data and I'll work on a chart. I love charts and graphs."

"Me, too," I joked, and Maddie laughed even harder than she did at Spy Girl.

———

I TOOK a glass of iced tea to the atrium where it was a little cooler than in my bedroom. I rolled back the skylight and looked up at the night sky. For most of our married life, Ken and I lived in this house. The open Eichler design was his choice and I loved it—four bedrooms, kitchen, dining, and living areas built around an atrium large enough for my ficus, a jade tree, and a generous border of cyclamen. Ken had spent his last days here under the skylight in a hospital bed. Now, Ken was everywhere in the house, from the studs in the walls to the cherrywood hutch he'd built for the dining room. Almost every bit of home décor was personal to us—the photos of our son growing up, graduating many times over on his way to a career as a surgeon; the oil paintings by our daughter-in-law, the refrigerator drawings and grammar school crafts of our granddaughter.

This evening, when some of the chatter had revolved around Bev and Nick's wedding, there had been a glance or three from Bev, as if to ask me, "Are you the next bride?" Once, she looked deliberately at me then at Henry, back and forth, with a questioning look. That interaction happened to coincide with phrases they were tossing around, working on their vows, about comfortable love and companionship and the joy of sharing the rest of one's life with someone special. Subtle.

Not that either Henry or I had brought it up, but there were times in the last year when I'd asked myself, what if? Could I marry again? Before Henry, I would have dismissed the idea out of hand. I'd had wonderful years with Ken and never dreamed of more with another man. But now...

*Dum dum, da da dum, da da dum.*

A call from Skip mercifully took me away from useless musings about the future. I knew what Skip wanted, but I clicked On anyway.

"Hey, Aunt Gerry, Fred says you haven't called him yet about giving your statement," he said, without preamble.

"I got involved with Maisie Bosley and sort of forgot." I looked at the empty chair across from me in my atrium and was glad Skip wasn't sitting there as he often was at this time of night. He'd have been able to tell at a glance that I was shaving the truth.

"That's not like you," he said.

"Your mom and Nick had been watching Maddie all afternoon, and I didn't want to keep them any longer."

"That's different from forgetting."

"It was a little of both."

"Or something else entirely."

"Oh?"

"Here's what I think. I think you're trying to do a little investigating on your own before you go on record."

"Why would I do that?"

"And, you want to be able to ask Fred some questions yourself."

"Well, if that's what you want me to do, sure, I'll be glad to."

Skip let out a loud sigh. "Why do I bother?" I smiled, with only my plants as audience. "Can I tell Fred you'll be there first thing in the morning?" he asked.

"How about early afternoon? I need to bake some cookies."

"That's low. Okay, I'll tell him one o'clock. And at least bring me cookies as proof of your schedule," he said.

"You got it," I said, on my way to preheat my oven.

WHO bakes cookies late at night? Me, when I don't want to waste valuable daylight hours that can be used for interrogation and research. Since ginger cookies are my staple, I always have the ingredients, including three types of ginger, on hand, so it took only a few minutes to whip up the batter. In between batches, I gave some thought to Maddie's plan. It couldn't hurt, and it would bring some cheer into the life of my conflicted little granddaughter.

I grabbed a notebook and started with Megan, recalling my chat with her. I coded my knowledge of her whereabouts as:

*Megan/KenTucky Inn/coffeemaker, ice bucket, and drinking glasses shook*

I began to see how Maddie was going to construct her chart. I thought back to Catherine's comments during Skip's grilling (my term) and to Jeff's answer when I gently (my term) asked his location during the rattler:

*Catherine/Ken Tucky Inn/hotel clock shook*

*Jeff/inside his store/games toppled from west wall*

Another data point (I felt so erudite) came to me, and I added:

*Maisie/her home/no movement*

Bebe, of course, by confessing, essentially claimed to be at the crime scene's ground zero during the earthquake. I still needed to fill in the rows for Leo and Bebe. Maybe charts could be fun, after all.

MY last chore, after packaging the cookies, was one of my (not quite) nightly rituals of cleaning out my purse in preparation for the next day. I had no plan yet for tomorrow and my need to gather information, except to go face to face with Leo, the only one for whom I was missing an alibi. I wasn't sure what about him intimidated me, other than his size and manner, but if I was going to complete my data for Maddie—ironically, my only hope of progress at the moment—I needed his input.

I pulled my purse onto a chair in front of me in the atrium, emptying out tissues and wrappers, piling up receipts. Apparently it had been more than a couple of days since my last decluttering operation.

I extricated copies of the flyers that listed upcoming Super-Krafts workshops. In my frenzied state on hearing Bebe's confession, I'd forgotten to give her a copy of the announcement. I realized this pointed to another flaw in her story. She'd said she was angry about Craig Palmer's cutting her out of the schedule, but here was proof that he hadn't. I couldn't believe she didn't know about the arrangement. I supposed the workshops could have been cancelled after the flyers were printed, but I doubted it.

A tiny light went on. The flyers could be my way into Leo Murray. For all he knew, I'd been commissioned by the leaders to confirm the schedule with him, and by the way, where was he during the earthquake?

I was nearly finished with my purse reorganization task. I pulled out the fabric lining to shake out various crumbs (I hated to think from what or when) and pieces of lint. And, it turned out, a lovely multifaceted blue-green bead, which rolled to the end of my small area rug and across the atrium floor, settling in a line of grout near the entryway. I retrieved the bead, which I'd picked up in SuperKrafts earlier today, and placed it in a bowl on the table. It sat there, all glittery, next to a dull set of keys, a roll of mints, an old watch headed for repair, and a miniature (one half inch) Bundt cake that didn't make it to the dollhouse I'd taken to the store for the raffle.

I turned off all the lights, feeling as though I was shutting Skip off from cookies. It served him right for badgering me about my statement. Still, I felt like a bad aunt as I headed for bed. I checked the clock in the hallway. For a change, it was before midnight on the same day I'd gotten up.

# Chapter 11

MADDIE WAS MORE CHEERFUL on Monday morning. "I don't need any breakfast," she said. "Uncle Skip called me this morning. He called direct to my cell phone."

"That's pretty special," I said, returning one bowl to the cabinet and pouring cold cereal for myself.

"You know, cops get free tickets all the time, and yesterday he got coupons for Willie's and he wants to take me there for breakfast. Sometimes he gets them for Video Jeff's and Sadie's."

Free tickets for food and games. That was enough reason in itself for a little girl to aspire to be a cop. "That sounds like a lot of fun."

"Did you put him up to it?" she asked.

"What? Why would I do that?"

"To get rid of me, because you have something to do for the case."

I let out a relieved breath. So far, Maddie hadn't caught on to Skip's agenda for today. When the chips were down, I wondered if Skip would really broach the boy talk.

"I'm not sneaking around you," I said, eating my cereal while Maddie drank from a small glass of juice.

She'd changed her mind and made herself a piece of toast also. I watched her remove the bread from the package, toast it, butter it, add blackberry jelly, place the nicely prepared breakfast on a plate. All with great dexterity. Did her ability to move around the kitchen like a grown-up, manage her own meals and often mine, qualify her as old enough for a boyfriend? Abso-totally-lutely not. She was still a little girl.

"What are you going to do today?" she asked.

"I'm going to work on the data for your alibi chart. When I see you this afternoon, I should have the input ready for you."

Maddie laughed. "Data and charts and inputs. It sounds so funny when you say it."

I needed to improve my math image with the preteen set.

SKIP came to pick up Maddie at about nine-thirty. She was wide-eyed with excitement. Not so Skip, who seemed to be straining under the assignment I'd given him. A lot had changed over the years. Usually this would be the moment when Skip would grab her and swing her around in the air while she pretended to want him to put her down. But lately with Maddie's meteoric rise in height, he'd been settling for a big hug, as he did today.

Before they left, Skip gave me a droopy, helpless look that told me it was touch-and-go whether this brunch date would yield any information on the source of Maddie's angst. I was hopeful, and also grateful to have my precocious granddaughter out from under me so I could use my next hours in a productive way before my police interview.

I needed an excuse to talk to the SuperKrafts principals. Catherine, Megan, and especially Leo, for whom I didn't have an alibi I could record on my data list. Or whatever it was called. The idea of confirming the workshop schedule seemed lame once I gave it some thought—I could confirm by phone or email. I resented the fact that I couldn't simply call a meeting, as any one of them could. Neither could I call them up and start interrogating them as if I had an LPPD badge. I was stuck.

With the last gulp of coffee, when I'd almost given up, came an idea. On Wednesday, we'd have what the SuperKrafts team members were calling a "soft opening"—no fireworks, simply operational cash registers so townsfolk could shop. I figured there'd be a lot to do to prepare—only two days away—even without the balloons and party hats.

I picked up my phone and called the number I had for Maddie's former, and occasionally current, babysitter.

"Hey, Mrs. Porter, what's up?" Jeanine asked. "I'm in my car on my way to work so I shouldn't talk too long. I'm still saving up for a Bluetooth."

"Just a quick question, Jeanine. I was wondering if you needed any help getting the dollhouse display ready for the raffle. I could come down and work on that if you have other things to do."

"OMG, Mrs. Porter, that would be awesome. Would you do that? Two of the girls called to say they didn't feel well, so I'll be by myself. I'd even split my check with you."

I laughed. "Not at all necessary, Jeanine. I'd love to do it. Most of the houses are from the women in my crafts group and…well, never mind, you'd better get off the phone. I'll see you shortly."

"Thanks, Mrs. Porter. That would be a huge favor."

"The pleasure will be mine," I said, with more truth than Jeanine could have imagined.


A HALF hour later, in a déjà vu moment, I pulled up behind SuperKrafts and parked in the same row as Catherine's silver Taurus, Megan's red Camry, and Leo's Ford, an odd shade of blue. I figured the beat-up maroon Dodge, with a California license plate that began with a two, marking it as many years old, was a hand-me-down that belonged to a recent high school graduate—Jeanine Larkin.

I rang the bell. "Hi. Really, Mrs. Porter, this is so nice of you," Jeanine said, opening the back door for me. "You can't imagine how crazy it is here, with Mr. Palmer's…dying and all. Can you believe it? I mean, we hardly met him. Well, I hardly met him."

"It is hard to grasp, I know. I suppose the police talked to you?"

"Well, yeah, but like I told you, I didn't know him at all." She shook her head as if to remove the event from her consciousness, I imagined. "What about Mrs. Mellon? I heard the police have her in custody?"

"Not technically. I hope she'll be home soon."

Jeanine looked confused, and who could blame her. "Anyway, I've been neglecting the dollhouse setups and feeling really bad about it," she said.

"Just tell me what to do," said I, the magnanimous volunteer.

Jeanine led me past the meeting room. Through the window in the wooden door, I could see the three managers, sitting at the long table, sans community representation. I guessed there were no more issues requiring input from reps of the concerned citizens of Lincoln Point.

"What do you think they're meeting about?" I asked, wondering if a young associate would know.

"I heard them discussing a moment of silence or something on Saturday, to remember Mr. Palmer. I wish they'd stop fighting. It seems like every day there's another thing they don't agree on. If you ask me, they all need time-outs."

*From the mouths of babes.* We'd arrived at an area near the front of the store. Here and there, through the tinted windows and the flyers and giant neon-green SALE signs that covered them, I caught glimpses of faces and arms and legs. Passersby, but no one I recognized from body parts only. I stepped to the locked front door and peered across the street into Willie's windows, too far away for me to see through, but I imagined Skip and Maddie eating bagels—an "everything" for Skip and a blueberry for Maddie. In my thoughts Maddie was confiding in Skip, explaining that her issues with Taylor involved a disagreement over whether to watch the next spy girl movie on DVD or on their computers. It had nothing to do with the young males of the species, and wouldn't for a very long time. A grandmother could dream.

"There they are," Jeanine said. She tucked a strand of hair that had escaped her long ponytail behind her ear and waved at the miniature skyline of dollhouses. "I haven't even prepared the basket for people to put their tickets in and the furniture is a mess in some of them, all tipped over."

"As if there'd been an earthquake," I said.

Jeanine laughed. "Exactly."

"Where were you when it hit?" I asked, before I realized that

Jeanine wasn't on my list of suspects. This was practice, I told myself, and for the sake of completion on Maddie's chart.

"I went to meet some friends for coffee at Seward's after work and we were, like, in the middle of a conversation when there was this noise, and then this box of coffee filters fell onto our table and knocked my friend Bonnie's mug over. We laughed. We didn't have time to drop, cover, and hold like we learned, though. It was over in a sec."

I dutifully recited the facts to myself in the format of the alibi data I'd already gathered:

*Jeanine / Seward's Folly / package of filters fell from shelf*

"Well, I came here to be of use," I said. "Why don't I start by fixing the furniture arrangements in the houses and then I'll work on getting the raffle basket ready."

"Awesome, Mrs. Porter. I'll be back in Floral if you need me."

It didn't take long for me to get caught up in restoring order to the rooms in the dollhouses. I couldn't resist a little remodeling while I was at it. I knew that my friends and crafts group members wouldn't mind my fiddling with their creations. Gail would understand if I moved the television set in the living room of her split-level ranch to a less central spot and used her spectacular fireplace as a centerpiece instead. Karen's Cape Cod kitchen had lost its refrigerator, but I found it on the floor below the houses and placed it by a window covered in gingham. While I was at it, I adjusted the bedding and tacked down a mat in the bathroom. (Every crafter I knew carried a handy kit with a selection of sewing notions, glues and fasteners, and assorted small tools.) I made similar adjustments to Susan's Victorian half-scale and Betty's grand Tudor.

I was so wrapped up in the delightful task, I nearly forgot my reason for reporting to work this morning. Initially, I'd thought the meeting participants would come out for a break, but they were apparently still deep in discussion, or maybe fisticuffs.

I needed a pretext to go back to the room. I could claim extreme hunger and crawl, clutching my stomach, to the vending machines. Or dire thirst and fall, panting, on the sink and hold my head under the faucet. I hadn't taught Shakespearean drama for nothing. To aid in finding an alternative to melodrama, I visualized the room, the vending machines, the kitchen counter, and the general storage area for cleaning supplies while the janitorial closet was being painted. And lockers.

Lockers! That would do. We reps had been given keys to the same locker, to share its use on a temporary basis. Bebe always stashed her purse in there when she went for a power walk after a meeting; Maisie put packages in the locker if she'd gone shopping on the boulevard before a meeting. Other reps, including me, stored odds and ends if we were doing errands around the meeting time. There was nothing of mine in the locker at the moment, but there was bound to be something in it, anything from a pair of shoes to a lunchbox or a shirt from the dry cleaners.

Hadn't I left my other pair of glasses in the locker yesterday afternoon? It wasn't out of the question. That was my story and I was sticking to it. I headed back. On the way, I came upon Jeanine, tangled in oversized paper flowers with long stems.

"I hate these things," she said. "They're really cheesy. You can tell they're not real a mile away." Jeanine drew in her breath. "Oh, sorry, Mrs. Porter. I hope they're not, like, your favorite thing?"

I shook my head. "Don't worry, Jeanine. I don't like them either and I never use them."

I didn't lie about the fake flowers, though I did love the beautiful sculpted specimens I saw at miniatures shows, by talented artisans—tiny petals and leaves that looked so botanically correct one would swear they were real.

"How's it going up front, Mrs. Porter?"

"Everything's fine. I'm ready to prepare the raffle basket, except I think I left my glasses in our locker." I pointed toward the meeting room. "Do you think they'll mind if I just slip in and check?"

She waved her hand in a "no big deal" way. "I'm always barging in for something."

With permission from a nineteen-year-old, I strode confidently toward the future employee's lounge. A few feet away, I smoothed my dress and hair, as if I were about to make an important entrance. I still hadn't figured a way to isolate Leo of the Missing Alibi, but first things first. I approached the door, ready to tap on the window. Without warning, like an alarm or a siren, the main door to the parking lot flew open behind me and three men pushed in. I was left with my arm in midair as the men, one in a light summer suit, the others in LPPD uniforms, closed the gap between us. Were cops privy to a universal key code for such barriers as alarmed doors?

I thought they'd come for me. My delinquency in providing a statement weighed on me, the worry increasing when the man in the suit addressed me.

"Geraldine," said Fred Bates. An interesting choice of name for me. What did it mean that Detective Bates had abandoned the "Mrs. Porter" of our parent-teacher conference days when his son, Aaron, was my student? I searched the faces of the two younger men behind him, the ones equipped with radios, handcuffs, and guns, for signs of recognition, but I didn't know them. "Imagine seeing you here," Bates added.

I backed away from the meeting room door. I mumbled something about working on the dollhouse display and alluded to a phone call I was about to make to his office just before he walked in. The SuperKrafts managers responded to the new racket by exiting their meeting room, Leo in the lead.

"What's up?" Leo asked. I could have sworn his look lingered on me, as if I were the one who'd called in the cavalry.

Jeanine came up behind me. "OMG, I propped the door open for my Dumpster runs," she whispered. "Did I forget to close it?"

"Catherine Duncan?" Fred asked, in lieu of answering Leo directly.

Megan's face took on a relieved look, as did mine, as Catherine stepped forward, her eyes questioning, her body seeming to quiver as if the earth had shaken under her feet. "I'm her...she," she said, in case I was still grading her grammar. "What...what can I do for you?" she added.

Then it seemed as if someone had turned on a television set and a crime drama was being piped in. We were at the point in the show where the cop says, "(*Name here*), I'm placing you under arrest for the murder of (*name here*). You have the right to remain…"

Surely it couldn't be happening in front of me, in real life. In the next minute, the two uniformed officers were leading Catherine out the back door. Following the script in my mind, I had the urge to shout, "Don't say anything until you speak to your lawyer."

When I came out of my confusion, I heard Catherine's real voice calling out, "This is a mistake," or something close to that, as she was hurried away by the officers.

Fred Bates stood in front of me. "I'd like you to come to the station, Geraldine," he said. His voice had an authoritative ring.

I pointed to the front of the store. "I'm in the middle of—" I interrupted myself, feeling Bates's eyes on me. "I'll just grab my purse."

I CONSIDERED walking the short distance from SuperKrafts to the LPPD building, but once I hit the ninety-plus-degree air outside, I chose to drive. It also occurred to me that, if seen strolling south along Springfield Boulevard, I might be construed as having too casual an attitude toward the personally delivered call to appear. I started my car, counting myself lucky that I wasn't sitting in the back of a squad car.

The parking lot behind the LPPD building was nearly empty as I pulled into a spot close to the basement door about three minutes after leaving the crafts store. I smiled as I thought of what my old friends in the Bronx would say about my driving the short, easily walkable distance. I heard them in my mind: "That's so California."

A kind female officer at the desk led me back to the interview rooms and offered me a bottle of water, which I gladly accepted. It wasn't clear whether I should be happy or worried that Skip was nowhere to be seen inside the building.

To my surprise, I was assigned to the interview room that had housed Bebe for so many hours. A faint odor of nervous perspiration lingered. I wished I knew who deserved the nice interview rooms more than I did? Had I used up all my chits for preferential treatment as the aunt of a homicide detective? There was no end to my list of questions. Where was Bebe now? There was no doubt that Catherine was under arrest. I'd heard the words myself. But why? What evidence did they have against her? And where was my nephew? I wondered if he knew what was going on. I assumed he had the good sense not to leave Maddie alone at Willie's, but I wanted him here.

No one had told me I couldn't use my cell phone, but in fact, there was no service in the windowless interior room. If I had to guess, I'd say the signal was deliberately blocked.

I took a long gulp of water, then tried deep breathing, not my best talent. When I was in an agitated state, there wasn't much besides a resolution to the cause that could bring me down. Especially when noises, like those from the busy hallway, intruded. I could have sworn I heard someone say, "I'm innocent!" But it might have been my active imagination in highly volatile surroundings.

It seemed forever but was probably only fifteen minutes before the door to the stifling room opened.

"Glad you made it down," Skip said. He was in shirtsleeves and a loosened tie. Not my official interviewer, I gathered.

"Where's Maddie?" I asked, putting first things first.

"Not to worry. She's entertaining the troops in the reception area. Seeing old friends, making new ones."

At least someone was having a good day. "Can you tell me what's going on?" I asked. "You've arrested Catherine?" In case I really had been imagining the scene, I framed it as a question.

"Yeah, we staged all this just to get you down here and finally give us your statement."

I crossed my arms. "Not funny."

"No, it isn't."

"What's happened to Bebe?" I asked, starting down a different road.

"Her story didn't check out."

"Her story?"

Skip gave me a look that might have been interpreted as annoyed. "She confessed to killing Palmer. Apparently not for the first time. When were you going to let us in on your little talk with her yesterday?"

I shrugged and made a note not to trust Bebe to keep promises that involved the police. "You just said yourself, her story didn't check out."

"That doesn't mean you shouldn't have told us."

"I figured you were listening in."

"Not if she hadn't been charged."

"I checked. I had no legal obligation."

I couldn't believe I'd fallen for the trap. Skip had only guessed that Bebe had confessed to me. I'd obligingly confirmed that he was right. I was sure I made his day.

"I'm guessing that means you asked Henry to ask his daughter and son-in-law, the criminal lawyers."

I shook my head. "They're not criminal lawyers. They're both in mergers and acquisitions."

Skip smiled and pointed his finger at my face. "Exactly," he said, triumphant. Worse, he was still standing, forcing me to look up to him.

"You win," I said, tired of his games. I was conscious that Fred Bates would replace my nephew at any moment and I still had questions, aunt to nephew. "Why was Catherine arrested?"

Skip sat on the table "We got an anonymous tip, pointing to evidence."

"You're arresting her on the basis of an anonymous tip?"

"Did you hear the word evidence?"

"Yes, but you didn't say what evidence."

"It's nothing you have to worry about."

I waved in the direction of the shabby walls of the room. "And why am I in this room? It's the prime suspect's room." I let out a long sigh. "I've never seen anything like this. First Bebe is arrested—"

"Taken for questioning. Never charged," Skip corrected.

"Then, Bebe is let go and Catherine takes her place. Am I next? You're all acting like Keystone Kops."

"Who?"

Young people these days. No sense of history, I thought. "The Keystone Kops," I repeated, slowly. "Have Maddie do a search on Google. You'll find them there, right alongside Charlie Chaplin. They're comic police figures who bumble around trying to keep order and capture criminals." I left out how they'd become the catchphrase for any incompetent group. "Your maternal grand-father loved their movies." I drew in my breath, ratcheting back to my mention of Maddie. "Did you get a chance to talk to her about—"

A slight tap on the door interrupted me. The tap was simul-taneous with the door's swinging open, before anyone could call out permission to enter.

"I'll take it from here," Fred Bates said.

"Whew," Skip said, pretending to wipe his brow.

It was good that at least one of us was relieved.

# Chapter 12

I'D THOUGHT ABOUT asking Fred if I could have a few more minutes with my nephew. I had questions hanging, answerless—what was the evidence against Catherine, and how did the Skip-and-Maddie meeting go, especially vis-à-vis any boys on the horizon? A third question, "Who really murdered Craig Palmer?" also needed attention. And a fourth, addressed to me, was why had I done so little to aid an investigation that kept leading to my friends being detained? If I ever decided on a second career as a private eye, as Skip had facetiously suggested more than once, I'd fail the experience test.

In the end I chose to greet Fred with a silent, submissive smile.

He began with an apology, perhaps disingenuous, perhaps not. "Sorry about the shabby digs. It's busy, busy today." Fred, also in shirtsleeves, hiked up the waistband of his pants. He still had an ample shock of white hair but had added a few pounds since his son Aaron's high school days.

"No problem," said I, the obliging one.

"Is Geraldine okay?" he asked. At first I thought he was inquiring after my health, in the third person—like the irritating practice of some medical professionals I'd seen lately. But I soon understood that we were back at the how-shall-I-address-you stage. Many parents of my students had difficulty coming up with a proper salutation once I was no longer their children's teacher. Fred and I were about to come to terms.

"'Geraldine' is fine," I said.

"Good. Then let's go with Geraldine and Fred. You understand why we can't have Skip formally interview you?"

"Of course."

He took a seat opposite me, the seat I'd occupied while I talked to Bebe. I didn't like this new arrangement, with the battered table between me and the door. And I really didn't like the small recorder he set out. He pressed the On button casually, as if he were simply adjusting his tie. "Let's start with how well you knew Craig Palmer," he said, after stating the formalities of names, date, and time.

"Hardly at all," I said. "He came to Lincoln Point for the first time on Friday night, as I understand it, and I met him briefly on Saturday afternoon."

"What was your impression?"

"By briefly, I mean about five minutes, when he came into Sadie's—"

"The ice cream shop?"

"Yes." I realized how odd that sounded and explained the sequence of events on Saturday when Craig and Megan interrupted the peacekeeping sweet-tooth meeting among Catherine, me, and Bebe and Maisie, who'd already left.

"What was your impression of him?" he asked again.

I understood what Fred wanted, but hesitated to use words like "arrogant," "demanding," and "downright unpleasant" about a recent murder victim.

"My impression was that he was in charge."

"Had you heard about him before he arrived? Was there, you know"—intentionally or not, Fred leaned in closer to me and lowered his voice—"was there any four-one-one you want to share?"

"Excuse me?"

"Sorry, I reverted to jargon. Four-one-one is shorthand for 'information.' I really want to know if there was any gossip about the victim that preceded him."

In other words, we were getting chummy. "Gossip about Craig?" I asked, stalling.

"Yeah. You've been working with his employees, like Catherine Duncan and Leo Murray, for a while now. Correct?"

"Uh-huh."

"So have you heard any gossip from Catherine or Leo?"

To squeal or not to squeal. My silence after Bebe's confession to me had got me into trouble, but only a small amount, with Skip. All in the family. In retrospect, I'd kept Bebe's secret better than she had. Was it worth it? And wasn't it a little off-base for Fred, a police detective, to ask for rumors? I'd told Skip everything I knew about the New York–Lincoln Point decision that was a sticky situation between Catherine and Jeff, and even the one-time romance between Catherine and Craig. Had Skip told Fred? The LPPD assigned partners on a rotating basis, so it wasn't as if they'd been buds for years, going for beers after work. But if Skip had already told Fred what I said and I now told Fred I didn't know any rumors, would Fred…this was beginning to sound like a word problem in algebra, the bane of my existence during my own high school days in the Bronx: *If Bobby has twice as many apples as you had yesterday, what's the capital of Peru?* I could bring on a headache just thinking of the daily assignments.

I decided it was my turn to ask a question. "Did Skip share what I told him informally?"

Fred smiled, as if he were onto me, a civilian trying to hedge her bets, let alone discern the inner workings of the LPPD. "Why don't you just share it all with me now?" he said.

I knew Fred was only doing his job, but I felt he could have been more forthcoming instead of putting me on the spot with respect to what I'd told Skip. If Skip hadn't shared with Fred, Fred might hold it against him in some way. And if Skip had shared, Fred might be ready to compare our two stories, planning to come back at one of us with a discrepancy. All of which could have been avoided, if Skip had only told me whether he'd told Fred. I tried to follow the lines of communication and again got lost in the algebra of it.

Finally, I told all. One more time, I went through the issues of Leo's promotion, Megan's status, and the ever-present romantic tangle, including Video Jeff's part. It all weighed on me and I saw that my distaste for the exercise came through to Fred.

"I know you don't like telling tales, Geraldine, but you understand even more than the ordinary citizen does how important it is that we know as much as possible while we're trying to figure out who murdered a man in our hometown."

"But you've already arrested Catherine," I pointed out. "Are you looking for more evidence?"

Fred clicked his tongue. Not happy. "Anything else?" he asked. "Any confidences you're still reluctant to share?" He held up his hand. "I guess that's an oxymoron, right?"

"Close enough," I said, back to being an English teacher. "And no, there's nothing else." In my mind, I added, "...that I care to share." I had a ridiculous moment of satisfaction at not telling either Skip or Fred about Catherine's threatening notes. More than ridiculous once I realized that the police would soon find them as they were bound to search Catherine's room, car, and personal belongings.

"Then I guess we're done," Fred said. He handed me his card with the usual admonition to call him if I remembered anything else. I took the card, but doubted I'd be using it.

Fred stood, pushed his chair under the table, picked up the small recorder, and opened the door to exit. Before leaving, he turned and addressed me again.

"Say, I assume you remember the earthquake on Saturday evening?"

As Skip himself would have admitted, the ploy was "way too Colombo."

I was ready for him. "At six thirty-two, I ducked under my dining room table with my eleven-year-old granddaughter, Madison Porter, and my friend, Henry Baker, of number four-seven-six-one Sangamon River Road."

Fred gave me a salute. "Okay, then," he said.

After he left the room, I lingered a couple of minutes, going over the interview. I wondered if I should put my own alibi on Maddie's chart.

———

OFFICIALLY dismissed by Detective Fred, I was at loose ends. The morning was shot and though I'd had a wonderful time plying my craft with dollhouses, I was no closer to talking to Leo or to closing in on Craig Palmer's killer. I was close to giving up on both, acknowledging the wisdom of the LPPD, accepting the idea that Catherine Duncan was a murderer. I still wondered what possible evidence had led to her arrest. Skip was not answering his cell phone and the same LPPD officer at Reception who let me know that Skip and Maddie had left the building also told me that Ms. Duncan was not available for a visit. I was on my own.

I doubted Skip and Maddie would have gone back to Willie's, but I needed food, and this time decided that the short walk up Springfield Boulevard would do me good. I pulled a floppy white hat out of a tote in my trunk and headed off under the searing noontime sun.

I made it all the way to a seat in Willie's without interruption. No friends, current or former students stopped me for a chat, no suspected criminal or relative of a suspected criminal asked for my help. My uninterrupted walk might have been due to the brim of my hat, which hid my face; my businesslike (antisocial?) posture in the shop might have been what kept greeters at bay. I sat hunched over, a toasted sesame bagel in one hand, a pen in the other. For the most part, I wrote nothing intelligible to anyone else, but doodled on my notepad, an activity that often accompanied heavy thinking for me.

Suppose Catherine was innocent. What was I missing? (Represented by a series of circles in an array with some holes filled in, some open.) How could I get back on track? (I drew thin, straight lines running parallel, diverging, then coming back to parallel, but thicker.) Was it time for me to bow out, let the investigation take its course, and resume my normal life? (A collage grew on my notepad: wedding favors; guidebooks for returning students of English; a miniature police station and a tiny ice cream parlor in progress on my crafts table.) I thought back to the threatening notes Catherine had showed me. Could they have been sent by the killer, who was now trying to frame Catherine since she didn't oblige him by leaving town? (A row of envelopes, each in its own elaborate frame, ran across the page.)

After a few more questions and more elaborate doodles, I took out my phone to call Jeanine. Most of Willie's patrons this afternoon were older and I felt judged and embarrassed to use my cell phone in a restaurant, even though I was by myself and therefore not being rude to a companion. I held the phone on my lap while I entered Jeanine's number and resolved to add texting to my phone plan as my whole family had been begging me to do. I finally saw the great value of texting: letting my thumbs do the work surreptitiously, while I could assume a meditative look, no phone blatantly attached to my ear to give me away. For now, I lifted the phone to my ear and gave anyone who was paying attention an apologetic look.

"Mrs. Porter, what's happening?" Jeanine asked. "It's crazy here. Leo and Megan are back there arguing. Catherine is, like, gone, as you know. I'm the only one working and maybe I'm the only sane one here and that's pretty depressing."

"Would you like some help?"

"OMG, would I. It's not fair to you, but really, I'm going nuts here. I can split my check with you."

"I'm just across the street."

"Okay, thanks a ton. See you in a few. I'll prop the back door open." Jeanine paused. "Oh, maybe not," she said, probably remembering what had transpired the last time she propped the door open. "Just ring the buzzer, okay?"

I downed the last bite of bagel and drank the last slurp of coffee, gathered my things, and headed for SuperKrafts. I wouldn't dream of taking a penny from Jeanine's paycheck, but I thought it might be nice to have a logo apron. I hoped I'd have a chance to spend as much time shopping in the store as I had preparing for its opening.

THE imposing back door opened just as I was about to press the buzzer. The full bulk of Leo Murray stepped out and nearly knocked me over. My heavily laden purse fell to the ground with a clunk; I felt sorry for the ground.

"Sorry," Leo said, buttoning his suit jacket as if he were not about to walk out into one of the hottest days of the year. He continued on in a way that I associated with twelve-year-olds (not that Maddie would ever grow into that behavior). I made a wild guess that this would not be a good time to run after him and ask where he was during the Lincoln Point three-point-one.

I straightened myself out, and grabbed the door before it closed and locked. While my eyes adjusted to the relative darkness inside the store another figure came toward me. Jeanine, looking more harried than a nineteen-year-old should.

"See what I mean, Mrs. Porter?" Jeanine noted. "Leo storms out, leaving Megan practically in tears in the break room. Have you ever seen such madness? All I want to do is get the inventory on the shelves and have a few minutes with my boyfriend before we have to go to class tonight."

I snuck a look through the window into the meeting room and saw Megan with her arms forming a cushion on the table for her head. Except for Jeanine's comment, I might have thought she was napping. Not a bad idea. I wouldn't blame Megan for hoping her life at the moment was a bad dream. Her boss had been murdered; her colleague was in jail for the crime; her fate in her company was most likely up in the air.

I gave Jeanine a bright smile; I needed to help her before she became the next one to give in to tears. I'd have been glad to talk to Megan also, but didn't know her well enough to insert myself into her problems.

Jeanine and I worked for about an hour, unloading pallets, opening cartons, discussing the best arrangement for the various yarns for knitting and crocheting. Not having kept up with stitchery lately, I was amazed at the new materials now available. Like the yarn with pom-poms woven into the skein approximately every two inches.

"As you knit," Jeanine explained, "the pom-poms fall into place."

I recalled the days when I had to form my own pom-poms, by pushing my needle six or seven times into the same stitch in an ever-tightening loop. Another skein that caught my eye was made of strands that were wide bands of lace, giving a cascade effect when worked into a scarf.

"I can whip up a long, beautiful scarf in a couple of hours with this," Jeanine said, expanding a length of the yarn. "And it looks like you worked a really complicated pattern."

"But the work has already been done for you at the factory," I noted.

Jeanine nodded. "Cool, huh?"

We unloaded silk yarn, bamboo yarn, glittery yarn, textured yarn, and yarn so thick you could finger-knit. Now that so many options were available, maybe I'd pick up yarn crafts again. I smiled as I thought of the purists in my crafts group. The way they felt about kits for building dollhouses and furniture gave me a good idea of what serious knitters might think about the novelty yarns. I wondered if they might fall under the spell of the glorious new colors and decorative touches.

Young women like Jeanine were always a pleasure to talk to, and for a while I put worry about Catherine and the whereabouts of Skip and Maddie out of my mind. I learned of Jeanine's ambitious plans to transfer from community college to a state university and then on to graduate school.

"I was going to major in psychology," she said. "But I don't know. What's the point? Do we really know anything about human nature?" Fortunately, Jeanine didn't pause long, and I didn't have to answer, though I had little doubt what had prompted the heavy thoughts. "I keep thinking about Ms. Duncan. I can't believe someone I've known for almost a year actually killed a person. Do you really think she could have done it, Mrs. Porter? Did she kill Mr. Palmer?"

There was no way out of this one. We'd taken a brief break and were seated on two sturdy crates eating grapes from Jeanine's lunch bag. Megan was still in the back room but was now working on her laptop. I thought of inviting her to join this conversation. She knew both Catherine and Craig better than either Jeanine or I did. I discarded the idea.

"I know it's hard to deal with, Jeanine. And we may never understand why people kill each other, after so many centuries of what we call civilization." I took a breath, reminding myself that I didn't need to be making speeches right now. "As far as what went on right here in this store on Saturday, I can't bring myself to believe that Catherine, who was my student, is a murderer. Remember, we don't have all the facts yet, so let's just wait and see."

I couldn't imagine a more pitiful performance, but I was as befuddled as Jeanine, leaning more toward acceptance than I'd let on to Jeanine, that the case was closed. And wasn't that a good thing, no matter that I knew the accused? Wasn't it time for me to go shopping with my sister-in-law and granddaughter for pretty shoes for all of us?

"I've never known anyone who was murdered," Jeanine said, possibly unaware of my comments, which wouldn't have been a great loss. "My boyfriend and I were talking about it. It scares me that one of the people here could be a killer. Do you know that the other two girls who were hired were supposed to be here today? They called in sick, but I think they're just too scared to work here. Do you think I should quit?"

I asked myself, what would I have told Maddie? That the world was a mixed bag of good people and bad and that living scared wasn't the best option? I said as much to Jeanine. "By all accounts, this wasn't random. Someone wanted Craig Palmer dead and used the opportunity presented by the earthquake. No one broke in hoping to find a victim or wanting to steal a vase or some yarn. As soon as the police have analyzed the fingerprints and all the other evidence they've gathered"—the alleged evidence, I thought—"it will make some sense. Well, maybe not sense, but…"

"I know what you mean, Mrs. Porter. And I'm not a quitter in general."

"Who's quitting?" Megan Sutley had come up behind us and now made herself known.

"I'm just taking a short break, Ms. Sutley," Jeanine said. "I'm not quitting."

Megan waved away Jeanine's nervous explanation. "Mind if I pull up a crate?" she asked, while doing so. I'd noticed at the balloons-or-no-balloons meeting, and when I ran into her at the police station before her interview, that she'd shed her obsequious manner; she showed more confidence, almost relief, which was understandable given the kind of boss Craig Palmer seemed to be.

"This is the first time I've been this far into the store," Megan said.

"Ever?" Jeanine asked.

"Uh-huh. Remember I just got into town a couple of nights ago and then after the … the death, I couldn't bring myself to walk farther than the meeting room. But I overheard you chatting and I needed a little company. This whole thing is certainly outside any experience I've ever had."

"It's crazy," Jeanine said, her position on many things, I noted. "Ms. Duncan in jail? I mean, I didn't think Mrs. Mellon was guilty either. I don't know what to think."

"Here's what I think: The police around here are at a complete loss with an honest-to-goodness homicide on their hands," Megan said.

I threw my shoulders back, ready to pounce. I might have started with "What's so honest or good about a homicide?" but Jeanine saved the day. Perhaps she knew what I was capable of when it came to defending the LPPD in public, and was afraid I'd be nasty to a woman who was currently one of her bosses. "We've had lots of homicides here," Jeanine said. "Well, not lots, but we have the best detectives. Mrs. Porter's nephew is amazing."

I could hear the town council in a frenzy at Jeanine's defense of Lincoln Point, touting its ability to hold its own with a murder rate to be reckoned with.

"I believe it was my nephew who interviewed you at the station," I said, barely containing my pique.

"The cute redhead?" Megan asked with what might have been interpreted as a flirty grin. (*Hands off*, I thought.) Unlike Catherine, she had not abandoned her New York wardrobe and had been in black every time I'd seen her. Today's sleeveless linen two-piece outfit was the kind advertised as being able to go from the boardroom to the cocktail party with a quick change of accessories. Her purse was the third one I'd seen her with in as many days, this one black with enough silver grommets, rivets, and chains to support a small bridge.

I wanted to tell Megan she was definitely not his type, but in fact Skip's girlfriends over the years had all been of slight build with dark hair. They'd all been nice however, whereas Megan had been insulting, starting with her ridiculing the KenTucky Inn. So what if most residents also blushed at it; it wasn't fair game for a stranger. I liked her better when she was a meek gofer, padding along behind her boss.

"I guess we'll never forget when it happened," Jeanine said. "I'm afraid from now on every time there's a quake, I'm going to think of the murder." She sighed, resigned. "Did you feel it, Ms. Sutley? The earthquake, I mean?"

"I did, and some things broke in my hotel room."

Megan had already told me that she was in her room, and had shared all she knew about Leo's movements, that he'd stayed a little later at the store with Craig. How late, I wondered. I'd yet to find a way to determine Leo's timeline. If only I knew someone on the LPPD force who would tell me, I mused. That is, in case I decided not to butt out.

"What's a killer like anyway?" Jeanine was back on her psychology track. I didn't blame her. "I mean, do they look normal? Do they show up for class and work and all? Pay their tuition?" It was easy to figure out Jeanine's stage of life.

"I'm sure some of them do," I said.

"Unfortunately they don't wear labels," Megan added. "I read somewhere that under the right...or wrong...circumstances, anyone might kill."

Jeanine rubbed her arms. "That's creepy."

"I agree," Megan said.

"Are you going to stay around, Ms. Sutley? I mean, not to be nosy, but I'm wondering..."

"Who's going to be your boss?"

Jeanine nodded. "If you know and can tell and don't mind."

Megan's eyes seemed to cloud over as she looked out the

tinted window. At what? Her future? It was hard to tell. "I really can't even say who will be my boss, let alone yours, Jeanine." Megan waved her hand in the direction of the back room, as if Leo were still there. "We're trying to work it all out now. Ultimately, Corporate will decide, of course," she said, as if Corporate were the name of the person who held her fate in his hands. Joe or Jane Corporate, I thought, amusing only myself. Megan stood and brushed the back of her skirt, which was smaller than some dinner napkins I owned. She threw back her shoulders. "But you can bet I'll come out a winner this time." I wanted to ask what kind of game they were playing, what the prize was, but Megan seemed ready to leave and I didn't want to detain her. "Well, I'm going to take off," she said. "Can you lock up, Jeanine?"

Jeanine stuttered an "I guess so," and gave me a frantic look.

"I can hang around a while," I said.

"Beyond the call of duty, Gerry," Megan said, chummy now that we'd chatted on crates together, and wandered off toward the back exit.

"Thanks, Mrs. Porter," Jeanine said. "Usually, I wouldn't mind, but—"

But a murdered man and his killer occupied this very ground about forty-eight hours ago. "No problem," I said. "Let's finish the job. One more box to unload, and when you come in tomorrow you'll just have to put the finishing touches on the shelves. Tell me about your boyfriend. You say you met him at school?"

"Oh, yeah, Ethan. He's another story, Mrs. Porter. He writes poetry."

Uh-oh, I thought. Things were tough for people in the creative arts. I knew only a few people who could make a living at miniatures, for example. And even they had back-up finances handy, in the form of an inheritance or a partner with a more traditional nine-to-five job. The few miniatures stores that were left, shops my crafter friends and I would travel many miles to visit, had of necessity given over half or more of their space to other products, from soaps and sundries to vintage clothing.

"Does he have a job, besides writing poetry?"

"Uh-uh," she said, removing spools of ribbon from a carton.

Like the yarn, the ribbons were of many designs and materials. I read the names as I handed the products to Jeanine. Holographic, lacquered, metallic, moiré, flocked, raffia, and at least a dozen more coming up, all in different colors and widths.

"He won't even take any practical classes," Jeanine continued. "I keep telling him he has to earn a living, you know, but he doesn't seem to get it. He wants to follow his heart. He doesn't understand why I take jobs like this." Jeanine held up a spool of narrow red crimped curling ribbon as a sample of her job duties. "He self-published a couple of sets of poems. They don't make any money, but you might like them, Mrs. Porter."

"How interesting," I said. As a former English teacher, I hated to admit that I wasn't a fan of any poetry published after the nineteenth century, with the possible exceptions of T. S. Eliot and Robert Frost. And some days, Sylvia Plath.

"I'll write down the names for you," she said, stopping to take a small notebook from her pocket. As she wrote the titles, she explained that the Lincoln Point library refused to buy them, but Rosie of Rosie's Book Shop had agreed to keep a few copies on the counter.

I took the piece of paper she tore out of the notebook. "I'll have to check them out," I said, not mentioning when that might be.

"So, what do you think? Should I encourage him? Maybe you need to read the poems first? I confronted him again this weekend about the need to earn some money. Like, I don't mind paying for things when we go out, but he needs to start contributing." She sighed. "Then I think, maybe I'm stifling his creativity?"

This conversation wasn't what I had in mind. I couldn't face another lovers' quarrel or another case of mismatched couples. Fortunately Jeanine simply wanted to talk, and did so as we emptied the ribbon carton. She didn't wait for my advice, which was good, because I was fresh out.

# Chapter 13

AT THREE O'CLOCK on Monday, Jeanine clocked out and I guarded her while she locked up SuperKrafts. She hoped I'd like Ethan's poems and thanked me again for my advice regarding her boyfriend. If the word "advice" had been replaced by "listening," she'd have had reason to be grateful, but if she thought I did her some good, I didn't want to talk her out of it. We said good-bye and I headed home.

It felt good to have been productive in one area at least: preparing a retail store with my favorite kind of merchandise for business on Wednesday. I'd had a voice mail message from Skip telling me that he and Maddie were having a good day and would see me midafternoon. I thought "having a good day" might be code for "she's not into boys" or something else. Or maybe they were simply having a good day.

Not so Catherine Duncan, I suspected. I wondered how she was faring and if I'd be allowed to see her. Probably not a chance. I imagined some highly paid lawyer from the SuperKrafts staff was on a plane now, and that a criminal attorney would follow shortly. What if she'd already confessed? I couldn't make up my mind. Should I continue to try to tie up all the loose ends in my head, or was it time to consider the Craig Palmer murder case closed and go back to my life? Making minis, tutoring, and getting ready for the wedding of the decade. I knew in the end I wouldn't get much mental rest until I learned what evidence the police had against Catherine. It would also have been nice to know how Bebe was doing and if her brother was aware of her attempt to sacrifice her freedom for him, if indeed that had been what prompted her to confess.

As a token gesture, I decided to call Bev as soon as I got in and set a date for shopping. She needed help, she kept telling me. There were entirely too many pairs of shoes out there for her to choose among, even considering that she wanted to match her dress, a shade of green that was perfect for her red-highlighted Porter hair.

As I pulled into my driveway, I saw that I had company waiting. June Chinn was sitting on my front steps, outfitted for warm weather with a bright yellow tank top, cut-off denim shorts, and her black hair tied back in a ponytail. She gave me a big smile and patted the concrete next to her, a reasonably clean patch. I could hardly believe my eyes when I saw that she was eating packaged cookies.

"I've been staking out your place," she said.

"I hope the journey wasn't too rough on you," I teased. My petite next-door neighbor and I called each other Eichler cousins since my house was pale blue with dark blue trim, hers two shades of green and the mirror image of mine in layout.

I sat next to her, my stomach churning as I watched her chain-eat flat round vanilla cookies with a "crème" filling made of who knew what. I opened my mouth to invite her in for my ginger cookies, but from her strained expression I realized she wouldn't know the difference right now, and more important, she needed to be in control of this little visit.

"Skip and Maddie came by to pick up her swimsuit," she said. "Skip was going to take her to the pool at his club. I didn't think she liked swimming that much?"

"She doesn't, not since she discovered computers. But something's up. She told me she wished she had a pool in her yard."

"Hmm," June said. "Didn't you say that she and Taylor are on the outs this summer?"

"She hasn't said so specifically, but it seems that way, yes."

"Is there, by any chance, another girl in the group of friends around here who has a swimming pool?"

It took only a minute to absorb what June was saying. "Henry told me that Taylor went to a pool party this past weekend. And then it became a slumber party as well."

"Uh-huh, I've been there," June said, with a nod of her head. "A new girl with more resources moves in and before you know it, your BFF goes off and leaves you hanging. Then you're alone and your BFF feels guilty because you weren't invited, but she can't give up a party like that. Then the party turns into more parties, and on and on."

"You really have been there."

June laughed. "For me it was a pony."

"The other girl had a pony?"

"She did. A golden pony, as I remember it. I'll never forget Kimberley or the pony. She lived way on the other side of the tracks"—June stretched her short arm up and away from our spot on my steps—"and she offered certain girls rides and other girls not. Kim seemed to go for one member of a pair, like she was deliberately setting out to break up BFFs, though we didn't call them that at the time."

Something clicked in my brain. I'd suddenly remembered an important remark that Maddie had made right before the earthquake on Saturday. "Nobody likes me," I said out loud.

"What?" June asked. "Everybody likes you."

"Maddie said that the other day. Then the rattling and rolling started and it went out of my mind. It fits with what you're saying."

"Definitely," June responded. "That's how you feel when it happens. When your best friend hooks up with someone else, you feel like nobody likes you."

"Poor Maddie," I said, not intending the sentiment to come out, but June was the right person to hear it. She put her arm around my shoulder.

"The good news is that the situation takes care of itself eventually. My prediction: Taylor will come crawling back once she sees that the new girl is all about collecting trophies and Maddie is the real gem of a friend."

"Thanks," I squeaked, more impatient than ever for Maddie's return.

I was impressed by June's insight, but then, she was much closer to eleven years old than I was. I started to feel guilty that June might have solved one of my big problems, and I hadn't done a thing for her except allow her to gorge herself on an inferior snack. I had to own up.

"I'll bet you haven't been boiling in the heat, staking out my house, to share your childhood traumas and help me with Maddie's."

June let out a big sigh, and waited for a noisy pickup to pass on the street. "I was hoping to talk to you about Skip and me," she said, offering me a cookie.

I was afraid it would come to that. I didn't know which was worse, being asked for romantic advice or having a bag of store-bought cookies waved under my nose. I could smell the chemicals.

"Thanks," I said and took the cookie. "I'm really not a good one to ask for advice on matters like this. As you see, I can't even figure out what's going on with eleven-year-olds."

"But you know Skip best, maybe even better than his mom does."

"Skip isn't that complicated," I said. I heard how dumb that sounded almost immediately. Of course it was simple for me. I was his aunt; my only job was to root for him and provide nourishment now and then. "Can you explain what's wrong?" I asked, trying to redeem myself.

June told me her side of the story, which matched Bev's interpretation—that Skip criticized her for being a workaholic when he spent every bit as much time as she did at work.

"Do you think it's just an excuse, the work thing?" she asked, wiggling her toes in her flip-flops and studying the motion as if it were a science project, and a simple one compared to her emotional struggle.

"I don't know. I know his feelings for you seem genuine to me, and he's been with you longer than anyone I can remember." Lame, but the best I could do.

"Maybe we've been together too long? It seems like, just as things are going along super-great, he ups and picks a fight and we're off again. It's almost like he waits until nothing's wrong, and then he makes something wrong. Do you know what I mean?"

"Well, I—"

"Wow, I see it, Gerry," June interrupted, scooting over and turning to face me. "He gets scared when things are too good, and he has to do something to aggravate me so I'll call it off. What do you think?"

"Well, I—" I started again.

"Especially with his mom's wedding coming up. I'll bet he thinks if everything is smooth with us, I'm going to push him into a wedding, too, and really I'm not in any more of a rush than he is. That's it," she said, exultant. "I'll just make sure he knows that." She stood and bent over slightly to hug me. With my height and her lack of it, the embrace worked perfectly. "Thank you so, so much, Gerry. I knew you could clear it up for me," she said, and skipped off to her green Eichler in a trail of thank-yous.

I pulled a tissue from my purse and wrapped the rest of the so-called cookie in it, in preparation for tossing it in the garbage. "You're welcome," I called after her.

If only the other problems on my list would work themselves out the same way.

I THOUGHT it was about time I tried to reconnect with my granddaughter. I tried her cell and Skip's, with no luck. Maybe cell phones were banned from the swimming pool area of Skip's club. At least I could dispense with all the bad images that had crowded my mind. Before I'd heard Skip's message and gotten eyewitness testimony from June, I'd envisioned a toxic bagel at Willie's, an automobile accident, a mugging (not so far-fetched now that the town had chalked up a murder to start the summer).

Overgrowths of weeds among the strips of flowerbeds at the end of my walkway had been nagging at me and I walked over to get rid of them. Maybe next time I'd let my landscaping guy use some of the eco-friendly poison he was always touting.

I was distracted by the noise of an oncoming car—a van, in fact, with Video Jeff's logo. Jeff exited one side of the van, Bebe the other. Jeff looked forlorn, probably torn between relief that his sister had been released and panic that his girlfriend had been arrested. Bebe wore her usual frown and tense expression.

"Hey, Mrs. Porter," he called as they walked toward me. Bebe waved, as if we were a great distance apart and her voice wouldn't carry.

"How are you two?" I asked.

"We thought we should come in person," Jeff said, with no assenting nod from Bebe, and giving me no clue as to what precipitated this unprecedented visit.

"Would you like to come in for a cold drink?"

"If you don't mind." Jeff again.

"Follow me," I said, wondering if Bebe would ever say anything. It was possible that her last allocution to me, that she'd murdered Craig Palmer, had done her in.

We talked only about the weather—the hottest first week in June ever, a bad summer for water coming up, with rationing likely—until we were all seated in my atrium with chilled glasses of iced tea in hand.

"I sure made a mess of things, didn't I?" Jeff asked.

I could think of a couple of things that might be messed up, from Bebe's confession (definitely) to Catherine's arrest (maybe). "What did you have to do with the mess, Jeff?" I asked.

"Look, I realize I have no right to ask you for anything, Mrs. Porter, but now Catherine's been arrested."

"I know that."

"It changes things."

"And I'm very sorry about that, but if you're asking me to do something about it, I'm afraid—"

"I know where you're coming from. The last time I asked you to help, I know you got into a little trouble. Bebe told me she had to tell the police that she confessed to you and that made you look bad with the cops."

An interesting way to put it. "Well, it all worked out," I said.

"I know my sister went off the deep end trying to protect me. I never expected that."

"What did you think I'd do?" Bebe, at last, more mellow than I would have predicted.

I still wasn't sure why the siblings had arrived on my doorstep, but I thought I might as well clear up some points for myself. "Jeff, did you say or do something that caused Bebe to believe you killed Craig?" I asked.

"Other than that the two of them were fighting over a woman who should have stayed in New York and left us all in peace?" Bebe asked.

Jeff scratched his head, thinking. Or trying to get his story straight? "I told her I was there and I hoped the police didn't find out."

I gulped. "You were where?"

"I went looking for Catherine. Our last date, you might call it, didn't end well, and she wasn't answering her phone. She has Caller ID, you know, so she was obviously mad at me. I went to the store to find her, and…"

"And?" I prompted.

"And I saw Craig, on the floor."

"How did you get in?"

"That back door was propped open. It was really hot inside so I figured she was in there, finishing up, and needed some air. I called out to her but no one answered. I walked in, and all of a sudden, I saw him. Craig Palmer. I'd only seen him for a minute when he was on his way to meet you guys in Sadie's that afternoon."

"You saw us in Sadie's? Were you following Catherine?" I asked.

"I wouldn't say following exactly, but I knew he'd come into town and I was curious, you know, even to see what he looked like. Catherine had pointed him out in a picture she had of an office party. But I wanted to see him in the flesh."

"Pssh," Bebe uttered. Meaning what, I couldn't say.

Jeff continued. "Palmer and a younger woman came around

the corner by Seward's coffee shop, which is right across the street from my store, as you know, so I got a pretty good look as he walked by and continued on to Sadie's." He shrugged his shoulders and looked sheepish. "And I might have watched him walk down the street."

"And you recognized him when you went into SuperKrafts looking for Catherine later that evening?"

"Uh-huh. Even though he was on his stomach, I could tell the dead guy was him. That brown and gray hair. And who else would be wearing a black suit in June? He was sprawled out on the floor, this huge crate of pottery on top of him." Jeff closed his eyes and took a deep breath.

"Did you call the police? Nine-one-one?" I knew the answer, but I wanted to make a point.

"No, I knew how it would look. My girlfriend's ex-boyfriend is dead and I'm the only other one in the place. Or maybe not, you know? I wasn't interested in hanging around to find out if it was an accident or...whatever. What if the killer was still there? Besides, there was no question that he was dead. Nine-one-one wasn't going to be able to help him. Plus, I knew the cops would be making rounds all night because of the quake and they'd find him soon enough."

Bebe had been watching my reaction. "Oh, no, Gerry," she said. "You have that look, like all self-righteous. Are you going to tell Skip?"

Lately, Bebe seemed to have a never-ending number of ways to aggravate me. I tried to recall what her personality was like before the takeover (her term) by SuperKrafts. My assessment was: not that different; she'd always seemed to have a chip on her shoulder. I remembered her nasty divorce from Jake Mellon, a tax attorney who took his business to another state to get away from her, as well as other shop-related troubles with vendors and employees. Since I had no such worries, I cut her some slack and kept my composure. "What I'm going to do is tell Jeff to tell Skip," I answered.

"Kinda the opposite of what you told me," Bebe said. "You said not to tell the police."

"Because I didn't believe your story," I said, miffed again that I had to explain myself when all I'd tried to do was protect her. "Jeff, on the other hand, has valuable information."

"How can it help Catherine if I tell them I found Craig's body?" Jeff asked.

"You can help the police pin down the timeline. You know what time you were able to get in. You say the door was propped open?"

"You sound like you don't believe him," Bebe said.

"What time was it, by the way?" I asked, choosing not to acknowledge Mama Bear. I was also distracted by the idea that security at SuperKrafts did not befit a major New York–based corporation. Not only had they purchased inferior cameras that were recalled, but no one noticed the back door was open?

"It wasn't too late," Jeff said. "Before sunset, not long after I closed up, maybe seven-thirty?"

One hour after the earthquake, which was consistent with the theory that the killer had taken advantage of the quake to cover the murder. Also, if he was telling the truth, Jeff's alibi was still intact, that he'd been in his store at six thirty-two.

"That's a big piece of information," I said. "If you really want to help Catherine, that's how you can do it—talk to the police."

"I see what you mean," Jeff said. "And knowing the door was propped open, that matters, too, so absolutely anyone in town or three towns over could have gotten in and killed him."

"Including Catherine," Bebe said.

One could never say that Bebe didn't make herself clear.

I felt great relief when I heard the key turn in the lock on my front door, a few yards from where we sat in my atrium. Not only would I have my granddaughter back, but I would have gotten away without making a commitment to work on the Palmer case as if I were a cop, no matter whose friend or relative had been arrested for the crime.

IN the next few minutes, there was a significant regrouping in my atrium as Maddie bounded in, Skip following. Bebe and Jeff beat a hasty retreat after a cursory greeting to Skip. I could be-

lieve they'd had a big enough dose of the LPPD to last a while.
Skip stayed only long enough to explain that he simply wanted
to drop Maddie off and had to rush next door to June's "because
she texted and said we had something important to talk about."

I wondered what that could be?

I was happy to have Maddie to myself again but also eager to
know how Skip had fared with her. Had the swimming session
relaxed them both enough to have the open conversation I'd envisioned? Had Skip found it easier to deal with Maddie than with
June, or was he stymied by women of all ages?

As I was debating whether to broach the tender subjects of
Taylor and boys myself, Maddie came up with her own plan.
"Can we do the chart now?" she asked. "The one with the earthquake alibis," she added, responding to my confused look. Charts
were not something I chose to think about on a regular basis.

I rummaged in my purse among the detritus of the day—receipts, wrappers, tissues, Fred Bates's business card—to pull out
the odds and ends of notes I'd made on the reported whereabouts
of my little group of suspects. I felt a pang of guilt as I came across
the piece of paper Jeanine had given me with the titles of her
boyfriend's books of poetry. I doubted I'd ever follow through
and look them up, let alone read them. I'd have to come up with
an excuse, but not right now. I picked out the alibi notes and gave
them to Maddie to compile.

"You can probably put these together faster than I can," I said.

"I can't believe you did this by hand," she said, shaking her
head, causing a red curl to fall in front of her eyes. "You know,
if you had a smartphone, you'd be able to type right into a notes
app and then I could have just ported them and then…"—she
looked at me and caught me rolling my eyes—"Never mind,"
she said.

Maddie disappeared into her computer and came back to the
atrium table about twenty minutes later. She placed one printed
copy of a nicely laid-out chart in front of me and another in front
of her seat. "I made an extra copy for Uncle Skip," she said, while
lowering her skinny body to the chair. She brushed back her curls
and we were ready for a high-level meeting.

She allowed me a couple of minutes of silence to study the chart (sometimes the word itself caused my jaw to tighten). I observed first the headings for each column: NAME, LOCATION, WHAT HAPPENED, DIRECTION, and then read the entries:

| Name | Location | What Happened | Direction |
|------|----------|---------------|-----------|
| Megan | KenTucky Inn | coffeemaker/ice bucket shook, glass broke | ? |
| Catherine | KenTucky Inn | hotel clock shook and slid | ? |
| Jeff | inside his store | games toppled | W |
| Maisie | home | no movement | |
| Bebe | ? | ? | ? |
| Leo | hotel (?) | ? | ? |
| Jeanine | Seward's Folly | filters fell, coffee spilled | W |
| Grandma | home w/Maddie | vase and bowl fell and broke | W, W |

I smiled when I saw the addition of "Grandma," and my alibi. I understood why Bebe's and Leo's rows were incomplete—Bebe had now retracted her initial claim to have been at ground zero, and Leo had escaped any attempt on my part to obtain his alibi. But I was confused by the extra heading, DIRECTION, and by the question marks and the "Ws" in that column.

"You did an amazing job," I said, following my longtime rule as a teacher—always lead with the positive.

"What's wrong, Grandma?" Maddie asked. Her skills at knowing how I operated went way back to her toddler days. "What don't you understand?"

"Nothing's wrong, but I haven't seen this last column before."

"It means 'west.' That's the point of the chart," she said, with remarkable patience. "Remember, I told you that when the earthquake wave comes in, it has a direction, and things fall on one side of the room or another." She'd just begun and I was already struggling to understand her explanation, but that wasn't her fault (so to speak). I still had a hard time thinking of earthquakes as waves and not as underground explosions, which made more sense to me. Maddie continued as if she were teaching her slowest student. "So, like, the vase fell from the west side of our atrium and the bowl fell from the west side of the kitchen. Nothing fell from the east side of any of the rooms."

"So, if one of these people said something fell from the east side of a room, they'd be lying?"

Maddie's smile said I aced the quiz, but I had my doubts. "Is it really that simple?"

Maddie shrugged her shoulders. "My teacher says it's more complicated, but I saw it on TV once where the police solved a murder by figuring out which side got damaged. A husband pushed a bookcase on his wife, but it was the wrong wall."

It wasn't my place to question Maddie's TV watching, but it was possible that I'd bring it up with her mother at an appropriate time. For now, I sat back, wondering what we'd accomplished by developing the chart, other than involving Maddie and bringing her a bit of satisfaction during a rough time. Otherwise, it seemed to be a dead end, maybe even good content for a school report on the soon-to-be-famous three-point-one. But as an aid in a police investigation? I didn't see it. Still, I wasn't going to dash a little girl's hopes.

"I think we should fill in these question marks, don't you?" I said.

Maddie's reaction, a wide grin and a modest round of applause, told me I'd made the right choice.

"I know what the inside of Seward's Folly looks like and where they keep the boxes of filters. Remember I got a box of them for my mom once? They're on the side that looks out on Video Jeff's across the street, and that's west, right?" Right, but she didn't wait for my answer. "That's how come I could put the W where I did in Jeanine's row. But we need to find out which wall the stuff is on at the KenTucky Inn. I already looked online at their website. There's not much on it, just a picture and an address and how to make reservations and stuff. The big hotels, like the ones in Los Angeles or New York, they all have photos and you see the exact way the rooms look."

"Not you, too," I said, before I knew it.

"Huh?"

"Never mind. I'm sorry for interrupting. What were you saying about the big hotels?"

"They show you the layout of the rooms sometimes. But the KenTucky Inn just has stuff like whether there's a hair dryer or a coffeemaker. So, I was thinking, maybe we should go there and ask them. Or look at the rooms. Do you think they'd let us?"

Ah, a field trip. Maddie's favorite thing. Maybe that was what this whole chart idea had been leading up to. "Great idea," I said. "You know the people who run it are good friends of mine. We can go tomorrow. If they're too busy, we'll make another plan."

"Yeah, like, we could rent a helicopter and fly next to the windows and look in."

Why not?

# Chapter 14

SKIP DIDN'T SURFACE for the rest of the afternoon and early evening. So, over a "boring" dinner of roast chicken, green beans, and plain brown rice (I put my foot down against pizza again), I tried to get Maddie to talk about her time with him.

"Did you and Uncle Skip have a nice time at Willie's?" I asked.

"Yup."

"Did they have your favorite blueberry bagel?"

"Yup."

"Was it fun at the pool?"

"Yup."

Nothing. "I had a good day, too," I offered.

"You want to know what we talked about?" she asked.

"Yup," I said, getting a grin from her.

"Police work."

I tried to keep my fork steady in my hand. "You mean 'The Caysh'?" I asked, putting quotes in the air. We'd laughed often about how she'd loved to use the phrase "The Case" when she was still too young to get her sibilants right.

"No, not The Caysh," she said, smiling as if those days were eons ago. "I wanted to know what it's like to be a detective. Uncle Skip says a lot of what cops do every day is very boring, like writing reports and filling out lots of forms at a desk."

"That doesn't sound like much fun," I said, grateful to Skip for not making his job sound glamorous. Teachers do a lot of dull paperwork, too, I almost admitted to her, as well as doctors and artists, but if Maddie were weighing criminal justice against education or other alternatives, I wanted to tip the scales against the police academy.

"Yeah, but a lot of it can be fun, too," she said. "He talks to all kinds of people and he says that's the most important part of solving a case. If you do it right, they'll tell you what you need to know. And he says cops have to be counselors, sometimes, and peacemakers and coaches, and even stand in for parents."

"You think you'd like that part?"

"Uh-huh. Like, we hear about all the clues and everything, like fingerprints and DNA. But Uncle Skip says fingerprints are overrated, because you almost never get really good ones. When the crooks break in, they aren't going to roll their thumbs perfectly on just the right kind of surface, like we did when we got fingerprinted at school. You have to listen really carefully when you interview people and that's how you figure things out. I almost told Uncle Skip about our chart, because that came from talking to people, right?"

"It certainly did," I said. I'd heard this description of police procedure many times from Skip, but I was impressed at how well my granddaughter understood his message. Besides, it was clear from her long-winded, excited state, that Maddie was coming out of her funk. I hoped the letter to Taylor, if there were a letter to Taylor, would give her the response she needed and remove this latest obstacle to her happiness. I realized I couldn't protect Maddie from heartbreak forever, but surely I ought to be able to do it until she'd finished college. And graduate school. And perhaps became a grandmother herself.

"But the chart wasn't ready yet this afternoon," Maddie continued, "and anyway I want to surprise him."

Just as well that we didn't "surprise" Skip. I had mixed thoughts about how he'd handle Maddie's creativity. Would he humor her? Actually use the chart? I knew Maddie was as eager as I was to find out.

Maddie pushed a green bean to the edge of her plate and added about a quarter of a stick of butter to her rice. "You tried to get Uncle Skip to find out what I didn't want to tell you," she said.

She'd caught me off guard, but I managed to pretend I was pretending to be shocked, sort of like a double-agent ploy I'd seen in the spy girl movie. "Whatever do you mean?"

"I can't tell you yet, Grandma," she said, serious.

I was glad she was close enough for me to ruffle her curls. "That's fine."

"I didn't tell Uncle Skip either. But it was so much fun hanging around with him."

"I'm glad." And also dismayed that Maddie had to be in trouble before we'd arrange a nice day with her cousin-once-removed.

"I think I'll be able to tell you pretty soon, though," she added.

I wondered if her timeline had anything to do with mail delivery.

BY ten o'clock, when Maddie was tucked in (not that I ever let her hear me use that phrase) I was ready for quiet time with a new issue of a dollhouse magazine. Now and then I contributed ideas to this miniatures periodical and others. I decided that the project Maddie and I had worked on for a while after dinner might be worth writing up for their tips page. We'd decided that the imaginary surrogate who would occupy our tiny police department cubicle-in-progress should have a salad for lunch. We shaved crayons (three shades of green) to make realistic lettuce, and whittled cheese, chopped olives, and carrots, all from Maddie's abandoned crayon box. We rummaged in my "recyclables" drawer, full of cast-offs like toothpaste tube tops and bottle caps, and found a suitable salad bowl among them.

A good-night call from Henry came at the usual time, about ten-thirty, unless we were together.

"No mail yet," he said. "I'm thinking you should have slipped the letter to me somehow and I could have put it under Taylor's door to speed things up."

"It will all work out," I said, and recounted my conversation with June. I planned to consult June in the future whenever a Maddie issue surfaced, no matter what her future with Skip turned out to be. He'd proven useless along those lines so far.

I clicked off with Henry when a call came from Bev, which, like Henry's, didn't count against quiet time. I made yet another promise to go shopping with her tomorrow.

"Shoes and lunch," I said.

"I know you don't want me to go barefoot down the aisle," she said. "Although in this heat, who could blame me?"

We chatted for a while, covering Maddie's troubles (info to come, I told her) and Skip's whereabouts (his car was still parked outside my house).

When Bev and I hung up, I took up my miniatures magazine again, but found I was waiting for late-night company. Who would it be tonight? Probably not Leo or Megan pleading for my help with getting Catherine released. Neither of them seemed to care. All that was left to motivate me was my own curiosity (I liked to call it obsession with justice) and the fact that a woman I'd taught and later worked with for a year might be falsely accused of murder.

There was still a possibility that Skip would drop in. He was always welcome, but especially when I needed information from him. There had to have been something more than an anonymous call to have precipitated an arrest. What a disappointment, then, when I heard his car drive off around midnight.

*Dum dum, da da dum, da da dum.*

At least he was calling to say good night. "Hi, Skip," I said.

"Hey, Aunt Gerry, I'm just driving off for home. In case you had some cookies waiting, wrap them up, okay? I'm beat." Rather than remind him that I know the sound his car makes when it takes off from right outside my front door, I thanked him for letting me know. "And I wanted to say thanks for talking to June today. She told me what a huge help you were. I think we're back on track," he continued.

"How nice," I said. "Maybe we can barter for some information on Catherine Duncan's arrest."

He laughed, as if I hadn't meant it. "No, really, thanks," he said, and clicked off, leaving me frustrated, with a sigh no one could hear.

I wished I knew what I'd said to patch things up between Skip and June; I might be able to use those words again for another purpose.

In spite of Skip's lack of cooperation, for the first time in a while, I felt progress was being made, due solely to Maddie's chart. I was warming up to the trip to the KenTucky Inn and the potential of clearing up the life-and-death matters of Craig Palmer's murder and Catherine Duncan's arrest. I was a little disappointed to realize that since Skip had been with Maddie, then June, all day and evening, he wouldn't have been involved in the inevitable search of Catherine's room and belongings. Not that he'd been much use to me anyway lately.

I headed back toward my bedroom and noticed a piece of paper on the floor of the hallway. The note, with titles of books of poetry, must have fallen out of my purse when I retrieved the scraps of paper for Maddie's chart. I had to give Jeanine credit for trying to support her boyfriend's career goals. I supposed it wouldn't hurt me to give an hour to the young man's work and think up something positive to say about his poems. I looked at the titles of the three collections—"You Never Dream Alone," "Pretty Days," and "Yesterday's World Again." I wondered how long the books were. Maybe I could read just one, the shortest. It would be a good chance to visit with my friend, Rosie, who owned the book shop.

I smoothed out the paper. The handwriting looked familiar but I couldn't imagine when I would have seen it before. From her early days baby-sitting Maddie, Jeanine and I communicated by phone or e-mail. Something about the flourishes on the uppercase *Y* and *P* niggled at my brain. Each of those letters had more loops than necessary and more elaboration than was present in the rest of the words. It was almost as if Jeanine were trying to mimic an illuminated manuscript where the first letter of the passage was oversized and full of curlicues.

Just like the letters in the notes sent to Catherine, recommending in no uncertain terms that she get out of town.

When I finally grasped what the similarity meant, I was sure there'd been a crazy mistake. I wished I'd agreed to take custody of the notes as Catherine had asked. Surely, if I could compare the handwriting side by side, I'd see my misjudgment. Too late now, since the police had most likely found them.

I drew in my breath. Should I show Skip Jeanine's note to me? A series of *no*'s ran through my head. It was ridiculous to suspect Jeanine of writing the notes to Catherine. Jeanine was one of the most level-headed, mild-mannered young women I knew. Besides, she had nothing to gain by Catherine's leaving town. She'd hardly be affected at all by a shift in management of the store or its employees. It wasn't as if Jeanine were after a career with SuperKrafts. But wasn't it Jeanine who'd brought up the psychology of a killer during our last conversation? Had that been merely the curiosity of a future psych major? Or something else? I thought back to Maddie's chart and Jeanine's alibi. She'd said she'd been in Seward's Folly having coffee with some friends. That should be easy enough to check out. And if it didn't? I tucked the paper back into my purse. There's another explanation, I thought. Wasn't there?

I knew I'd have to talk to Jeanine about my suspicion. I had no idea how to approach her. I could email her, ask to meet. But my computer was in Maddie's room; I hadn't moved it from its position during the days when Maddie didn't bring her own laptop. I'd have to wait till morning.

I got in bed, knowing my peaceful night's sleep wouldn't come easily. I composed at least four versions of an email to Jeanine in my head, before drifting off.

ON Tuesday morning, I was as eager as Maddie was to start the day. We had the KenTucky Inn to visit, shoes to shop for with Aunt Bev, and the mail to check for a letter from Taylor. I also needed to contact Jeanine.

Maddie was up and ready to hit the road by nine. I stalled her a bit, wanting to arrive at the inn after their guests left for a day of business or sightseeing. Our police station replica held her interest for a while as we cut out images of police magazines,

glued them to foam board, and strewed them around the miniature cubicle.

"Uncle Skip has aspirin on his desk," Maddie noted.

"Easy," we said, in unison.

Maddie cut a label from a newspaper ad for aspirin, and
wrapped it around an appropriate-size plastic cylinder, gluing it
in place. Another small piece of plastic tubing served as a tumbler,
and Uncle Skip was on his way to pain relief. Who could deny
the pleasure of instant gratification achieved by doing miniatures?
No wonder it was often hard to reenter the life-size world.

MY stalling strategy worked. By the time we arrived at the Ken-
Tucky Inn, only a mile or so past downtown Lincoln Point, the
nicely paved parking lot behind the three-story Colonial was
nearly empty. I'd heard that the Olsons' son, now in his thir-
ties, had begged his parents over the years to forget his childish
mandate and change the name of the inn, to no avail. I'd gotten
used to zoning out as I passed the grammatically skewed sign and
hardly caught a glimpse of it this time. I smiled as I recalled a
science fiction device in a short story I'd read, and mentally sent
an electric pulse through the state of California, eliminating all
uppercase letters in the middles of words.

Innkeepers Loretta and Mike Olson had moved to town from
New Hampshire about the same time that Ken and I arrived from
the Bronx. Considering the relative distances, we felt we'd been
neighbors back "home" and became good friends. After a couple
of years, the Olsons bought a large abandoned home and remade
it into a near-replica of a New England–style inn. The white
clapboard building held up to twenty-five guests (which made
me question why SuperKrafts managers Leo Murray and Craig
Palmer thought they would have felt crowded here). The inn
was beautifully maintained, the house surrounded by two lovely
verandas lined with salvia plants, nearly two feet tall and densely
populated with red, pink, and lavender blossoms that filled the air
with a fruity scent. I remembered the advantages of salvia—low
maintenance and a great attraction for hummingbirds—and resolved to add a row of the plants to my front garden. It would be

a much more appropriate item on my to-do list than "find Craig's killer," I reminded myself.

I'd been to more than a few weddings here and knew that the interior was equally reminiscent of New England, with a cozy, dark-paneled library, handmade quilts on the beds in every room, and a lounge with a handsome but unnecessary-for-California fireplace. It was as if the Olsons had transported their homestead from three thousand miles away. Bev had wanted to have her wedding here, but occupancy laws limited the inn's gatherings to one hundred or fewer, and in the end, Bev and Nick couldn't whittle down their list. We were resigned to celebrating their marriage in San Jose, at a hotel the size my New York visitors would feel comfortable with.

"Wow," Maddie said, peeking through the fence, "they have a pool."

I scanned her face for signs of teasing, but found none. I might have to accommodate to this new hydrophilic Maddie.

We entered the lobby, which was more like a living room, with groupings of sofas and easy chairs in soothing fabrics and patterns. I wasn't surprised to see Loretta herself at the desk; she'd always wanted to stay close to the everyday operations. Her intense blue eyes were focused on a computer screen, though the desk seemed better suited to a large, leather-bound ledger with blotchy signatures in dark ink. In fact, the picture Loretta presented was not an unusual one these days—a gray-haired woman pecking away at her laptop as comfortably as if she were stitching a HOME SWEET HOME needlepoint sampler for the entryway.

"Look who's here," she said, mostly to Maddie.

She came around to the front of the counter and gave us each a welcoming hug, then made a call that brought a young woman from the back room, ready to take over reception duties. The new woman looked so much like Jeanine, the same age, with a slight build and long hair, that I nearly excused myself to call the poet's girlfriend and ask to see another sample of her handwriting. In particular, I would have requested a few more upper case *Y*'s and *P*'s. When had I become so easily distracted? And suspicious? And impatient? Instead of listening to what my old friend was saying, I proceeded to rehash my conversations with Skip, wondering why he hadn't gotten back to me about what led them to arrest Catherine.

Therefore, I missed most of Loretta's narration on the way to the screened-in porch that she suggested for our visit. I tuned in again as we passed an old-fashioned game room with a Ping-Pong table and pinball machines. Another "Wow" erupted from Maddie as she stopped for a glimpse into the past.

"Would you like to play in there for a while?" Loretta asked Maddie. "There are some new video games in there, too."

Maddie shook her head. "No, thank you. I'll stay with Grandma."

I let Loretta think how sweet and loving it was that Maddie chose me over a game room. She wasn't aware of The Chart, which I now thought of in initial caps, much as I did The Case, Maddie's designation from years ago. Loretta couldn't have known that no mere entertainment center, new or old, would steer Maddie away from her goal of filling in the rows and columns of her latest fixation.

On the porch, Loretta directed Maddie and me to seats at a wooden table encircled by weathered chairs. Large fans at either end, plus a plastic container with weedkiller and assorted small gardening tools, disrupted the pastoral setting a bit. But the much-needed cooling effect was worth the blight on the décor from the fans, and I knew all too well the necessity of unpleasant substances to keep the beautiful plants and flowers growing.

"I'll be right back," Loretta said, and disappeared into the inn.

"When are we going to ask her about the earthquake and what broke in the rooms?" Maddie whispered when we were alone.

I was aware that Maddie and I hadn't talked about exactly how we'd present our question to Loretta. "What do you think?" I asked her, also whispering, although the nearest people were in chairs three tables over—a young couple who were clearly not interested in what we were talking about.

"We can start by asking if she felt the earthquake."

"Good idea," I said. "And we also can try to learn what the police found when they searched Catherine's room."

"I forgot about that. What if they already found out something. Like, that she lied about her alarm clock?"

"Maybe she didn't lie," I offered.

"Yeah, but maybe she did."

I had a frightening thought. "Maddie, you're not hoping Catherine Duncan lied, are you?" What I meant was, *I hope you're not glad there's a murder to solve.*

Maddie's face took on a sheepish expression. "I'm sorry, Grandma. I know a man died and I should be sad about that. But sometimes I forget this is not just a homework problem." Maddie's eyes teared up, causing mine to do the same. We shared a quiet hug. Something told me my granddaughter was sorting through quite a few confused feelings, and that her tears were probably about all of them.

In the few minutes we had before Loretta returned, we pulled ourselves together and engaged in a round of "Love you/Love you more," with a promise to talk again when we were home. We also agreed to move slowly toward getting the information we needed from Loretta.

The aroma of warm apple pie preceded Loretta onto the porch. "I hope you don't mind leftovers," our hostess said. The young woman, now introduced as Dana, placed a tray on the table and distributed slices of apple pie and glasses of iced tea.

"Mmm," was all that could be heard as we tasted the delicious "homemade goodness" that store-bought pies only write about on their wrappers.

"There were a few pies left over from an event over the weekend. A big baby shower on Saturday for the daughter of a friend in Palo Alto."

"That's where I live," Maddie said.

"I know."

"Did the people at the shower feel the earthquake on Saturday?" Maddie asked. I gave her a raised-eyebrow look that was meant to slow her down.

"The earthquake? I almost forgot. It must have been the smallest I've ever felt. But the shower was long over by then." Loretta took a sip of tea.

"Did anyone else in your guest rooms feel the earthquake? Or did things break?" Maddie persisted.

"Nothing that I know of. If we'd lost anything significant, the housekeepers would have reported it."

"Even if it was just a glass?" Maddie asked.

Loretta paused, and came up with what would have been a natural question for a normal eleven-year-old with a tiny earthquake still on her mind. She put her hand on Maddie's. "Did the quake scare you, honey?" Loretta asked.

"Uh-uh. My teacher told us all about them and how to protect ourselves," Maddie said. She leaned over to me. "Can we see the rooms now?" she asked in a low voice, pointing to where The Chart rested in my tote bag, which I now secured between my ankles.

"In a minute, sweetheart," I said. I turned to Loretta, who, thankfully, was so involved in removing a glob of apple from her bosom that she missed Maddie's question. "How's Mike doing after his surgery?" I asked quickly.

Maddie fidgeted like a child half her age as Loretta reported that Mike was progressing better than the doctors had expected, after an operation on his knee. We moved on to an update on Garrett, their son (he who gave the inn its name), who was now a successful realtor in San Francisco; and then on to my son, Richard.

"Your dad's a surgeon at Stanford," Loretta said to Maddie, with an uplift in her voice that suggested she was impressed.

"Uh-huh, and my mom's an artist," Maddie added, surprising me. I'd expected her to blurt out our reason for being here.

But I knew Maddie couldn't last through too many additional rounds of family talk, and decided to veer off in our self-serving direction. "We have something in particular to ask you about, Loretta," I said. Maddie's legs started moving, her "tell" when she was excited.

Loretta banged her forehead with the palm of her hand. "I should have known," she said, with a grin that was incongruous with her next utterance. "The murder. The man from New York who was killed during the earthquake. And our guest who was arrested for it. Of course. You're up to your old tricks, aren't you, Gerry?"

"Tricks? What kinds of—" I began.

"Shall we review the number of times you've inserted yourself into—"

"No need to do that," I said. "We're just here to—"

"I meant nothing bad, Gerry. You've been a huge help to the—"

"Not really. I've simply—"

"And you're teaching your granddaughter now. I love it!"

Maddie, who looked like she was about to explode, took advantage of the interruptions with a turn of her own. "We need to ask you some questions about where the coffeemakers and ice buckets are in the rooms upstairs," she said.

Loretta looked amused and confused. I was nervous about showing her The Chart, not wanting to put her on the spot in case the police came fishing. I managed to get one more interruption in, when Maddie said, "We have a chart that shows—" I broke in with, "If we could just see the rooms upstairs, Loretta, we'd be really grateful."

"Certainly, I'd be glad to show you." She grinned. "Anything to help you with your—"

"I have no tricks," I said, grinning back.

# Chapter 15

LORETTA, AS TALL as I am, but always considerably heavier, lumbered up the carpeted stairs, holding onto the white wooden banister. Maddie and I followed behind. From the grin on Maddie's face, an observer unfamiliar with my granddaughter might think she'd won a ticket to the Grand Opening of the world's greatest theme park, or to a wonderland where pizza and ice cream were free and served at every meal.

We reached the KenTucky Inn's second level, the first of two floors of guest rooms. "I can't show you Catherine's or Megan's actual rooms, of course, but I can take you to ones just like them," Loretta said.

"Did you happen to notice if the LPPD took anything away?" I asked, as we walked three abreast down the long, wide hallway.

"The cops didn't take very much," Loretta said. "Just one box full of stuff, like a computer paper box, uncovered, with some brown bags sticking up. They wouldn't tell me what they were looking for, but they were in there for quite a while."

"So they didn't leave with a suitcase or piles of clothes over their arms?" I asked.

"Nothing like that. And believe me I was waiting at the bottom of the stairs the whole time."

"In case they carried out an antique dresser or a vintage rag rug?"

"Exactly. You can't trust the cops." She smiled and added, "Except for your venerable nephew, of course." She leaned toward me. "As a matter of fact, Amelia overheard something interesting."

Amelia Reyes was the Olsons' supervisor of housekeeping, whose daughter I had tutored in English a couple of years back. "Do tell."

"Not that she was eavesdropping, but she was checking the room adjacent to Catherine's, and even though the connecting door was closed"—Loretta shrugged her shoulders and displayed her palms—"sound carries."

I tried not to seem too eager. Maddie had her pencil ready, poised over her clipboard. "Amelia couldn't help it if they were talking loudly," I prodded.

"Apparently they found a piece of a ceramic pot or something that they were looking for. I guess they'd been tipped off."

It fell into place. The anonymous caller Skip had mentioned pointed the police to a piece of the vase that was the murder weapon. Skip had held back for some reason, but I trusted Amelia's report, which was staggering. But I didn't believe Catherine would be arrested based only on a shard that anyone could have planted in her room. Not as easy as slipping notes under her door, but still doable. Didn't anyone in the LPPD wonder why she would bash Craig Palmer over the head and then take a piece of the weapon home with her? What was I missing?

"Are you going to keep the room available for Catherine"— I gritted my teeth—"in case she's able to come back?" I asked Loretta.

"I couldn't get any information from the cops on that, either, but I hate to just leave her in the lurch. I'm going to have House-keeping pack up her room and put her things in the storage area downstairs. We're not that busy yet, but this coming weekend we have a tour coming through, and then it will pick up for the rest of the summer."

When we reached the door identified by lettering on a wooden plaque as Room 213, Loretta took a set of keys from the pocket of her smock and unlocked it. "Even though Catherine is…uh…indisposed at the moment, I'd feel uncomfortable taking you into her room, which is right above us. But, as I said, this one has the same layout."

"That's what we expected. We appreciate this," I said.

"Does it have an alarm clock?" Maddie asked.

Loretta nodded her assurance. "All the guest rooms have clocks. Also, this room is the same layout as Megan's, which is number three-eleven, upstairs. Unless you want to come back tomorrow when she'll be gone? Then I'd be able to show you her exact room."

*Gone?* "Megan is checking out?"

"Yes, she told me she'll be leaving tomorrow, after the store opens, sometime in the afternoon."

"But the Grand Opening isn't until Saturday," I said, as if Loretta would know why that mattered.

Loretta shrugged. "I guess she doesn't have anything to do with that."

It didn't make sense. One of Megan's prime duties as Craig's admin was to oversee the program for SuperKrafts' Grand Opening. Granted, the gala had been moved from tomorrow to Saturday, but I'd have thought Megan would stay on. She could have a good reason for needing to get home tomorrow as originally planned. A family event, for example, or important meetings at another store location. Or she could simply want to get out of town before she was the next one to be hauled in by the LPPD. I tucked away those thoughts in my mind, the way the inn's guests tucked themselves into the charming beds, I guessed.

Maddie had printed out several pieces of paper with a grid on them and fastened them to a clipboard I'd lent her. Her intention was to sketch the layout of the room. "I have some real graph paper at home," she explained, lest someone think she was not well-equipped. "But I didn't bring it with me. I found out you can print the lines from online images, though." I was glad I was off the hook for having to provide tools that smacked too much of math.

"Here we are," Loretta said, with a flourish.

She had every right to be proud of her establishment. We stepped into a large, lovely bedroom with matching bedspreads, headboard covers, and draperies, all in greens and pale yellows.

An area rug in complementary colors filled the room to within about a foot of the walls, leaving highly polished dark wooden floors visible around the edges. Picture-book, I thought, and vowed that never again would I be embarrassed to send people here just because I didn't like the way they spelled the name.

Maddie began sketching, drawing different sizes and shapes of boxes to represent the beds, two chairs, two luggage racks, a dresser, and two end tables with lamps. I had a vision of Maddie entering her grandfather's profession, designing rooms and buildings. I chided myself, as if she could see into my mind. If she did know what I was thinking, I hoped she'd realize that I'd always love her, no matter what path she chose.

As if we'd all heard the same command, we walked closer to the end table that held the alarm clock. "This is the west wall," Maddie said. Loretta nodded, a questioning look on her face. Maddie wrote a large uppercase *W* in the last column of Catherine's row on The Chart, which I'd slipped under the drawing paper, out of sight. So far, so good, for Catherine. Except for a tiny flaw.

I picked up the clock and checked its bottom, which had four rubber feet. "This isn't likely to slide," I said. Star reporter (also an acceptable career) Maddie nodded and made a note on her drawing.

Maddie wandered around the spacious room, looking under some things, over others, as if she were just in from Scotland Yard. She tapped her clipboard. "Where's the coffeemaker?" she asked.

"No coffeemakers," Loretta answered. "We like to encourage the guests to use the common dining area. The idea of a B-and-B..." Loretta covered her mouth with her hand, pretending to have made a mistake, and not the same point I'd heard many times over the years. "Oops, we're not supposed to call it that. Lincoln Point's zoning laws say it's too big for a B-and-B, and is technically a hotel. Anyway, a smaller hotel offers a family atmosphere, where people can meet other travelers and congregate in all the rooms downstairs. The restaurant opens at six in the morning, so there's not a long wait for coffee."

"Are guests allowed to bring their own coffeemakers?"

"Oh, yes, and some do. One thing we don't have on a regular basis is room service. Until the city or the county tell us we have to, that is." Loretta paused. "Say, Gerry, why don't you get yourself on the Downtown Committee and use your influence to relax some of the laws for Lincoln Point businesses?" Just what I needed, but fortunately, Loretta wasn't waiting for an answer about my political future. "Anyway, if things are slow and we happen to have someone available to take a tray up, we're happy to accommodate."

"How about an ice bucket and glasses?" Maddie asked, on the job.

Loretta pointed to the bathroom and we followed her to the doorway of the small room, which included a full bath with shower. "We have a small plastic container for ice, but no ice machine on the residence floors." I was surprised she didn't add "until the government forces us to have them." "There's a lounge downstairs, a full bar, open till midnight, and guests are free to take ice from there. There are plastic cups in the bathroom."

"No glass glasses?" Maddie asked.

"No glass at all, for safety reasons, only paper or plastic cups."

"Hmm," Maddie said as she added another note to the official record.

Back in the bedroom, Loretta straightened a perfectly straight quilt on its rack, adjusted the lampshades and the positions of the chairs, and made other minute changes in the look and feel of the room. Maddie chewed on her pencil, a serious look on her face, the face I'd seen while watching her do her homework.

As for me, I leaned against the wall by the bathroom door and thought about what we'd learned. It occurred to me that we could have gotten answers from Loretta without the tour, but what fun would that have been? We might not have been alerted to the fine point of the rubber feet on the inn's alarm clocks. A deal breaker for Catherine's alibi? Not if she'd brought her own travel alarm clock, which I always did. They tended to be smaller than standard-issue hotel clocks and one might easily have shaken and slid across the end table.

It was Megan who seemed to have struck out. No coffee-maker, regular ice bucket, or glasses that could break. But several defenses came to mind. She might have brought her own coffeemaker. Loretta had no rule against it, and it was a common practice, either because of coffee snobbery or because some travelers needed coffee before saying "Good morning" to a stranger. As for the ice bucket, Megan might have seen the small container in the bathroom shake on the counter. The broken glass was a problem, however. I pictured Megan's row on Maddie's chart and also remembered two different versions of her earthquake experience. When I ran into Megan at the LPPD station, she'd told me that a glass broke; but she'd told Jeanine during our SuperKrafts chat that "things broke." A glass and what else? Two glasses? How likely was it that she'd brought her own glass tumbler—tumblers?—and one or both fell to a tile floor during a three-point-one? I sighed, questioning my analysis of Megan's remarks. My thoughts were sailing far beyond the question of east wall versus west wall. Megan wasn't under oath when she was relating her first earthquake experience. Who didn't elaborate on a story now and then? Only an English teacher or an editor would be literal and so picky. Or maybe a cop?

Loretta had finished her white-glove test of Room 213. "Ready to go?" she asked, waving her hand in front of my eyes. Apparently she was aware that I'd virtually left the scene a few minutes ago.

"One more question, if you don't mind, Loretta? Would the housekeeper report a broken glass in the room?"

"Well, as I said, there aren't any glasses in the rooms. So, unless a guest brings her own, there's no glass to break. And why would anyone bring a glass?"

"What if some people would rather drink out of glass glasses?" Maddie suggested.

Loretta shrugged. "To each his own. Do you want me to find out if Amelia found any broken glass-glass"—she winked at Maddie—"in the trash from this room?" she asked me.

"From Megan Sutley's room, please," I said, having a hard time believing my luck. I'd have to send Loretta a thank-you gift, maybe a miniature of the KenTucky Inn lounge area. I couldn't wait to rummage in my carpet samples drawer to find a piece that would match the burgundy hue I'd admired on the floor below.

I had another thought. "Oh, and one more last-last question?" I asked, getting into the spirit of double words. "Do you know anything about envelopes that were hand-delivered to Catherine's room? Slipped under her door?"

"No, she asked us about that. I'm sorry to say our cameras don't cover every inch of the property. We have keypads on the stairway doors and other measures in place, but certainly someone who was intent on getting up to the other levels could do it."

Hearing Loretta's borderline-defensive tone, I decided to quit while we were still good friends. We walked back through the house in something close to companionable silence and reached the front door. Loretta invited us to stay for an early lunch, but even as a tempting aroma wafted from the kitchen, I declined.

"I promised Beverly we'd go to lunch and shop for shoes," I said.

"Ah, the big wedding is coming up," Loretta said. "Say, Gerry, it's not too late. You can still talk Beverly and Nick into getting their list down to a manageable size so they can get married here."

"I'm afraid that's not going to happen." I looked out at the lovely property, richly landscaped, and remembered the perfectly prepared dinners and elegant decorations for events I'd attended. "Though to me it's the perfect setting," I said, before thinking through the many implications.

Loretta gasped. She leaned in to whisper to me, out of Maddie's earshot. "Gerry! You and Henry Baker? Are you ready to—"

My gasp was louder than Loretta's. "No, no, no," I whispered back.

Loretta's laugh suggested that maybe I protested too much.

MADDIE and I had a little time to stop at home before we were to meet Bev at a restaurant in San Jose, near a large retail center with many options, from high-end shops to outlet stores. Many weeks ago, I'd recommended that Bev buy white shoes and have them dyed to match her dress.

"That's what our mothers did," she'd said. "I never liked the way they looked. You could always tell by the streaks in the satin that it was a fake color."

"They have new technology now," I'd said, having no idea if there was anything new in the shoe-dyeing industry.

"Well, anyway, I can't even find any white shoes that I like," she'd added, thus ending the conversation, but not the hunt for the perfect green wedding slipper.

As soon as we got in the door, Maddie grabbed a handful of cookies and headed for her computer, her usual practice (though the snack varied), having nothing to do with the current situation regarding Taylor. I could never figure why it was necessary for a preteen to have an email account at all, or to check it so often, certainly more often than I checked mine. Were there job offers with a time value? Contracts to review? Bills to pay? Our ground mail, as we now called it in my circle, didn't arrive until midafternoon, so we'd have to wait a while if Taylor chose to respond that way.

In many ways I'd embraced the electronic age, but I decided to call Jeanine by old-fashioned landline and ask to meet with her. I sat in my atrium rocker and punched in her cell phone number.

"Hey, Mrs. Porter," she said. Uh-oh, I'd been hoping to leave a message. I wasn't ready with a reasonable script. "Mrs. Porter?"

"Hi, Jeanine." Fortunately, I caught myself before saying, "This is Mrs. Porter," and pulled myself together. "I was wondering if I could see you today, just briefly. There's something I need to discuss with you." I heard traffic noise in the background but no answer from Jeanine, so I rattled on. "I can stop by the store if that's easier for you." A heavy sigh came over the line, along with the honk of a horn. I hoped I wasn't the cause of a rare bottleneck in downtown Lincoln Point. "Or I can wait until you're off work."

Finally, Jeanine's voice: "No, I can do it now. Are you home?

I'm in my car on my way to do some errands but I can just go to your house." Doubt filled my mind as I realized how unlikely it was that Jeanine was the author of the get-out-of-town notes slipped under the door of Catherine's hotel room. I nearly withdrew my request to the young woman who'd been nothing but respectful and an enormous help to me the last few years—until I heard her final comment. "Let's get it over with," Jeanine said.

My feelings exactly, except, sadly, now I thought I knew the outcome.

JUST how patient and forbearing was my sister-in-law? I put the question to the test by calling Bev with yet another postponement.

"Anyone would think you hated shopping for life-sized things, Gerry," she said.

I explained that I wouldn't be asking for a rain check unless the meeting was truly important. I told her I really was looking forward to spending time with her, which was true even if it did involve going in and out of stores.

"This is about the case, isn't it?" Bev asked.

"Are you channeling Maddie?" I asked, and we both chuckled.

"I can't imagine you're sitting around while the specter of murder lingers and a former student and now coworker stands accused."

"When you put it that way… Any breakthroughs you can share, by the way? Or even any breakdowns?"

"Nothing major, except they found some threatening notes in Catherine's stuff and they're trying to figure out who sent them." I drew in my breath, but Bev didn't seem to notice. "Hasn't Skip talked to you yet? He was going to get in touch this morning, but then I saw him head for an interview room with that big guy from SuperKrafts."

Notes? Big guy? Too much all at once. "You mean the manager, Leo Murray, was there for an interview?"

"Yeah, I guess so. You can't miss him. He reeks of New York.

Who wears suits in the summer around here? Not even the car salesmen. And believe me that was no car-salesman suit."

My curiosity was flaring. What did the police think of the notes? Why was Skip reinterviewing Leo? Unless it wasn't Leo. There were a lot of tall guys in town. But not many who wore designer suits on ninety-degree days.

"Do you know why he brought Leo in?"

"No, but I do know that as soon as Catherine's lawyer gets wind of it, he's going to be clamoring to get her released. That is, unless Skip thinks this guy has some kind of evidence against her."

"And the notes? Any word on those?"

"They're back from analysis but I don't know what the results are. Tell you what, Gerry, why don't I pick up some lunch and bring it over and we can chat some more."

"What about your shoes?"

"We can go later. We'll see how it goes. Will you be free in about an hour?"

"Perfect. Thanks. I don't deserve you."

"What I always said."

*Buzz, buzz. Buzz, buzz.*

My doorbell. "That's my..." I began. What to call Jeanine? I looked at the clock. Almost noon. "My twelve o'clock is here," I told Bev.

I figured either Jeanine would be on her way out by one o'clock, with my profound apologies, or I'd be visiting her in jail later. Either way, I'd need a lunch.

# Chapter 16

I LED A VERY NERVOUS Jeanine Larkin into my atrium. She wore a short, bolero-type sweater over a white tank top, with the outer garment pulled tight across her chest. She looked about ten years old. I hated to leave her, but I needed to check on Maddie, realizing she might not be able to wait until one o'clock for lunch. Besides that, my granddaughter had been silent and nonintrusive all through my phone call with Bev and even through the doorbell. Something was amiss.

"Please have a seat, Jeanine," I said. "I just have to check on Maddie. I'll be right back."

Jeanine's "Okay" was weak.

I'd placed the paper with the poetry titles on the table and left it there for Jeanine to mull over. I steeled myself against her anguish and walked the few steps back to Maddie's bedroom at the front of the house. I wasn't prepared for what I found—I couldn't remember the last time I saw Maddie crying. Not teary eyes or a sad face, but lie-on-the-bed, full-out sobbing. I went to her immediately, sat on the bed, and rolled her into my arms.

"I'm here, sweetheart. What is it?" I fought back my own tears.

"There's nothing from Taylor. Or anybody else."

"The mail isn't here yet."

"There's no email and no phone calls."

"Is there someone else you're waiting to hear from?"

"Erica and Samantha, my friends in Palo Alto. They're supposed to let me know about the bus we're taking on the scouts' museum trip."

"When is that trip?"

"August tenth."

"That's a long time from now, sweetheart."

Jeanine appeared in the doorway. "Is everything okay?" She knew my house very well from years of baby-sitting and could probably hear us from her seat in the atrium. She seemed to have shed her own anxiety in favor of concern over Maddie's. A point in her favor, if I was keeping score.

"We're fine, thank you," I said, shaking my head "no" as to whether she should come into Maddie's bedroom. Jeanine nodded and turned away.

Maddie buried her head on my shoulder. "You can go, Grandma," she said, magnanimous.

"Jeanine is here about the case," I said. "Would you like to join us?" Was I really coaxing my granddaughter out of her depression with the promise of participation in a murder investigation?

"No, that's okay." No? Now I was really worried. "I'm going to stay here in case I get an email," she said.

I took another minute to tell Maddie the good news about lunch being delivered by her Aunt Bev.

She sat up. "I'm good now, Grandma. I just got, I don't know, sad or something."

I thought of calling June and asking for more of her insights into preteen relationships, but in fact, even if my own social traumas were in the distant past, I'd been witness to enough similar experiences with my high school students—a girl misses a phone call from a guy she thought was her boyfriend; a guy isn't invited to the coolest party of the term; a girl is left out when there's a drastic regrouping at lunch. I knew Maddie would eventually forget the reason she cried today, but that didn't mean she wasn't suffering right now, and I considered it my job to help her out of it.

It didn't take much. Already, Maddie was drying her eyes and sitting up. "I'm fine, really, Grandma. I don't know why I got this way."

"Maybe you didn't take enough cookies. And did you notice the ice cream sandwiches in the freezer?" I figured I wasn't the only grandmother who saw food as a cure for emotional distress.

"You mean I can have one before lunch?" she asked, grinning now.

"Absolutely."

She was out of my arms in a Lincoln Point minute.

I wanted more than anything to call Henry to hear what was going on at his house. I'd had notification of a voice mail message from him on my way to my car from the inn, and wished I'd taken the time to return the call. Had Taylor been crying also? Or was she swimming again with the new girl that June had postulated? No time now, with Jeanine waiting. I left Maddie to her own devices at the freezer while I tended to a more serious problem in my atrium.

JEANINE was wandering around the entryway, pausing to look at the objects on my table and to fiddle with the leaves of my ficus. The slip of paper with titles of her boyfriend's books of poetry was on the atrium table. When she saw me, she took a seat in front of the telltale note.

"I'm sorry I didn't even offer you a drink, Jeanine," I said. "But you know where they are, right?"

She nodded. "I'm good, Mrs. Porter." She moved the paper toward me. "I'll bet you don't want to talk about Ethan's poetry."

"I've seen this handwriting before, Jeanine. In a very unlikely place."

"I should have known better. I thought it was a strange thing to do, but she said it was just a prank."

"Who said what was a prank?"

Jeanine's breathing was labored, each word seeming to weigh on her, dragging her down. The sunlight coming through my atrium skylight, filtering through the ficus, did nothing to lighten her mood or soothe her, as she continued to hold her sweater closed tight around her.

"Mrs. Mellon," she said.

"Bebe Mellon told you these notes were a prank?"

Jeanine ran her fingers through her loose, long hair, tucked it behind her ears, then crossed her arms around her body again. "She told me she and Ms. Duncan were playing this game, sort of, like they were going back and forth with little pranks on each other. And she had this idea to write these notes and they were supposed to be part of the joke. But, she said Ms. Duncan would know her handwriting, so she asked me to write them and deliver them."

I sat back, trying to take in Jeanine's story. Was she telling me the truth? If not, it was a tale worthy of a creative writing major. Why would a smart young woman engage in such a game, or joke, or prank or whatever it was? For that matter, why would a smart middle-aged woman talk her into it?

"She offered me a lot of money," Jeanine said, answering my unspoken question. "And all I had to do was this simple thing. Mrs. Mellon had the words all written out for me, and she wanted me to make the grammar mistakes just the way she wrote them."

"And you also delivered them?"

Jeanine shook her head. "No, I was afraid to try to sneak into the inn the way Mrs. Mellon wanted me to. But I know Dana real well. We were cheerleaders together." She looped a stray strand of hair back behind her ear. "I know, cheerleaders. Pretty silly, huh? But it was a big thing for us." I was still trying to figure out who Dana was when Jeanine clarified. "Dana works at the KenTucky Inn, so she could just slide a note under any door at any time."

Sweet-looking Dana, who'd taken over Loretta's desk duty today. Dana was in on the note game? One just never knew who was serving tea and pie.

"I split the money with her," Jeanine said, as if that made everything all right. "One hundred dollars each, for just that little bit of work. I wrote all four of the notes out at once and gave them to Dana, and she put them under Ms. Duncan's door at the times Mrs. Mellon gave me. Oh, Mrs. Mellon doesn't know that I got Dana to do the delivery. Are you going to tell her?"

"Is that what matters to you?"

"Well, she paid me to do both jobs. Do you know how many hours I'd have to work at SuperKrafts or baby-sitting to make that kind of money? Or how many hours Dana would have to put in at the inn?" Jeanine wiped her brow, as if to indicate the hard labor that would have been required to legally earn one hundred dollars.

"It didn't seem too easy to you? Two hundred dollars for a practical joke, when you must have known that Mrs. Mellon and Ms. Duncan didn't get along? You didn't wonder if maybe something was off?"

"Well, sort of. But Mrs. Mellon seemed to be having fun, you know, not like her usual cranky mood. So, I thought, what the heck? But then Mrs. Mellon was arrested." Brought in for questioning, I thought, but figured the fine point was not worth bringing up. "And we were going to go to the police, but she was released."

"How convenient." I was beyond caring if I hurt Jeanine's feelings. I felt myself getting angry as I did sometimes when a particularly good student did something to sabotage her grades. Or her future.

"I know it sounds crazy, Mrs. Porter, but honest, we didn't mean any harm. Me and Dana talked about reporting it, but we didn't know anything for sure, like whether the notes had anything to do with why Mr. Palmer was killed. Then when Ms. Duncan was arrested, I figured I should tell someone and I almost told you when we were working together, but I didn't want to get Mrs. Mellon in trouble."

"Or yourself," I suggested.

Jeanine's eyes filled up. Her face went back to sad, after the relatively confident expression while she was defending her choices. "I know what you must be thinking. That I'm a really bad person." I didn't think that, but I also didn't think it was the time to console her. Not until I was sure she was going to do the right thing now. "The whole thing is making me dizzy, first one suspect, then another," she continued. And possibly another, I mused, as I thought of Leo, now in the hot seat at the LPPD.

"Are you planning to go to the police now?" I asked.

"Do you think I should?"

I breathed out a long, frustrated sigh. I'd have thought that would have been obvious, but I humored Jeanine. "Yes, you should never withhold information that might have relevance to a murder investigation." Or run with scissors, I thought, feeling like her nanny.

"I guess you're right, but…one question?"

"Yes?"

"Do you think we'd have to give back the money?"

At last, I was speechless.

ONCE Jeanine showed her mettle, seeming to care more about the money than the ramifications of her actions, I called an end to our meeting. I ushered her out the door, getting no promises from her about taking her story to the police, and giving none myself about keeping her secret. For now, I had a worthy grand-daughter to take care of.

Maddie was at her computer playing a math game, a decid-edly Porter choice, with no genetic input from me. I saw not one, but two, empty ice-cream sandwich wrappers on her desk. She gave me a grin. "They're smaller than they used to be," she said, echoing her Uncle Skip's declaration about my latest batch of ginger cookies. "So don't worry, I'm still hungry for lunch."

*Buzz, buzz. Buzz, buzz.*

Maddie jumped up to answer the door while I stayed behind and stripped her bed. I didn't want sheets with leftover tears to disturb her sleep tonight.

I expected to hear Bev's voice with a call to lunch, but Mad-die came back to her room alone. "It's the tall man from Super-Krafts," she said.

Leo Murray? At my house? "Did you let him in?"

"Uh-uh. I checked the peephole like you always say to do and I didn't know if I should let him in. He looks kind of scrungy."

That description didn't fit Leo, but maybe a couple of hours in a police interview room could scrunge up even a Madison Avenue New Yorker. "Good choice," I said.

I walked around to the entryway, with Maddie trailing, and looked out the window. There was Leo Murray's rental car, its unmistakable shade of blue sending rays of sun in all directions. What would he be doing in this neighborhood? Obviously the police cleared him and sent him on his way, but why was he here? To find out, I'd probably have to let him in. I couldn't figure out why I was reluctant to do so, other than that I was rattled by the events of the past days. Bebe Mellon's confession about her confession, Catherine Duncan's arrest, my interrogation at the mercy of Fred Bates, concern for Maddie and Taylor, ditto for Skip and June, and most recently, Jeanine Larkin's fall from grace.

I had no basis for being afraid of Leo, however, and as long as he didn't hit me with a love interest problem or a cruel joke he'd played, we should be okay. I prepared myself for another counseling session and opened the door. One of these days, I really should remove the shrink shingle from my house.

"Leo, what a surprise to see you here."

"I hope you don't mind." He pointed toward the interior of my home. "Would it be okay if I came in? I'm roasting in this weather."

Leo had never looked worse, slumped over, his face sunken, his suit rumpled, and his forehead deeply furrowed. It was as if some cloud of transformation had settled over SuperKrafts, changing Megan from the wimp I first met at Craig Palmer's heels in Sadie's to an unflappable force ready to take her career into her own hands, and changing Leo from the storming exec who presided over meetings to someone who looked like he couldn't manage his own dry cleaning.

"Of course," I said, stepping aside to let him in. Leo walked by me, into the atrium. Maddie stayed close to me, but in plain sight.

"I didn't know where else to go," Leo said.

"Apparently, there isn't anywhere else," I said.

"Huh?"

"Nothing."

Leo took a seat and Maddie, likely judging the situation to

be less interesting than the resources in her bedroom, took off. "I just came from a grilling by your nephew," Leo said.

"He's good at that."

I wasn't proud of myself, that I was enjoying having this upper hand over Leo, after all the meetings where he was king. But when I noticed his jacket and shirt sleeves were soiled, probably from the less-than-sterile interview room furniture, I felt a stab of pity.

"It's the craziest thing. The cops think I wrote some threatening notes to Catherine," he began.

How to get my attention, Leo! Confusion set in quickly as I considered whether I'd dreamt the recent visit with the confessed writer of the notes. Did Skip have different notes from the ones I'd seen in Jeanine's handwriting? Maybe Bebe paid several people to write notes, backup in case one didn't have the nerve to follow through. Was there another set of notes, written and sent by Leo? A set Catherine hadn't bothered to tell me about?

"Did you write notes to Catherine?" I asked.

Leo straightened his shoulders and looked at me, a glimmer of his old, in-charge self coming through. "No, I didn't write them. The cops think I did. They found notes in her room, telling her to get out of town, or else. Why would I do that?"

"Why do the police think you did, Leo?"

He hung his head, slumping down again. "It was my stationery. The notes were written on my personal stationery. They're right about that."

I'd never given a thought to the stationery, other than to wonder about fingerprints. It had seemed to me rather ordinary kind of paper from a notepad, off-white in color, standard size, about four by six inches, unlined.

"How did they trace the paper to you? Are your prints on it?"

"I have a watermark on each sheet of my notepads."

Imagine that. Everything about Leo was status and class. Why was I not surprised? Didn't watermarks go with gold cufflinks, designer clothes, a high-end briefcase? I wondered if watermarks were registered, but didn't want to ask and risk sounding like the plain-Jane, small-town folk I'd become. I hoped Leo would explain, but he must have assumed I had my own watermark and knew all about them.

"What can I do for you, Leo?"

"Well, I'm okay for now. I convinced them that I leave my pads around and anyone could have lifted one from the meeting room at the store or from my briefcase or my hotel room. It's not like I have document control on the sheets. It's just a notepad."

A very expensive notepad, I guessed. Not like the small ones I picked up at the dollar table in an office supplies store. I still didn't have an answer to why Leo was sitting in my atrium in the confessional seat, where Catherine, Bebe, and Jeanine had sat before him.

"The police must have believed you if they let you go."

"Yeah, but these guys, the cops in this town, they..." Light dawned as he saw the folly of insulting the person he'd come to for help, the cherished aunt of one of the cops. "I'm just afraid it's not over—I'm sure they're trying to tie the notes, and me, to Palmer's murder, and I'm alone here. I have an attorney at home, of course, but I need someone on my side. Someone local."

"You'd be surprised how little that matters."

Leo leaned toward me, his dirty elbows on my table. "Listen, Geraldine, I'm at a loss here. I know how it works when everyone knows everyone else. I don't mean to keep disparaging your town but don't you see that the cops have been going down the list, accusing anyone associated with Craig? First one of your own, then Catherine. Well, she's still their top one, I guess, since she's still in jail, but as soon as her lawyer gets wind of how they questioned me, he's going to have her out of there. The cops are acting like, like..."

"Keystone Kops?" I said.

"Who?"

"Never mind. I still don't see what I can do for you, Leo. You're free."

"And I want to make sure I stay that way until I can get myself back home. All I want is for you to corroborate my position that"—Leo held up his fingers and ticked them off—"one, you saw my pads all over the store, especially the meeting room; and two, I had no reason to harass Catherine, especially no reason to want her out of town. I just wanted *me* out of town. I'm much better off if Catherine stays here forever. I'd love for her to settle down with her Video Jack."

"Jeff," I said. "The man's name is Jeff Slattery."

Leo didn't acknowledge my correction. I didn't even blink, so accustomed was I to the SuperKrafts managers' culture of the New York way or the highway. Nevertheless, I'd have no problem supporting Leo in his two assertions, if it came to that. I had certainly seen Leo's notepads, though I'd never noticed a watermark (so what was the point of the personalization?) and as far as I knew, Catherine and Leo had shown no more animosity toward each other than any other two SuperKrafts employees, all of whom seemed to be at each others' throats more often than not. But I didn't have to make it easy for Leo. Since he was on my turf, and here to beg a favor, I thought I might as well bargain with him.

"I can certainly make sure Detective Gowen knows about the ubiquity of your notepads and I can tell him about the interactions I observed at meetings," I said. "In return I'd like to ask you a few questions."

Leo sat back and threw his palms open in the space between us. "Go ahead."

I wished I'd had a little warning and time to prepare for this cooperative spirit on Leo's part. I thought of Leo's row on Maddie's capital-C Chart. She'd put a question mark under his location; all I had was hearsay that Leo and Craig had stayed in the SuperKrafts building after the afternoon meeting ended. Filling in the Leo row seemed as good a place as any to start. "Where were you during the earthquake last Saturday?" I asked.

"You mean while someone else was bashing in Craig Palmer's head?"

"If you need to put it that way, yes."

"Sorry. That sounded pretty bad. We had our disagreements, Craig and me, but I'd never wish that on him, or anyone." He shook his head. "It was a horrible way to go."

"The earthquake hit at six thirty-two. Where were you?" Gerry the interrogator, not easing up—I'd learned from the best.

"I was at a 'gourmet'"—here he'd drawn quotes in the air—"supermarket near my hotel in San Jose picking up dinner. And yes, I have a receipt because I turn everything like that in with my expense sheets."

I supposed Leo had already been through this with the LPPD, but I needed to evaluate him for myself. And for The Chart.

"Did anything in the supermarket fall over during the quake? Anything break?"

Leo gave me a confused look. I didn't blame him. "No, it wasn't that big a deal. That's what the locals down there said, too. The dude at the register called it 'puny.'"

Not even our earthquakes measured up to Leo's standards.

I was out of questions. As pushy as Leo had been since I'd met him, I had a hard time labeling him a killer in his current state. Maybe that was his plan all along. Maybe I should join Jeanine in her psych courses.

I was about to let Leo out, without even offering him a drink, I realized, when Maddie crept up beside me, her clipboard in her hand.

"What's the name of the store?" she asked Leo.

Leo looked flustered for a moment. Perhaps Maddie was more intimidating than the LPPD? But he recovered, and before I could react, he bent down, too close to Maddie's face, I thought. I pulled her back from him. "One of those chains with a big orange sign and a take-out section in front," he said.

I would have expected him to use the word "chains" with more fondness, given his association with one. Leo turned and walked down the driveway toward his car, his off-putting strut resurfacing. Maybe he'd already forgotten he'd come for my help.

# Chapter 17

BACK IN THE ATRIUM with Maddie, I looked over her shoulder and saw that she'd filled in Leo's row with "San Jose Store."

"Should we call the store and check it out, Grandma?"

I was sure we could figure out which orange chain was closest to Leo's hotel, but was it worth it? Leo had been grilled and re-grilled by Lincoln Point's finest and I was sure they were more than capable of checking his alibi if they hadn't already done so. A call more pressing to me was one to Jeanine to learn more about the Curious Case of the Watermarked Paper.

*Buzz, buzz. Buzz, buzz.*

Saved by lunch? Surely it was Bev this time. Maddie hopped to the peephole and I used the time to punch in Jeanine's number.

"Hey, Mrs. Porter." Jeanine sounded rightfully anxious over the phone. I would have bet money that she and Dana had made no plans about taking their story to the police.

"Jeanine, I have a question for you."

Her hesitant "Sure" sounded the opposite.

"Where did you get the paper for the notes you wrote to Catherine?"

"Oh, I thought you were calling to ask if I'd contacted the police yet."

*How smart is it to remind me?* I wanted to ask. Jeanine was still losing ground on my list of favorite teens. And Dana, her co-conspirator, had never made it to the list. I thought of calling Loretta at KenTucky Inn to let her know that one of her employees had taken advantage of her position to collude in what might now be construed as a crime. Wasn't it stalking to slip a threatening note under someone's door?

"It's Uncle Skip, Grandma," Maddie called from the entryway.

Not what I wanted to hear until I'd decided when and how I'd share what I knew about the notes. And besides, I was expecting his mother, with lunch.

"Mrs. Mellon gave me the paper," Jeanine said.

I drew in my breath. The notes were taking on a life of their own.

"Hey, Aunt Gerry," Skip said, then when he noticed I was on the phone, "oops, sorry."

I gave him a smile, turned my back, counting on Maddie to entertain him, and whispered to Jeanine. "Mrs. Mellon gave you the paper for the notes?"

"Yes, she was very specific about that, too. I thought I told you. She said it had to be on that paper. That was part of the whole joke, well, not a joke." Jeanine chuckled, then turned it into a cough when I didn't join her.

Bebe certainly had access to Leo's fancy notepads. It must have given her quite a thrill to see his personal paper used for her purposes—framing Leo for sending the notes to Catherine—Bebe's only possible motive being to hassle both her perceived enemies with one shot. She couldn't have had Craig Palmer's murder in mind at the time, but she got a dividend when Palmer was killed and the notes were seen as connecting Leo to the crime. I was embarrassed for my fellow citizens. Bebe, Jeanine, Dana. Could I blame the influx of New Yorkers for what some of them had turned into?

"Aunt Bev says to tell you she's running late but she'll be here soon," I heard Skip tell Maddie. "And June's coming over, too." I gave a thumbs-up to that though no one was watching.

*Beep, beep. Beep, beep.*

A call from Henry, waiting. I was through with Jeanine anyway, in more ways than one. I thanked her for answering my question and switched to Henry's call.

"I left a message for you this morning," he said. "Figured I'd try again."

"It's been a kind of hectic day." If you can call a parade of people hectic.

"No problem. Are you and Maddie home now?"

"Uh-huh."

"Okay if we come over?"

"'We'? You mean…?"

"Taylor and me."

I looked at Maddie, playing some kind of slap-my-hand game with Skip, a big grin on her face. Did I want to spoil things? "Uh…"

"It's all good," he said.

Because I trusted Henry, I relaxed and a smile crossed my face. "Have you had lunch?"

"Thought we could take you to lunch. That was my message earlier."

"Hold on, Henry." I covered the phone mic and said to Skip, "Can you call your mom back and tell her to bring lunch for seven?"

The day was looking up.

I GAVE Maddie the task of setting the dining room table. I was on pins and needles about the Maddie-and-Taylor reunion (which sounded like an album I used to own) and about telling Skip what I knew about the notes. Leo Murray was the last person I ever thought I'd be defending, but even though I wasn't legally bound to share what I knew, I felt obligated in every other sense.

With Bev, June, Henry, and Taylor on the way, this was my best chance to pull Skip aside. Before I talked myself out of it, I motioned for him to step into the atrium while Maddie was clattering around between the kitchen and the dining room with plates, glasses, and silverware.

Skip took a seat and crossed his legs. "Is this about me and June?"

"Should it be?"

"Uh-uh. We're good, thanks." He made a circle with his thumb and index finger: A-OK. Just like that? If he could move on, so could I. "You want to know about my day with Maddie?" he asked.

"Eventually, but not right now. Tell me about watermarks," I said.

"Ha. You first," he said.

"Okay, we don't have a lot of time. I had a visit from Leo Murray."

"Of course you did."

"Why are you always saying that to me? Am I that predictable? Never mind. Before Leo came, I entertained Jeanine Larkin."

"Who?"

"I'm sure you've met her. Maddie's baby-sitter, now a Super-Krafts employee." Skip nodded. "She's the one who wrote the notes to Catherine Duncan."

I always enjoyed surprising my nephew. He looked at me intently and scratched his head. "What? I'm all ears."

I gave Skip the short form of Jeanine's story.

"Way too weird," Skip said. "If this is true, Bebe needs help. If she can't eliminate her enemies, she pits them against each other?"

"It looks that way. Are you going to check it out?"

"You bet."

"Are Jeanine and Dana in a lot of trouble?"

"Don't worry. You absolutely did the right thing telling us this time."

"This time?" I asked.

"I'm assuming you saw the notes, before we did."

I cleared my throat. "What makes you say that?"

"From the way you talked about them. You didn't say, 'Catherine got some notes,' or 'There were some notes.' You talked about them as if you'd already dealt with the fact that the notes exist. Jeanine was telling you who sent them. Leo was just giving you information about the paper. My guess is that Catherine showed them to you right when she got them. How am I doing?"

"I told Catherine immediately that she should take them to you. I didn't—"

Skip held up his hand. "I'm sure you tried to get her to do the right thing. We'll check out Jeanine's story, but it's looking like some stand-alone unfortunate play on Bebe's part, taking advantage of a couple of unthinking teenagers only too willing to accept easy cash. There doesn't seem to be any connection to Palmer's murder."

"So all we need to do now is find out if Catherine really is guilty."

"Aunt Gerry, when I say 'we' I don't mean you and me."

"Point taken. I'm still curious about the watermark. How did you find it?"

"Through the usual analysis, looking for prints or any distinguishing marks on the paper."

"Why would anyone use one in the first place? I thought they were for security, like on passports or bank documents or something official."

"Also for status. You'd be surprised how many we see." Skip started to laugh. "Want to know what Leo's mark was?" I nodded. "The head of a lion with his initials, *L.M.* making a wreath around its neck. Gotta love those proud, roaring New Yorkers."

I tried hard not to, but ended up joining in Skip's laughter. We were having such a good time, I almost forgot that Catherine was still in jail. Our loud glee brought Maddie running. She'd been so intent on getting the table set up perfectly, she'd forgotten she was missing something big in the atrium.

My guilty pleasure, making fun of Leo's personality traits, was cut short when I realized I hadn't told Maddie that Henry and Taylor were coming to lunch. I revisited my invitation to them, especially with other guests here, familiar as we all were with each other. Maybe I'd been too quick to respond, before I knew what Taylor had in mind. How sure was Henry that Taylor was ready to make up, and not simply about to make things worse with the equivalent of a Dear John letter?

"I have something to do in my bedroom," I told Skip and

Maddie. I needn't have worried; they'd already picked up their hand-slapping game. As I passed the dining room I noticed the long table set for five. I told myself that making room for two more would be a very happy task.

I sat on the chair next to my bed and punched in Henry's number.

"We're on our way," he said. "I stopped to pick up some dessert. That chocolate cheesecake that Maddie likes, from the Swiss bakery."

"Henry, I have to ask—"

"I don't blame you for being anxious, Gerry. But I promise. If Maddie will accept Taylor's apology, everything will be fine. Taylor was very moved by Maddie's letter and she wants to tell her in person. Oh, and, by the way, no young males involved. Whew."

"'Whew' is right. Okay, see you soon."

I hung up feeling a little better—the word "apology" sounded better at least than "discuss," which was too much like the ominous "We have to talk." I still wasn't sure whether I should give Maddie a warning.

*Buzz, buzz. Buzz, buzz.*

My doorbell and phone were making lots of decisions for me lately. If that marked me as a faltering, irresolute character, so be it. I heard shouts of "Welcome" as I walked toward the front of the house and saw Bev and June arrive together, each carrying a sack.

"Good thing I was handy," June said. "Bev brought enough food for an army."

"Or for seven hungry people," I said, causing everyone to either raise eyebrows or count or both.

I made a decision and this time it was Maddie I coaxed to the side. I led her to her bedroom, watching her eyes grow larger and more wary with each step. She sat on her bed, leaving the rocker for me.

"Taylor's coming?" she asked. Smarter than I was ready for, every time.

"Is that okay? Uncle Henry told me she'd like to apologize."

Now I was worried her eyes would never go back to normal. "Really?"

"Uh-huh. It might be a little tricky with everyone here, so that's why I wanted to let you know ahead of time."

"Wow," she said.

"Do you want to talk about it?"

*Buzz, buzz. Buzz, buzz.*

Maddie jumped as if we were sitting on the epicenter of at least a seven-point-five.

"You might want to wait—"

But Maddie was already on her way to answer the door. I felt like hiding in her room until peace had descended on all couples in the universe.

COWARD that I am, I waited a few minutes in Maddie's bedroom, pretending to be busy at my computer. Hadn't I done enough for all the affected parties out there, buzzing around my house? I'd come forward with key information for Skip regarding Catherine Duncan's notes; June and Skip thought I'd been a big help with their relationship issue; and I was providing my home for a reconciliation lunch for Maddie and Taylor. I'd earned a little respite.

I'd had about two minutes of it when Maddie, Taylor, and Henry came to find me.

"Grandma, we were looking for you," Maddie said.

"I was just a few steps away," I said, with what was probably a foolish grin.

Taylor gave me a big hug. "Aunt Gerry, I missed you. Thanks for inviting us to lunch."

"Let's go eat," Henry said to me.

I took his arm, mock-formal, and we left the room, leaving the girls behind. So far, so good, but I expected a full report at bedtime with Maddie. Then Henry stopped to hug me, and all was well.

———

THE lunch fairies, led by Bev, had rummaged in my cupboards for platters and bowls and had arranged sandwiches and enough sides to fill a deli counter—fruit salad, potato salad, leafy greens, a tomato and mozzarella mix, and a creamy cole slaw. In the center sat a huge chocolate cheesecake.

In the kitchen, I helped Beverly prepare the drinks. "It looks good for Taylor and Maddie, huh?" she whispered. I nodded and showed her crossed fingers.

Bev was six years younger than her late brother Ken and I, but with her fair skin and her hair a lovely shade of red, she looked at least ten or twelve years younger, as I'd often told her.

"It all comes in a bottle now, Gerry," she'd say whenever I complimented her hair especially. "You, too, can be gray-free."

"Maybe on my next salon visit," I'd say, though we both knew I'd never spend the time and energy on hair maintenance. I'd stick with admiring the outcome on someone who did.

Conversation around the table was understandably rife with cross-talk, making it fun, but difficult to follow one thread for very long.

"Where's Nick?" Skip asked his mom.

Bev raised her chin and looked at me. She delivered her answer smoothly. "He's out buying shoes."

"Funny," I said.

From another corner I heard Maddie and Taylor.

"Really?" Maddie had just said.

"Yeah, and I'll use yours for a week," Taylor replied.

"Grandma, Taylor said we can swap phone cases for a week. Hers is really cool." She held it up for me to see. "It has all these really sparkly crystals."

"It's beautiful," I said, dutifully.

Skip and June, at the other end of the table from me, shared their plans with whoever was listening.

"We're going to take a vacation as soon as the Palmer case is closed," Skip said. June nudged him. "And also, matching the time to June's workload," he added.

Bev gave a thumbs-up to her son. "Where are you going?" she asked.

"Tahoe," Skip and June said together. A good sign.

The very large Lake Tahoe, a four-hour drive from Lincoln Point, was once ranked "Best Lake in America" though I still preferred the Finger Lakes of upstate New York, where Ken and I had visited often. But Tahoe was handier, and offered all the water sports Skip and June loved.

The impromptu lunch party, which started at about two o'clock, ran into late afternoon. No one was in a hurry to leave, and I liked that. When the break came, we went off in twos and threes. Henry and the girls went in one direction, toward his home workshop where he'd been helping them make jewelry boxes. "Grandpa is going to show us how to use the sander on a piece of wood," Taylor told me, giving me a good-bye hug. She'd been especially affectionate toward me all afternoon. I could hardly wait to get the backstory at Maddie's bedtime.

Skip and June went in the other direction, but not before Skip whispered to me, "I'll be ba-aaaack," imitating a character in a movie, I thought, but couldn't think of which one. "Will you be up around eleven?"

"For you, any time," I said, though his visit would really be for me.

Before I knew it, Bev whisked me into her car and drove us to a mall. "At last," she said. "I feel like I haven't talked to you in ages."

"You have a lot going on," I said, as we pulled into a parking spot. "Once you have your shoes, you'll feel a lot better." I couldn't remember another time when I'd recommended retail therapy instead of ice cream and cookies to relieve stress.

Bev hit the buttons to lower the windows and parked her SUV. She reached around to the floor behind her and brought up a plastic bag with a shoe box inside, not saying a word. She opened the box and I peered at a pair of elegant sling-back sandals—green shoes, the same shade as her dress, as near as I could recall.

"What's this? I love them. When did you buy these?"

"Two weeks ago. It was never about shoes, Gerry. I just needed to talk to you."

Was I that hard to get? "What's up? Are you okay?"

The first thing that always came to mind when Bev was fa-
tigued or indicated that a serious conversation was coming up,
was her physical well-being. Although she looked fit and healthy,
she carried with her the remnants of childhood scarlet fever,
which had weakened her heart. Too many times in our life together as sisters-in-law, I'd sat in a hospital waiting room with
Ken after one of her episodes. We were more optimistic now
because of advances in heart surgery and medicine, but the worry
was always there.

Bev waved my concern away. "It's not health-related," she
said. "It's wedding-related."

"Tell me," I said, dreading what I'd hear.

"I'm getting married," she said. I waited for real news. "I'll
have a new husband." Still nothing I didn't know. "My son will
have a stepfather who's a guy he used to work with on the force."
More waiting. Finally, after more obvious announcements, like "I
love Nick," Bev asked me a question. "Do you think it's okay?"

I didn't know where to start. Should I remind her that it had
been twenty years since Skip's dad died? No one could accuse her
of being quick to replace him. Should I mention that Skip clearly
loved and admired Nick? I could bring up the fact that Skip had
tried to set Nick and me up before it became clear where Nick's
attention was focused.

"How could it not be okay?" I asked. "Everyone who knows
either of you is thrilled."

Bev's eyes teared up and her voice was sad. "But I'll be a
happy wife."

*But?* "And you don't deserve it?"

Bev shrugged. "It's hard. Skip lost his dad."

"Through no fault of yours."

"He'll never get his father back."

"He knows that," I said. "And he's not replacing him with

Nick. You're all adults. Skip doesn't really need a father now. He'll be one himself before we know it."

Bev's head snapped up. "Really? Do you know something?"

I laughed, in spite of the heavy air in the car. "No, I didn't mean to imply that. I meant 'eventually,' not necessarily 'soon.' But the fact is, you're marrying Skip's friend, and we know he's happy about it. He'll have a good buddy who's also part of his family. How great is that? Any more questions?"

Bev shook her head and ran a wad of tissues over her face. "No more questions. I guess I just needed to hear you say it."

I couldn't believe I'd said anything I hadn't been saying since she and Nick started dating. But I'd do or say whatever it took, as many times as necessary, to set Bev's mind at ease. I knew she'd do the same for me. Not that I'd ever need her to.

# Chapter 18

I ARRIVED HOME after a brief shopping spree during which Bev picked up the personalized jewelry she'd ordered for her attendants—too late for me to recommend watermarked stationery. The number 2 blinked on my landline answering machine. Only one message, from Maddie, came up when I turned my cell back on. I'd wanted to be fully available to Bev during our heavy conversation.

The message from Maddie was a simple notice that she'd be having dinner with Taylor and the Baker family and I was invited and please come. She sounded so happy, I thought of capturing the recording and saving it, along with the one or two (or three hundred) other precious items I'd collected over her short span of life. I talked myself out of keeping the recording, mostly because I didn't know how to do it. I also talked myself out of joining them for dinner. Not only was I still full from the late lunch, but I needed some time alone to arrange all the pieces of information I had that involved SuperKrafts and the murder of one of its managers.

I sat at my kitchen counter and punched the button for my voice mail. As I waited for the first message on my landline, I sorted through the mail from the post office, relieved not to be searching for a letter from Taylor. Loretta Olson's voice came through the speaker.

"Hi, Gerry. It was great to see you and Maddie at the inn this morning. You'll have to come back for lunch some time. I talked to Amelia and she assured me that no broken glass was found in any of the rooms the day after the earthquake. Or ever, that she can remember. Hope that helps. Whatever. See you."

No broken glass. Whatever. I dug around in my purse for The Chart. I had the older, unedited version that Maddie had printed out for our trip to KenTucky Inn, but it would do. Megan was listed as telling me that a glass broke, and I remembered that later she'd told Jeanine that "some things" broke. But so what? Megan Sutley exaggerated. We were all in trouble if a little hyperbole was a crime. Especially when we talked about earthquakes. "Nothing happened" is not a good story (though that was Leo's); a little fiction makes things more interesting. I remembered allegedly true stories that were passed around during the meeting of my crafts group a few days after the last major quake to affect the San Jose area. Some anecdotes rivaled what might have been depicted in a movie version.

The only thing that concerned me about Megan was that, according to Loretta, she was scheduled to fly back to New York tomorrow. I'd have to check with Skip, but I would have thought a "don't leave town" rule would apply to all persons of interest in an open homicide case. Maybe the police had already decided they weren't interested in Megan.

I put on water for tea as I listened to the next message, from Jeanine.

"Hi, Mrs. Porter. This is Jeanine. Um, you probably know my voice. *(Chuckle)* I want you to know that me and Dana are going to the police station tomorrow morning. I also forgot to tell you that when I was waiting for you in your atrium I saw a crystal that I think is the one Ms. Sutley lost from her cell phone case. She's been looking for it and I told her I thought you might have it. So, in case she calls you, that's why. Um, thanks for everything today. I'm at work if you need to reach me."

*Too little, too late*, as far as turning themselves in, but I was glad "me and Dana" had come to the right decision. Whether—as a result of my snitching—Skip would contact them before they got to him, remained to be seen. I couldn't worry about it. In other circumstances, I'd have called and offered to help Jeanine if she needed help with last minute tasks before tomorrow's informal opening. But now I had no desire to see her or talk to her in person until I knew what would transpire with the police, if it hadn't already.

Bebe was another story, and I intended to ask Skip what he planned to do about her. I hadn't decided what I would do about her either. She was beyond reasonable discussion as far as I was concerned. After hearing of her crazy scheme to hassle Catherine, I couldn't put anything past her. Even murder. Her false confession might have been another scheme. Distract the police with an obviously unlikely story, so they wouldn't look more closely.

While I let my tea sit a few minutes, I paid a visit to the blue-green bead I'd found at SuperKrafts while I wandered around the store on Sunday afternoon. I hadn't looked closely at the bead since I'd noticed it in the dim light of the store. I picked it up now and turned it around in my hand. I saw that the bead was indeed a crystal that might have been glued to the case. Crystals were not my field of expertise, but even so, studying it now, I could tell this item was more pricey than the crystal-like beads on the racks of SuperKrafts or on Taylor's phone case. No wonder Megan was looking for it. I placed it back in the bowl, far from my crafts room where it might not be seen again for years.

*Dum dum, da da dum, da da dum.*

Maddie on my cell phone. I hoped they weren't holding dinner for me.

"Where are you, Grandma?"

"I just got home, sweetheart."

"Uncle Henry said he'd pick you up if you want to come for dinner."

"Thank him very much, but I think I'll pass. I'm beat."

"You're never beat."

How nice that I presented an unbeatable image. "You're right. How about 'a little tired' and 'need a little rest'?"

"Okay, I get it. Uncle Henry said he'd drive me home in a little while if you didn't want to come. Do you want me to stay away longer?"

"Of course not. I just need to sort out all these things I bought for you."

Maddie giggled and gave me her new good-bye. "Mwah," she said, which was so much better than the "Nyah" she'd begun her visit with. I was eager to call Mary Lou and tell her that Maddie's funk was over, that it wasn't boy-time yet, and that Maddie and Taylor had reconciled, but I wanted to wait until I had more specifics. Since Mary Lou and Richard were in the same time zone, I could safely wait until later this evening. I doubted my son was even aware of the trauma. He'd married well.

I poured the tea over a large glass of ice, stirred, and took a refreshing sip. I had an idea I wanted to work on for the miniature police station scene—stationery with the LPPD letterhead, inspired by Leo Murray's watermarked notepads. Though computer tasks were usually Maddie's job, I thought I could handle searching online for the LPPD logo and shrinking the image to fit mini correspondence paper.

*Dum dum, da da dum, da da dum.*

Maddie again. It might have been a better idea to simply succumb to the invitation.

"Hi, sweetheart."

"I didn't want to bother you, Grandma, but if you want to study The Chart some more before I get home, you should use the latest version. It's in the printer tray. I put in all the new stuff we learned at KenTucky Inn and what the guy said who came over this morning. Then I forgot to give it to you because it got so busy. Maybe that's why you're beat."

"I'm fine now."

"Did you find all the things you bought me?"

"Uh-huh, there's a really fancy dress, and a—"

My granddaughter blew a raspberry at me before clicking off. Imagine.

I abandoned the mini-stationery project, since computer-based crafts weren't my favorite anyway. Instead, I retrieved the newest chart from my printer and looked it over.

UPDATED THE CHART

| Megan | KenTucky Inn | coffeemaker/ice bucket shook, glass broke | Not |
|---|---|---|---|
| Catherine | KenTucky Inn | hotel clock shook and slid (? Maybe) | W |
| Jeff | inside his store | games toppled | W |
| Maisie | home | no movement | |
| Bebe | ? | ? | ? |
| Leo | San Jose store | nothing happened | |
| Jeanine | Seward's Folly | filters fell, coffee spilled | W |
| Grandma | home w/Maddie | vase and bowl fell and broke | W, W |

The speed with which Maddie had updated the chart—I loved the title—even in her misery over her social life, was impressive, but I'd ceased to be amazed at the wonders of my granddaughter.

I took The Chart and my iced tea to a soft chair in my living room. In retrospect, it might have been a mistake to lean back and stretch my legs out. Soon after I propped a pillow behind my neck, the lines on the sheet began to blur and the slippery paper slid off my lap and onto the floor.

"GRANDMA, Grandma." Maddie's voice came to me out of a deep hole. I opened my eyes to see that the sun had set and I'd missed anyone's idea of dinnertime. "You fell asleep, Grandma."

"Hi, sweetheart," I managed, trying to focus.

Henry emerged through the shadows in my head. He very thoughtfully ran the atrium light up slowly through the dimmer switch. "I guess you really were beat," he said.

I smiled. "How did you come up with that term?"

"It's all the rage in the Baker household right now."

I rubbed Maddie's head, which happened to be on my lap as she knelt on the floor in front of me. "Thanks for taking care of her dinner."

"Our pleasure," Henry said.

"Can I get you a drink?" I asked, making no move to leave my overly comfortable chair.

"Thanks, no. I'll be moving along. Are you going to be first in the door at SuperKrafts tomorrow?"

Tomorrow. Wednesday. Opening day, albeit an informal beginning. "Probably."

"Shall I pick you up?"

"That would be great."

"See you at nine-thirty."

He leaned over and kissed me. All was well. Maddie let Henry out, in deference to my slow wake-up.

"Do you want me to make you some dinner while you get out my presents?" Maddie asked.

The great negotiator. "That sounds perfect." I knew eventually I'd have to leave my chair and its cushions.

"What do you want to eat?"

"Surprise me."

While Maddie prepared my surprise meal, I forced myself out of drowsiness and gathered my shopping bags. It was about time I sorted through the loot I'd purchased. I'd learned long ago that it was physically impossible for me to spend a couple of hours shopping and not buy things for Maddie. I took the bags in the dining room, spread the contents on the now clear table, and began the process of separating the boring items from the more exciting purchases.

Under "boring" I had bought Maddie new summer pajamas. I found a pair with a black-and-white image of headphones hanging down the front of the pajama top, as if she were actually wearing them. Also under "practical" were badly needed socks and a few school supplies. I'd also fallen victim to the strategically placed hair clips by the cash register. Under "exciting" (I hoped) was a medium-sized metal chest marked EMERGENCY SUPPLIES in stenciled letters across the front and back, that contained a booklet on safety for earthquakes, floods, and other disasters, and a list of common things that should be stored for such times. I thought it would be fun to fill the chest. I had a ready supply of water and flashlights, but not a complete kit and not everything was in one place. Our next project could be to put together a chest full of blankets, canned food, bottles of water, extra clothing, a battery-powered radio, and so on, down the list.

"Ready!" Maddie called, summoning me to the atrium where she'd set the little table with a plate of leftovers—a ladleful of fruit salad, and one scoop each of potato salad and a rice-and-cheese dish from not too long ago. On another plate, in front of her seat, was a slice of pizza she must have found in the depths of the freezer.

Since nothing was going to spoil, we agreed to check out the purchases first. She pulled the pajama top over her head immediately, a sign of acceptance, and clapped at the sight of the official disaster kit. I'd done well.

There wasn't too much time between my late dinner and Maddie's bedtime, but we squeezed in another session in the crafts room. As I expected, Maddie whipped up an LPPD letterhead in no time, and I took pleasure in my contribution of folding tiny pieces of paper into the shape of envelopes. We'd made an L-shaped desk–computer station combination from a block of Styrofoam covered with adhesive paper, and placed the stationery in strategic spots.

"Did you talk to your mom today?" I asked, using my fingernail to firm up a fold in a miniature envelope that had sprung open.

"Yeah, I called her and said good night, and I told her that I had a good day today. I wish I didn't make her worry."

"She knows it's hard to talk about things sometimes. But as long as you know that we're always here, and there's nothing you can't tell us if you want to, everything is fine."

Maddie gave me a sweet smile that said my feeble attempts at parent talk were at least passing. It seemed so much easier when her dad was her age, but then Ken was around to take up the slack of what I might have missed.

AT our bedtime chat, we had a lot to talk about. I praised her work on updating The Chart and she praised my shopping skills on her behalf.

"I'm glad you had a good day with Taylor," I said.

"Uh-huh. She said she was sorry she left me out of some

things. I didn't want to complain to my mom or you or anything, but there's a new girl in Taylor's class, named Sierra, and she has a swimming pool. It's right down the street."

"You don't say?" I asked, with a tip of an imaginary hat to June, who'd nailed it.

"Taylor and all the other kids have been talking about it and even sent around a picture of the pool before we got off school."

"But you weren't invited to join them?"

"Uh-uh. Taylor said she asked if I could come and Sierra said she only wanted kids from their school right here."

"You mean Lincoln Point Elementary?"

"Uh-huh, no one from out of town, like Palo Alto. But all Taylor's other friends like me, so I guess it's okay that one person doesn't."

"You've never even met her, have you?"

Maddie shook her head. "Uh-uh, just emailing with the group."

"If she knew you, she'd love you," I said, tickling the right spots for maximum laughter.

When she calmed down, Maddie continued to explain. "Taylor said she was sorry and she should have at least told me instead of just ignoring me."

"And I assume you accepted her apology?"

"Yeah, and I was thinking that instead of being mad at her, I should have been happy that she was having a good time in the pool and all. Like a grown-up would."

I hesitated to tell her how few grown-ups would have responded differently.

TIRED as she was from what must have taken an emotional toll on her, Maddie convinced me to read from one of her favorite kids' books. I had the feeling she was seeking comfort by revisiting a simpler time, and I thought how tempting it was to wish we could keep her trouble-free for at least a few decades. When she finally dozed off, I went to the atrium to make my own call to Mary Lou who, I knew, was a night owl.

"Hey, Mom," she said, in a soft voice.

Uh-oh. I'd forgotten that Richard had flown to LA to join her on Sunday for his own medical convention. She'd now be in a hotel room with my son, decidedly not a night owl. More like the man who is early to bed, early to rise. "Sorry, I hope I didn't wake Richard."

"No, I'm just a little hoarse today. Too much sales pitching to get people to appreciate, that is, buy, the gallery's pieces. Believe it or not, Richard's actually downstairs now schmoozing with his bosses."

"I thought he was the boss."

"There's always another boss."

"Good point. I'll bet he's having a great time with hail-fellow-well-met."

"Oh, yeah, you know how he loves to do that." She paused. "Not. But he has to meet and socialize with the funding agencies and all the people who support the hospital."

"I know Maddie called you. I'm sure you're relieved."

"No kidding. Thanks for facilitating that. Whatever you did worked."

"I can't take credit. Skip spent the day with her. And she didn't just mope. She took some action to help her own cause by sending Taylor a letter—contents unknown, but it worked."

"Whatever. I'm still calling you for the next crisis."

I could hardly wait.

# Chapter 19

ELEVEN-THIRTY seemed to come too soon, but that's what happened when a long nap and a very late dinner took over a good part of the evening. I began to wonder if Skip was going to come back as he'd threatened. I had the new, updated chart ready for him, as well as a fresh batch of larger-than-usual ginger cookies.

I needn't have worried. I heard his car pull up shortly after I set glasses out and made sure the pitcher of iced tea in the fridge was full enough to get through the night. I opened the door for him, preempting his knocking or ringing the doorbell. I credited my next-door neighbor for the spring that was back in his step.

He scraped his shoes on my welcome mat, as he always did, as if he, too, had once lived through messy rain and snow in the Bronx. My nephew glanced at the atrium table and studied the two places set with glasses of ice and copies of The Chart, plus an extra sheet at my place with a list of agenda items.

"I think those months of SuperKrafts meetings have turned you into a top-ranking administrative assistant," he said.

"I don't want to forget anything," I said, taking my seat across from him. I lowered my voice, in case there was a sleepwalker sneaking out of her room. "First, thanks for whatever part you played in Maddie's rehabilitation."

Skip shrugged. "Once I figured out that it was a swimming pool and not a young buck at the center of their struggle, it was easy. I just told her about the time my best buddy in sixth grade dumped me for a new kid whose family took him and a few other kids to Tahoe skiing, and left me behind. And then when the letter to Taylor worked, well, everything was good."

With June it was a pony; with Skip a ski trip to Tahoe; with Maddie a swimming pool. Was I the only one without a story of abandonment at an early age? "Is that a true story? You got left behind?"

"Yeah. You don't remember? Uncle Ken's the one who sat me down and put it in perspective. Plus, he bought me my own plane." When my eyes got wide, Skip explained that he was referring to the kind of plane that smooths wood.

I had to restrain myself from calling Richard immediately and asking if he'd ever been left behind because a new kid had something he didn't have. I was glad it hadn't fallen only on me to notice such traumas.

It was time to move on to matters of life and death. I reached for my copy of The Chart and directed Skip to do the same.

"Wow, this must be the squirt...oops, I better stop using that even when she's not listening...this must be Maddie's doing."

"What makes you say that? I could do charts." We both knew how far off that idea was.

I explained the significance of the *W*s in the DIRECTION column and did my best to explain the east/west wall rule of earthquakes. "You know how earthquakes come in a certain direction and affect things on one wall but not the one across from it?" I asked, as if I knew what I was talking about.

"Always?"

"Uh, I don't know. Don't you have a seismologist on staff?"

"I guess we should."

While we were waiting for the final word from a scientist, I pointed out the consistency of the reports of games (from Jeff), and coffee filters (from Jeanine) falling from a west wall, and Catherine's claim that her alarm clock at the inn slid.

"Catherine had the right wall," I explained. "The 'maybe' in her entry is due to the presence of rubber feet that would have made it harder for the clock to slide. But I've been thinking, and it's possible that the housekeepers polished the table that morning and even got some polish on the feet of the clock, so it slid easily. I can check that with Loretta. Whereas, Megan's report is all off. Amelia, the head of housekeeping at the inn, says there has been no broken glass in any of the rooms."

"You're saying that because Catherine's clock is on the west wall and Megan may have lied for dramatic effect, we now know that Catherine is innocent and Megan is guilty?"

Was it that obvious that I wanted my friend Catherine to be innocent?

"Of course not," I said. "We still don't have Bebe's alibi or Maisie's. Do we?"

"There's that 'we' that I love to hear." If Skip weren't eating my cookies with a happy grin, I'd have thought he was being sarcastic. "In fact, we have Bebe buying bagels to go at Willie's and Maisie calling her daughter in Los Angeles from her landline minutes after the earthquake. Neither of them could have made it to SuperKrafts to fit the timeline. And by the way, thanks to you, Jeff Slattery came in and helped us confirm what we thought about the time of death."

"Thanks for sharing. I'm sure you've considered how unlikely it would be that Catherine took a piece of the murder weapon back to the hotel with her?"

"It might have gotten stuck to her clothing or something."

"To her sundress? It doesn't make sense. Someone framed her."

I seemed to have made this determination on the spot. I remembered clearly a time when I'd been somewhat relieved to hear that the LPPD had finally arrested Craig Palmer's killer, with hard evidence to back it up. Whatever was churning in the back of my brain to change my mind hadn't fully revealed itself yet.

Skip pointed to the second sheet of paper on my side of the table.

"Anything else?"

I scanned my list. "One other thing. Loretta mentioned that Megan is going to check out tomorrow and head back to New York. Isn't she supposed to stay around until the case is closed?"

"There's no reason to ask her to."

"Given that you have the killer."

"Given that it's likely, yes. We can't keep people here if we're not charging them."

I was frustrated, but I saw no use in going forward with Case talk until I could figure out what was bothering me, other than what I'd already expressed, all of which Skip was able to wave away.

We turned to talk of The Wedding, which I thought deserved an initial-caps designation as much as The Case did. Skip was resigned to wearing a tux and had even been talked into a lavender pocket square to match June's dress.

"What are you wearing?" Skip asked.

"It's a secret."

"You don't have it yet."

"That's the secret."

"I can't wait for the day."

"Really?" It was too late at night, actually too early in the morning, for me to discern truth from tongue-in-cheek.

"No kidding. I mean, not that I like all the fanfare, but I'm blown away by the fact that those two found each other. My mom so deserves a guy like Nick."

"Have you told her that?"

"She knows how I feel."

"It wouldn't hurt to remind her."

"You think?"

"It would be the best present you could give her."

*Tap, tap. Tap, tap.*

Someone knocking on my door at twelve-thirty in the morning? Not that it was unheard of. Skip gave me a questioning look. Was I expecting another guest? I shook my head, no. He got up and checked the peephole, which seemed a strange thing for an armed man to do. He opened the door to Megan Sutley, in a navy linen pants outfit, who looked as surprised as I did.

"I saw your lights on," she said. "I didn't realize anyone else was here. Good evening, Detective Gowen."

"G'morning," he said, stifling a yawn. For real or to make a point, I couldn't tell.

"Come in," I said. And while she was getting her bearings, presumably adjusting to Skip's presence, I offered her a glass of iced tea.

"Oh, no, I just…well, Jeanine said you might have something that belongs to me."

"The crystal?"

"I didn't mean to disturb you. I can come back another time."

"No problem," I said, walking to the table that was against the wall. "It's right here." I looked into the small bowl where I dropped my keys and small odds and ends that I don't want to lose, or that I'm too lazy to return to their proper place. I wiggled my fingers through the contents—keys, mints, paper clips, a mini-coffeepot that was part of a tiny metal camping set. I jiggled things around again. More clips, and a hat pin. In what decade had I worn a hat pin last?

Megan had crept up and peered over my shoulder. "Did you find it?"

"It's not here. I can't imagine what happened to it. I saw it earlier today when I put my keys down." I lifted the edges of the cloth under the bowl and shook it. Nothing fell out. I looked on the floor under the table. Nothing. "I'm sorry. It doesn't seem to be here. Maybe in the light of day, it will show up."

Megan folded her arms across her chest and chewed her lip. She gave me a strange look, as if she didn't believe me, as if I had the crystal and planned to keep it for myself. She glanced at Skip. I had the feeling she'd have railed at me if he wasn't standing there, observing. "Well, I'll get out of your way for now. If you do find it, you can just bring it to the store tomorrow." She walked toward the door and Skip let her out.

"Weird," he said. I agreed. "What was that about?"

I gave him a brief account of finding the crystal, hearing about it from Jeanine, and now losing it.

Skip got down on his hands and knees and gave the floor a more thorough going-over. Nothing.

I convinced him to let it go and get some sleep. The plastic bag of cookies-to-go was an incentive and he left.

I went to bed, wondering where the bead was and why I cared, and hoping the supine position would help my brain sort things out before it was too late to get Catherine out of jail.

I SPENT about fifteen minutes on my hands and knees on Wednesday morning, and another few looking at eye level for the accursed bead. No luck. I decided I'd buy Megan another cell phone case if that's what it took to get the bead problem out of my life.

Henry and Taylor arrived on the dot of nine-thirty. The new plan was that Henry would return home and I'd take the girls to SuperKrafts with me. After that we'd make a girls-only trip to San Jose. The second shopping day in a row for me. My head was spinning. And we'd agreed that the trip wouldn't end until all three of us had wedding outfits. I had permission from the mothers of both girls to use my judgment in making the final decision on their outfits. The responsibility weighed heavily.

"Good thing my old suit is still in style," Henry said.

"Hmm," I uttered.

"Oh, no," Henry said. Pretending to block his ears, he rushed out the door, leaving three females laughing.

SUPERKRAFTS sales were in full swing. I'd have sworn that every woman I'd ever seen at a crafts fair was in the store, and a few men besides. There were sale signs, red tags, and one-time-only special deals on all the aisles. I wondered what was left for Saturday, other than balloons and cake.

I'd decided to play anonymous shopper today and not go near the back room, lest I be dragged into one last meeting concerning nothing I cared about. We began by roaming the scrapbooking aisles since both Maddie and Taylor wanted to make books for their parents' anniversaries, Maddie's in August and Taylor's in September. We checked out the plain burlap books that were held together by binder rings and ready for markers and stickers, and also the shiny cover stock useful for starting from scratch. Maddie was collecting things for a Los Angeles page, since Richard and Mary Lou were married there; Taylor had found a Scales of Justice page for her two-lawyer family.

Halfway through the sticker aisle, Megan showed up. She looked better than I did for having stayed up late, or maybe it was only an aura given off by her short, crisp dress and sparkly purse in matching dark blue. I was ready for a reprimand since I'd lost her precious bead, but she presented a friendly front, chatting with the girls, telling them she used to do scrapbooking herself. I had my doubts that she even knew what glue dots looked like.

"I looked all around the atrium again and I'm sorry I didn't find your bead," I said.

Megan waved away my concern. "Don't give it another thought. There are a million beads in the universe. One little crystal more or less won't make a difference."

I heard a gasp from a few feet down the aisle. "I have it," Maddie said. She and Taylor approached us.

"You have what?" I asked.

Maddie reached into the back pocket of her white shorts. "I took it to show Taylor and—"

"We wanted to buy more of them, so we brought it to the store to make a match," Taylor said.

It had never occurred to me to ask Maddie about the bead, though in retrospect, it would have been a smart thing to do. Who else was living with me at the moment? Who was attracted to shiny things and missed nothing, ever? Who talked about beads at the table yesterday? It was what Skip would have called a "duh moment."

"I'm sorry, Grandma."

"Me, too, Aunt Gerry. We thought it was yours and you were, like, getting rid of it. That's where my mom puts things she eventually throws out."

"I'm just glad we found it. Right, Megan?"

"You bet," she said, as she took the bead from Maddie. She

pulled out her cell phone and showed us the empty spot where the bead belonged.

The girls were wide-eyed at the dazzling case. They trotted over to the bead section, but I had the feeling nothing in the SuperKrafts aisles would measure up to Megan's crystal.

"I hear you're leaving today. Going back to New York," I said, pleased to chat with Megan now that another crisis had been averted.

"Yes, things are going smoothly and there's no reason for me to stay. In fact I need to run an errand in town before my trip and I wanted to ask you for a favor. Is there any chance you're going to be around here for about an hour, in case Jeanine needs help? Leo's back there, but he's useless." She pointed to the girls, who'd moved down the aisle. "There's punch and cookies up front in case they get hungry."

"Sure, we're just getting started. Just call my cell when you get back."

Megan went off, full of gratitude, trailing her lavender scent, and I continued down the aisle, filling my basket as I went.

The girls came back to the sticker aisle, studying each different theme for possible use in their projects for their parents—puffy stickers for the fifty states, flat stickers for the Fourth of July, 3-D stickers for Halloween, rolls of stickers with images for the seasons, animals, and sports—so I knew we weren't going anywhere fast.

We filled a cart plus a basket with merchandise from every section of the store. I paused to admire the dollhouse display, of course, and couldn't help tweaking a few pieces of furniture. We were ready to check out and I still hadn't heard from Megan. With some reluctance, I wandered to the back of the store where Leo was dealing with one of the maintenance crew.

"Excuse me, have you seen Megan?" I asked Leo, giving the man in coveralls an excuse to tip his gray-and-white striped cap and leave.

"Far as I know, she's gone."

"On an errand, you mean."

"Nope, she's gone, as in back home. She had her luggage loaded in the rental when she got here this morning."

"That's strange."

"It's what she planned."

"But she asked me to stay around for an hour in case Jeanine needed anything, and that was"—I checked my watch—"an hour and ten minutes ago. I assumed she was coming back."

Leo shrugged, oblivious. "I have no idea why she gave you that impression. I don't expect to see her again in California." His turn to check the time. "She was scheduled for the twelve-ten flight. It's a half hour to the airport, and she had to return the rental, so I assumed that when she left here around ten-fifteen, ten-twenty, she was headed there."

There was no use stressing about it. "I'll be leaving now," I said to Leo.

"No problem," he said.

I wished I could have said that it was the strangest thing that had happened in the last five days, but it wasn't even close.

IT hadn't been hard to talk Henry into meeting us at Willie's Bagels. "Sustenance for the road," I'd said, cell phone to cell phone.

"And for buying dresses, I'll bet."

"That, too," I'd admitted.

The four of us were seated in Willie's, made hungrier from the aroma of bagels, fresh out of the oven. I detected the aromatic presence of cinnamon, blueberry, and chocolate, and had a hard time deciding.

I related the Megan Sutley story to Henry, then posed my questions. "First, why would she be so obsessed last night with a single bead, crystal or otherwise? It's not as though it was museum quality, though admittedly it was a cut above the crafts beads in those packages on the SuperKrafts racks. And then today, she acted as though it was nothing, until Maddie produced the bead."

"If you say so."

"And second, why did she lie to me today? If she had a

twelve-ten flight, then her so-called errand when she left me at SuperKrafts was to get to the airport."

"Maybe she didn't want you to know how long you'd really be covering for her. Or maybe it was Leo who lied?"

I thought about it. "I should call Loretta," I said. I pulled my phone out. "Do you mind?"

Henry gave me a head shake that said he wanted the answer, too. The girls were occupied, head to head, with some app on their phones. I punched in the number.

"KenTucky Inn. How can we help you?" I was happy to hear Loretta's voice. I wasn't ready to deal with Jeanine's friend Dana until I knew she'd cleared herself in the eyes of the law.

"It's Gerry, Loretta. I have a quick question for you."

"Yes, we're available for your wedding."

I acknowledged my friend's clever opening, hoping Henry didn't notice the flush it brought to my face. "Did Megan Sutley check out this morning?"

"Yes, she did, as planned. First thing. Paid in full. Is there a problem?"

"No, and thanks for letting me know about the glass, or lack of it, after the earthquake."

"Okay, and hey, make sure you keep that wedding guest list down to one hundred or less so we can handle it. Ha, ha."

"Ha, ha to you, too, Loretta."

"What's that about?" Henry asked.

Our bagel orders arrived just in time for me to avoid his question.

"Good to have confirmation," I said when we'd thanked our waitress. "Megan checked out first thing this morning."

"Well, that's the end of it, then, right?"

"Right," I said. But it didn't feel right.

# Chapter 20

HENRY TOOK OFF for his own errands (not involving a cross-country flight, I hoped) while the girls and I discussed ordering brownies to go and taking them on the shopping trip. We got one for Aunt Bev, of course.

*Dum dum, da da dum, da da dum.*

The LPPD on my cell phone. Not Skip's number, however. "Mrs. Porter?" A young woman's voice. "This is Pam Blake from the LPPD."

"Yes?" My heart pounded as I thought first of Bev. Was it her heart? Had the stress of the wedding gotten to her? Was I to blame for postponing and rescheduling over and over?

"Mrs. Porter, we had a report from a neighbor of someone leaving your home, possibly after breaking in. We've sent a car and we've just reached Skip, also, but you might want to check it out."

"Uh, thank you very much. I'll do that."

I tried to keep my voice level for the sake of the girls. I was never so glad Maddie and Taylor had each other and their electronic baby-sitters. On the other hand, I had to deposit them somewhere safe while I went home. I tried Henry's cell and got no answer; the same for June's. My third idea worked, as Rosie, my friend and the owner of Rosie's Books, just down the street, agreed to have preteen company.

"Of course, Gerry," Rosie said. "You can drop Maddie off any time, you know that."

I sent effusive thanks her way. "This is a bit of an emergency.

And she has a friend with her."

"Any friend of Maddie's…"

I pulled money from my wallet and dropped it on the table. "Something's come up," I said to the girls and led them out the door before they could question me.

Following only a moderate grilling on the way to Rosie's, Maddie was astonishingly cooperative about staying put, and I attributed her compliance to the reunion with Taylor. After nearly a week apart, there were endless things to talk about and an infinite number of games to play. The other reason she wasn't making a fuss might have been that my face, as I saw it in my rearview mirror, was as white as the cheapest vanilla ice cream.

Rosie was waiting at the door to her shop, as planned. I let the girls out of the car, gave Rosie a quick wave, and drove in the other direction toward my house. I wished I'd thought to ask Pam, whom I knew from the LPPD reception desk, a few questions. Who had called in the report? What did the burglar look like? What kind of car was he driving? And about a dozen other things. Burglaries were not at all common in my Eichler neighborhood where neighbors looked after each other. My own home did not present a great challenge to someone who wanted in. My spare key was tucked into a tiny space under a large planter near my front step. One of the three most common places anyone ever kept an extra key, I imagined. High on the list with "under the welcome mat" or "at the top of the doorframe."

I tried to stay at the speed limit, but it was difficult not to race through the streets to my usually peaceful neighborhood.

*Blare, blare. Blare, blare.*

A car, rightfully honking at me as I nearly missed a stop sign at the bottom of my street. What was I doing? When had my life gotten so out of control? There was nothing in my home of great value, except to me—pieces of china that were my mother's; a brooch given to me by Ken's mother at our wedding; various drawings and crafts from Maddie from kindergarten on; photos, of course. I certainly valued all my crafts supplies and ongoing projects, but not to the point of being devastated if they were stolen. Then again, who would steal crafts projects?

I slowed down as I approached my house, breathing better when I saw a patrol car, and one other, parked in front of my house. The beige sedan looked like it could have come from the police's small fleet of unmarked cars. Should I consider it good news or bad that Skip might be here? I parked in my driveway and walked to the door, now held wide open by Skip, with Henry at his side.

THE next half hour went by in a blur as I sat in my atrium with Henry and Skip while uniformed cops wandered about my home, in and out of doorways, looking for trouble. "We'll go through it when they're done," Skip told me.

"Who called the station?" I asked. "Esther Willoughby?"

"Beige with brown trim," Skip said, up to the minute on Eichler shorthand.

Esther, a lovely woman in her nineties, lived across the street. Everyone within a couple of blocks in either direction counted on her to take a delivery if we were away, to tell us if children from the nearby grammar school were eating lunch on our lawns, to make sure everyone's garbage was picked up when it was supposed to be. Esther kept track of new owners and reported anyone who didn't belong. We all loved Esther.

"The trouble is with her eyes," Skip said.

"I know. Did she describe the person?" I asked.

"According to Pam, Esther first reported that it was a young boy, but she told the uniforms who responded that it might have been a short, thin woman. And the car has gone from blue to black."

The uniformed officers came back from their tour of my home. "Nothing," said one of the young cops, by which I hoped he meant, "Nothing has been disturbed" and not, "There's nothing left."

Once the officers were gone, Henry and Skip walked me through the rooms. I checked my jewelry boxes, the drawer where I keep a small reserve of cash, Maddie's laptop and my computer.

Nothing was missing that I could see. My furniture hadn't been moved, and neither had my books. My closets were intact, some less neat than others, through no fault of the maybe-burglar.

Back in the atrium, we analyzed what we knew and tossed around all the possibilities in rapid fire.

"A kid from the school up the street?" from Henry.

"Not if he was driving," from me.

"Esther didn't necessarily see the person get in the car," from Skip.

"Why would someone break in and not take anything?"

"You don't know that for sure."

"It's possible something will turn up. Or not turn up."

"We could sweep for a bug."

"Know any national secrets?"

"How about SuperKrafts secrets?"

"I know what color balloons are ordered for Saturday."

"Maybe one of those door-to-door people found your door open."

"And thought, 'Why not?'" from Skip.

"They usually travel in twos," from me.

"True," from Henry.

"Did you lock your door when you left this morning?" from Skip.

I wanted to block my ears. My head was splitting. "Yes, I always lock my door. Does any of this matter?" I asked. "I should just be grateful that no one was hurt and nothing was taken."

I should have been grateful, but I wasn't.

BY the time I recovered from what was apparently not a burglary, it was midafternoon and I had no heart or energy for shopping or for much of anything. I should have known my wonderful family and friends would come to my aid.

Henry offered to pick up the girls and take them to his house. "They're due for a sleepover," he said.

"If you're sure—"

"Kay and Bill love having them. Why don't you take a little

down time?"

Nothing sounded better. And between Bev and June, I had more casseroles and take-out than I could eat.

Skip promised to go back to talk to Esther himself to try to psych out what aspects of the incident stayed in her mind in a consistent way.

"Are you sure you're okay by yourself?" each one asked in one way or another.

"Yes, it was a non-burglary, remember? Just like the non-earthquake."

I suppressed the fact that someone had been murdered during the most recent non-earthquake.

I puttered around my house, still checking for signs of a stranger's presence. I looked through my shelves for bookmarks or notes that may have fallen from books that were tampered with. I opened each kitchen cabinet and studied the arrangement of the mugs, the spices, and the boxes of crackers. I opened dresser drawers and counted my pajama sets and pairs of sandals. For a moment, I felt my heart skip—where were my blue terrycloth slippers?—until I remembered they were in the wash. I wished my furniture and rugs could speak to me and tell me if anyone undesirable had passed through today. I wished my clocks would stop ticking.

Finally, with not another inch of my house left to scrutinize, I poured a large glass of iced tea, gathered up loose periodicals and mail and took everything to my atrium. I seldom allowed myself such a treat, to sit and leaf through magazines and catalogs, to play with the crossword puzzle in the Sunday (it didn't matter from which week) newspaper. I browsed through catalogs from a kitchen store, a museum, and a "creative toy" company, sipping tea in between.

*Ring, ring. Ring, ring.*

A call from Bev on my landline, checking in. "I figured if you were sleeping, you wouldn't hear the phone," she explained.

I pulled the phone back to my chair, as far as the cord would reach. "I was just reading, feeling a little sleepy."

"Good, that's good. Let yourself sleep. But I have to tell you, the funniest thing happened. Megan Sutley's car was stolen. Either that or she just dumped it instead of turning it in."

"Strange. So you guys are looking for it?" I knew that in her capacity as civilian volunteer, Bev worked on all matters related to lost, stolen, and abandoned cars and was closely connected to leasing and rental companies.

"No, they found it. It was a rental and they found it even before Megan could report it missing. The car was at the San Jose airport. Where it belongs, sort of, but it wasn't turned in to the company. You know how the rental companies cruise the lots in case someone abandoned one of their vehicles or dropped it at the wrong spot." I did now. "So, Megan's car was just sitting in one of the private lots off the freeway and they tried to call her. But, of course, she's in the air on the way to JFK. I'm sure they don't really care since they must have her credit card number and that's all they care about."

"The weirdness won't quit."

"No kidding. Well, I'll let you rest."

We signed off but the call had wakened me a bit. I left the phone on the floor and my mind wandered back to Megan and her strange lie about the errand and her important bead. My head was fuzzy, in the middle ground between sleeping and waking. I took a gulp of tea. It tasted less fruity than usual. Maybe I'd mixed in a caffeinated brand by mistake and the stimulating properties were fighting with the relaxing effects.

My mind drifted to the start of the day, in SuperKrafts, and my surprise that Maddie had taken Megan's bead. I floated back, all the way to my first encounter with the shiny crystal. I'd been summoned to a meeting at the last minute, around three o'clock on Sunday. I became bored, or annoyed, or both, and left. I wandered through the store and saw the bead. I seemed to see it now. On the floor. In the retail section. At the border of the area where Craig Palmer was murdered.

Another neuron (not that I knew what that meant) kicked in. My head snapped up and I remembered with clarity hearing Megan tell Jeanine and me that she'd never been in that part of the store.

My head fell forward. Confused again. How did the bead from Megan's cell phone case get into a part of the store where she had never been? Unless she was lying. And unless she had entered the area on Saturday evening, arguing with Craig.

I heard noises in my atrium. My front door opening and closing. A chair scraping. An earthquake? Another three-point-one? I tried to stand but my legs were limp. I slammed back down on the cushion. Now someone was sitting in front of me. A scent of lavender. Megan? Had she landed already? Was I in New York with her?

No.

As muddled as I felt, it became clear to me that Megan Sutley was in my atrium. And it wasn't good.

What time was it? I couldn't keep my head up. I tried to focus on Megan, but I was disoriented.

Now she was holding up a key. My key. I reached for it, but my arm flopped down on the table.

"Nice of you to make it so easy, Gerry. Leaving the key in an obvious place." My head fell again. Megan lifted my chin. "Don't fight it, Gerry. Have some more tea."

The tea. Something in the tea had clouded my brain.

"Why…" I had a question for my guest, but I couldn't get the words through my thick lips.

I heard Megan's voice. "Why? Because you're too nosy, Gerry. And too smart. Talking to Loretta, asking about broken glass. At first, I thought if I got out of town with the bead, you'd forget about everything and it would be all over, but I realized that, sooner or later, you'd put it together. I'd be worried about you for the rest of my life."

Megan's voice was sharp. Why wasn't mine sharp? I tried again to speak but my head and everything in it was heavy. My thoughts were feathery and sticky at the same time. Was Esther on duty? Where was Maddie? How soon would Skip get here?

Megan's voice droned on. "Or maybe you want to know why I killed Craig? I'll tell you. Craig wanted to leave me here. In Lincoln Point. It's a point all right, like the dot at the end of the world. He knew I loved him and this was his way of rejecting me.

A double rejection. A twofer. He wanted to destroy both me and my career. Well, California came through for me." She laughed. "An earthquake just when I needed one. At least I could salvage my career."

"Not from prison," swam around in my head. I didn't think I should say it, even if I could have overcome the puzzling lump in my throat. Something must have come out, however, since Megan got angry.

"You need to drink more tea," she said.

She stood and picked up the glass. She came around to my side of the table and aimed the glass at my mouth. Her face was close to mine. More lavender invaded my nostrils. I shouldn't do it. I shouldn't drink more tea. I summoned all of my strength and raised my arms. I grabbed the glass with both hands and poured whatever strength I had into pushing it toward Megan's face. I hit her nose and sent tea splashing into her eyes.

"No," she screamed. "Look what you've done." She grabbed a napkin and wiped her face. "What have you done?" She ran behind me, toward my kitchen. I heard her mumble, as if her mouth were as clogged up as mine. "Have to wash my eyes… need to get more tea…in the fridge…finish this job…meet this goal. My eyes…can't see."

I fell to the floor and picked up the phone that I'd left there. The activity spurred me on a little bit. I heard water running. Megan in the kitchen, barely audible. I punched Redial. I couldn't remember the last call I'd made on my landline. I hoped it wasn't for pizza.

"Hey, Gerry." Bev's voice. "I was just going to call you. Skip is on his way there. He found out that Megan never boarded that flight this afternoon."

No kidding. "She's 'ere," I said, my voice sounding drugged.

"What? What's wrong, Gerry? Gerry? Oh, no!"

More noise. Megan cursing. I crawled across the atrium, down the entryway, toward my front door. Megan yelling. The door opening. Skip's voice: "Aunt Gerry, can you hear me? Aunt Gerry?"

Then nothing.

# Chapter 21

BY THE TIME SuperKrafts had been open two weeks, I could hardly remember when the giant source of crafting goods wasn't part of our landscape. Leo Murray and Catherine Duncan (minus Video Jeff) were back in New York City, and strangest of all, Bebe Mellon was named manager of the new store.

As a favor to me for (in her opinion) helping catch the real killer, Catherine Duncan declined to press charges against Bebe and her co-conspirators, who were responsible for the upsetting correspondence slipped under her door.

"Everyone's suffered enough," she'd rightly said.

It had taken the brilliant detectives of the LPPD a little while to extract Megan's confession. She'd stolen Leo's car because it was a distinctive blue that someone would remember, making Leo blameworthy for whatever she did while driving it, thus buying her a little time. She needn't have bothered, since Esther was lucky if she could distinguish blue from green. Megan had dumped her own car at the airport and taken a cab back to Super-Krafts, counting on Leo to have stayed put at the store. On such a busy first day, she was safe in that assumption. She'd entered my home and spiked the pitcher of tea in my fridge. No wonder we'd seen no signs of burglary.

Now Megan was safely in jail in Lincoln Point. What irony. If she thought the town was boring when she was a free woman, what did she think of it now?

I wasn't sure I wanted to know the details of what Megan had used to spike my tea, but Skip was determined to tell me.

"You'll just ask me a week from now, and I'll have forgotten," he said.

I listened, along with the rest of the family and friends assembled in my living room, while Skip described a mixture of a roofie, sleeping pills, and alcohol. In a large enough dose, the combination was lethal. Megan had come back to be sure it worked.

"The doctors who pumped your stomach said it was a good thing you'd had enough to eat, and also you have a pretty strong constitution," Bev said.

"I knew that."

"I thought they fixed it so that any clear liquid turns blue when a roofie is dropped into it?" Henry said.

"Only some formulas. There are generic versions that don't have that property," June said. "I saw it on TV." June was now the proud owner of a miniature police station, thanks to Maddie's idea.

"So she'll think of Uncle Skip whenever she sees it," Maddie had said.

Eventually, all the girls in the extended family, including Maddie and me, found a time to go shopping together. We'd come home with enough clothes, shoes, and accessories to outfit a seriously large bridal party. Even Maddie chose a dress—a blue silk sleeveless with a wide gold belt, sparkly, of course, and identical to Taylor's dress, the same style in fuchsia. I thought I'd never want to look at a shiny bead again, but I got over it once the girls modeled the very "in" creations.

With less than two weeks to go, there seemed to be no end to wedding talk. Who would sit where? Had all the music been selected yet? Was there time to add another dessert to the menu?

Henry leaned in to me on the sofa. "Once this wedding is over, we should talk," he said.

"Don't we talk?"

"I mean really talk."

"Should I be worried?"

"Not unless you'd mind one more shopping trip for wedding clothes."

I looked at my BFF and saw in his eyes exactly what he meant. We inched closer and clasped hands.

"Do you think we can keep it below one hundred guests?" I asked.

He smiled and kissed my cheek. I knew it was time to call Loretta at the KenTucky Inn. I wondered if she'd be willing to take her sign down for just one afternoon.

———*oeoeoe*———

# *Gerry's Miniature Tips*

Gerry shares her tips for making dollhouse furniture and accessories from everyday objects.

## Lollipops
Don't toss that old hairbrush away. If it has the kind of bristle that's a stiff plastic rod with a little "knob" on top, cut to size and put a few of them in a holder.

## Glasses, containers
Use a colored or transparent stiff drinking straw cut to size for a drinking glass (no bottom needed unless you're going to show it tipped over), or as a holder for lollipops (above) or pencils (toothpicks).

## Purses
Use binder clips! Remove the metal prongs. (It's easier than you think—simply squeeze together the ends that run along the track of the clip and they'll slide out.) Cover the body of the clip with fabric of your choice, or (the easy way) buy clips with designs already printed on the metal. Add a handle: a chain or a thin strip of leather. You're ready to go shopping!

## Bathroom scale
A disposable razor makes an excellent start for a doctor's-type scale. Stand it on its end and glue to a base of the same color. Add a strip of numbers to the top along the razor, either from printables or drawn yourself.

## Springs

The small springs found in ballpoint pens have many uses. Stretch one a bit and attach it to a screen door for a realistic look; place it on the floor of a child's room as a Slinky. You can also bend it into an arch and glue the ends down for another typical Slinky look.

## From Stickers to Props

Check the sticker aisles of office supply and crafts stores. Many have a 3-D look and can be used as is. Flip-flops are a common sticker item and can simply be stuck to the floor of a dollhouse bathroom, a porch, or the towel in a beach scene. Give three-dimensional musical instrument stickers extra depth by gluing to a piece of foam board, cut to shape. Lean a guitar against the wall in the retro-hippie's room.

## Charms to Go

See above, on stickers, and apply to charms. Even more designs await in charms. But, since charms are most often silver, gold, or pewter, they're better when painted, for a more realistic look. Also, jump rings and other jewelry findings may need to be removed or hidden.

## Toys to Go

Many types of toys and games make great material for furniture. Dominoes, for example, offer twenty-eight identical blocks that can be used to build the familiar style of open-work entertainment center with shelves for books, electronic equipment, or objects of art. They come in different colors, and the dots can be painted to match or covered with paper or fabric. Some small toys, like cars, balls, and board-game tokens can be placed in a nursery or child's room as is, with no additional labor.

## About the Author

Margaret Grace, author of six previous novels in the Miniature series, is the pen name of Camille Minichino. She is also the author of short stories, articles, and twelve mysteries in two other series. She is a lifelong miniaturist, as well as board member and past president of NorCal Sisters in Crime. Minichino is on the staff at Lawrence Livermore National Laboratory, and she teaches science at Golden Gate University and writing at Bay Area schools. Visit her at www.minichino.com and on Facebook.

# More Traditional Mysteries from Perseverance Press
*For the New Golden Age*

**Albert A. Bell, Jr.**
PLINY THE YOUNGER SERIES
*Death in the Ashes*
ISBN 978-1-56474-532-3

*The Eyes of Aurora (forthcoming)*
ISBN 978-1-56474-549-1

**Jon L. Breen**
*Eye of God*
ISBN 978-1-880284-89-6

**Taffy Cannon**
ROXANNE PRESCOTT SERIES
*Guns and Roses*
Agatha and Macavity awards nominee, Best Novel
ISBN 978-1-880284-34-6

*Blood Matters*
ISBN 978-1-880284-86-5

*Open Season on Lawyers*
ISBN 978-1-880284-51-3

*Paradise Lost*
ISBN 978-1-880284-80-3

**Laura Crum**
GAIL MCCARTHY SERIES
*Moonblind*
ISBN 978-1-880284-90-2

*Chasing Cans*
ISBN 978-1-880284-94-0

*Going, Gone*
ISBN 978-1-880284-98-8

*Barnstorming*
ISBN 978-1-56474-508-8

**Jeanne M. Dams**
HILDA JOHANSSON SERIES
*Crimson Snow*
ISBN 978-1-880284-79-7

*Indigo Christmas*
ISBN 978-1-880284-95-7

*Murder in Burnt Orange*
ISBN 978-1-56474-503-3

**Janet Dawson**
JERI HOWARD SERIES
*Bit Player*
Golden Nugget Award nominee
ISBN 978-1-56474-494-4

*Cold Trail (forthcoming)*
ISBN 978-1-56474-555-2

*What You Wish For*
ISBN 978-1-56474-518-7

*Death Rides the Zephyr*
ISBN 978-1-56474-530-9

**Kathy Lynn Emerson**
LADY APPLETON SERIES
*Face Down Below the Banqueting House*
ISBN 978-1-880284-71-1

*Face Down Beside St. Anne's Well*
ISBN 978-1-880284-82-7

*Face Down O'er the Border*
ISBN 978-1-880284-91-9

**Elaine Flinn**
MOLLY DOYLE SERIES
*Deadly Vintage*
ISBN 978-1-880284-87-2

**Sara Hoskinson Frommer**
JOAN SPENCER SERIES
*Her Brother's Keeper*
ISBN 978-1-56474-525-5

**Hal Glatzer**
KATY GREEN SERIES
*Too Dead To Swing*
ISBN 978-1-880284-53-7

*A Fugue in Hell's Kitchen*
ISBN 978-1-880284-70-4

*The Last Full Measure*
ISBN 978-1-880284-84-1

**Margaret Grace**
MINIATURE SERIES
*Mix-up in Miniature*
ISBN 978-1-56474-510-1

*Madness in Miniature*
ISBN 978-1-56474-543-9

**Wendy Hornsby**
MAGGIE MACGOWEN SERIES
*In the Guise of Mercy*
ISBN 978-1-56474-482-1

*The Paramour's Daughter*
ISBN 978-1-56474-496-8

*The Hanging*
ISBN 978-1-56474-526-2

*The Color of Light*
ISBN 978-1-56474-542-2

**Diana Killian**
POETIC DEATH SERIES
*Docketful of Poesy*
ISBN 978-1-880284-97-1

**Janet LaPierre**
PORT SILVA SERIES
*Baby Mine*
ISBN 978-1-880284-32-2

*Keepers*
Shamus Award nominee, Best Paperback Original
ISBN 978-1-880284-44-5

*Death Duties*
ISBN 978-1-880284-74-2

*Family Business*
ISBN 978-1-880284-85-8

*Run a Crooked Mile*
ISBN 978-1-880284-88-9

**Hailey Lind**
ART LOVER'S SERIES
*Arsenic and Old Paint*
ISBN 978-1-56474-490-6

**Lev Raphael**
NICK HOFFMAN SERIES
*Tropic of Murder*
ISBN 978-1-880284-68-1

*Hot Rocks*
ISBN 978-1-880284-83-4

**Lora Roberts**
BRIDGET MONTROSE SERIES
*Another Fine Mess*
ISBN 978-1-880284-54-4

SHERLOCK HOLMES SERIES
*The Affair of the Incognito Tenant*
ISBN 978-1-880284-67-4

**Rebecca Rothenberg**
BOTANICAL SERIES
*The Tumbleweed Murders*
(completed by Taffy Cannon)
ISBN 978-1-880284-43-8

**Sheila Simonson**
LATOUCHE COUNTY SERIES
*Buffalo Bill's Defunct*
WILLA Award, Best Softcover Fiction
ISBN 978-1-880284-96-4

*An Old Chaos*
ISBN 978-1-880284-99-5

*Beyond Confusion*
ISBN 978-1-56474-519-4

**Shelley Singer**
JAKE SAMSON & ROSIE VICENTE SERIES
*Royal Flush*
ISBN 978-1-880284-33-9

**Lea Wait**
SHADOWS ANTIQUES SERIES
*Shadows of a Down East Summer*
ISBN 978-1-56474-497-5

*Shadows on a Cape Cod Wedding*
ISBN 1-978-56474-531-6

*Shadows on a Maine Christmas*
(forthcoming)
ISBN 978-1-56474-531-6

**Eric Wright**
JOE BARLEY SERIES
*The Kidnapping of Rosie Dawn*
Barry Award, Best Paperback Original. Edgar,
Ellis, and Anthony awards nominee
ISBN 978-1-880284-40-7

**Nancy Means Wright**
MARY WOLLSTONECRAFT SERIES
*Midnight Fires*
ISBN 978-1-56474-488-3

*The Nightmare*
ISBN 978-1-56474-509-5

## REFERENCE/MYSTERY WRITING

**Kathy Lynn Emerson**
*How To Write Killer Historical Mysteries:
The Art and Adventure of Sleuthing
Through the Past*
Agatha Award, Best Nonfiction. Anthony and
Macavity awards nominee
ISBN 978-1-880284-92-6

**Carolyn Wheat**
*How To Write Killer Fiction:
The Funhouse of Mystery & the Roller
Coaster of Suspense*
ISBN 978-1-880284-62-9

**Available from your local bookstore
or from Perseverance Press/John Daniel & Company
(800) 662–8351 or www.danielpublishing.com/perseverance**